"[A] fabulous
—*The Best Reviews*

Praise for the
Kendra Ballantyne, Pet-Sitter Mysteries

Howl Deadly

"Mystery readers and animal lovers alike will find much to enjoy in this mystery series. The mystery is tightly plotted and a bit of a departure this time around, making the story feel fresh while we follow Kendra, who always has the animals' best interests at heart." —*CA Reviews*

"Fans will enjoy Kendra's latest who-done-it as her energy, élan, and love of animals (as well as Dante) make for an appealing investigative story." —*The Mystery Gazette*

Never Say Sty

"Ms. Johnston continues to make Kendra Ballantyne a likeable character with a sense of humor . . . Perfect in today's world . . . *Never Say Sty* is well thought out and an enjoyable read." —*My Shelf*

"The pacing is solid, the dialogue crisp . . . Animal lovers will adore this series for the mystery as well as the animals." —*CA Reviews*

D0032795

continued . . .

Double Dog Dare

"An incredible writer who creates believable, intelligent characters. *Double Dog Dare* has a fun-filled, suspenseful story line that contains intrigue, mystery, murder, lots and lots of animals, and humor. Ms. Johnston's wit, pacing, and dialogue make this cozy entry into the Pet-Sitter series a surefire winner."
—*Fresh Fiction*

"[A] fast and fun read."
—*New Mystery Reader*

The Fright of the Iguana

"Wonderful . . . I always enjoy the pet-sitting antics in this series. The author has done a great job of making the reader care about the animals. Plus their personalities really shine through. The Southern California [setting] is enjoyable as well."
—*Mystery Lovers Corner*

Meow Is for Murder

"A humorous, cleverly constructed murder mystery . . . Intelligent . . . with an eccentric cast that infuses the plot with a sense of jocularity and pets that readers would love to adopt."
—*Midwest Book Review*

"Kendra is such a fun . . . likeable character. [There's] plenty of humor along with a well-plotted cozy mystery."
—*Mystery Lovers Corner*

Fine-Feathered Death

"A wonderful new addition to the ranks of amateur detectives . . . The well-timed humor . . . sets it above the current crowded crop of cozy mystery series. Johnston's ability to blend pet love, mystery, and romance into one well-wrapped package makes this a summer treat for mystery and pet lovers alike."
—*Front Street Reviews*

"Exciting . . . Johnston is a creative storyteller who not only writes a fascinating mystery but also creates a deep character study."
—*Books 'n' Bytes*

"A fast-paced who-done-it . . . Kendra is a fun character, and her supporting friends and assorted critters make an enjoyable read."
—*Fresh Fiction*

"You'll laugh out loud! Don't read it when you have to be quiet!"
—*Mystery Lovers Corner*

Nothing to Fear but Ferrets

"Linda O. Johnston has a definite talent for infusing humor in just the right places . . . Pet lovers and amateur-sleuth fans will find this series deserving of an award as well as a place on the bestseller lists."
—*Midwest Book Review*

Sit, Stay, Slay

"Very funny and exciting . . . Worthy of an award nomination . . . The romance in this novel adds spice to a very clever crime thriller."
—*The Best Reviews*

"A brilliantly entertaining new puppy caper, a doggie-filled who-done-it . . . Johnston's novel is a real pedigree!"
—Dorothy Cannell

"Pet-sitter sleuth Kendra Ballantyne is up to her snake-draped neck in peril in Linda O. Johnston's hilarious debut mystery *Sit, Stay, Slay*. Witty, wry, and highly entertaining."
—Carolyn Hart

Berkley Prime Crime titles by Linda O. Johnston

SIT, STAY, SLAY
NOTHING TO FEAR BUT FERRETS
FINE-FEATHERED DEATH
MEOW IS FOR MURDER
THE FRIGHT OF THE IGUANA
DOUBLE DOG DARE
NEVER SAY STY
HOWL DEADLY
FELINE FATALE

Feline Fatale

Linda O. Johnston

BERKLEY PRIME CRIME, NEW YORK

THE BERKLEY PUBLISHING GROUP
Published by the Penguin Group
Penguin Group (USA) Inc.
375 Hudson Street, New York, New York 10014, USA
Penguin Group (Canada), 90 Eglinton Avenue East, Suite 700, Toronto, Ontario M4P 2Y3, Canada
(a division of Pearson Penguin Canada Inc.)
Penguin Books Ltd., 80 Strand, London WC2R 0RL, England
Penguin Group Ireland, 25 St. Stephen's Green, Dublin 2, Ireland (a division of Penguin Books Ltd.)
Penguin Group (Australia), 250 Camberwell Road, Camberwell, Victoria 3124, Australia
(a division of Pearson Australia Group Pty. Ltd.)
Penguin Books India Pvt. Ltd., 11 Community Centre, Panchsheel Park, New Delhi—110 017, India
Penguin Group (NZ), 67 Apollo Drive, Rosedale, North Shore 0632, New Zealand
(a division of Pearson New Zealand Ltd.)
Penguin Books (South Africa) (Pty.) Ltd., 24 Sturdee Avenue, Rosebank, Johannesburg 2196,
South Africa

Penguin Books Ltd., Registered Offices: 80 Strand, London WC2R 0RL, England

This is a work of fiction. Names, characters, places, and incidents either are the product of the author's imagination or are used fictitiously, and any resemblance to actual persons, living or dead, business establishments, events, or locales is entirely coincidental. The publisher does not have any control over and does not assume any responsibility for author or third-party websites or their content.

FELINE FATALE

A Berkley Prime Crime Book / published by arrangement with the author

PRINTING HISTORY
Berkley Prime Crime mass-market edition / July 2010

Copyright © 2010 by Linda O. Johnston.
Cover illustration by Monika Roe.
Cover design by Rita Frangie.
Interior text design by Stacy Irwin.

ISBN: 978-0-425-23554-6

BERKLEY® PRIME CRIME
Berkley Prime Crime Books are published by The Berkley Publishing Group,
a division of Penguin Group (USA) Inc.,
375 Hudson Street, New York, New York 10014.
BERKLEY® PRIME CRIME and the PRIME CRIME logo are trademarks of Penguin Group (USA) Inc.

PRINTED IN THE UNITED STATES OF AMERICA

10 9 8 7 6 5 4 3 2 1

Acknowledgments

Many thanks to Donna Hollingsworth of Holly Sams, a delightful breeder of champion Samoyeds and a pet-sitter—and, especially, a dog show aficionado and expert who gave unstinting information about how breeders view the showing of the show-quality pups from their litters. If Linda nevertheless misstated anything, please chalk it up to poetic license; it's her bad, not Donna's.

Thanks, too, to Linda's delightful editor, Michelle Vega, for all she has done to help keep Kendra's series moving smoothly, and to her agent, Paige Wheeler, for all the excellent help she has given to her career. Linda would also like to particularly thank both of them, and all the appropriate folks at Berkley Prime Crime, for the opportunity to write the upcoming spin-off series about Lauren Vancouver, pet rescuer! Kendra reserves judgment about the new series, but she likes Lauren enough to wish her the best—especially if she, too, becomes a murder magnet.

And to Lexie and Mystie, Linda's current Cavalier King Charles spaniels. Mystie's penchant for elusiveness helped Linda describe the proclivities of Lady Cuddles, the escape-artist kitty in *Feline Fatale*. And, of course, kudos also to Kendra's Lexie.

And, as always, to Linda's husband, Fred.

Kendra Ballantyne/Linda O. Johnston

Chapter One

"Who are you?"

The woman who demanded my identity blocked my path up the narrow stairway. Her print pull-on pants seemed snug for her curvaceous figure, although her shocking pink knit shirt was loose enough to allow her to cross her arms as she glared down at me through black-rimmed glasses.

She'd appeared quite suddenly through the door to the third floor, exactly where I was heading. She startled me enough to cause me to grab the stair rail with one hand and my heart with the other as my large bag banged against my hip.

"Er . . . I'm Kendra Ballantyne," I said. "I'm a pet-sitter." Among other things. "One of your residents who does a lot of animal care around here asked me to take over while she's away for the weekend. Wanda Villa-real. Do you know her?"

It was nine in the morning. We were in the rearmost

of several residential structures at the Brigadoon condominium complex, in Burbank, California. Wanda was
a friend and fellow member of the Pet Sitters Club of
SoCal. Even more, she was the girlfriend of my dear-
est friend in the world, Darryl Nestler—owner of the
Doggy Indulgence Day Resort in Studio City.

They were off for a romantic long weekend, so of
course I'd agreed to step in and help Wanda out.

"Yes, I know her." The woman's chilly voice and
sneering smile made it clear she wasn't one of Wanda's
closest acquaintances. "Are you saying you're here to
take care of some residents' pets today?"

I nodded. "That's right. Wanda's caring for pets
in four of the condos here. She got the okay from the
owners for me to help out this weekend, and gave me
the keys. And a letter of introduction." And why I was
telling this nasty piece of work anything, without her
giving any indication she had authority to ask me questions, I didn't know.

Okay, yes, I did. It could save me a lot of time and
aggravation if she simply let me go on my way, instead
of keeping me standing there in the stairway.

But I didn't hold out much hope for her sudden
cooperation.

"Let me see that letter," she ordered.

"Sure." I ignored an urge to ram it between her large,
too-white teeth. "But let's go upstairs into the hallway,
where there'll be more light."

She didn't immediately move. I waited, feigning
patience. Worst case, I'd resort to returning to the second floor and finding an alternate staircase. But I suspected this unpleasant human obstacle would impede
my entry anywhere.

"All right," she eventually conceded, not sounding thrilled. "This way." She opened the door she'd emerged through, then glared at me, shooing me past her with her hand.

I considered spitting on it, but decided not to be so petty. After all, if I were in her position, living in a condominium complex where some stranger appeared and claimed to have a valid reason for strolling the stairway, maybe I'd be equally nasty till proof was provided. But I liked to think I'd at least pretend cordiality until the truth was established, one way or the other.

We stopped in a wide hallway, well-lit through roomy windows along one wall that revealed a small balcony. Along the other wall were several doors bearing numbers starting with three. Two doors were decorated with woven wreaths of tree branches trimmed with artificial, bright-colored flowers. Another was garnished with a gold and purple pennant extolling the Los Angeles Lakers.

I reached into a pocket of my roomy purse and drew out the letter Wanda had left with me. I'd reviewed it, of course, to ensure it appeared legitimate, legally speaking. After all, in addition to being a pet-sitter, I'm also an attorney. This wasn't a binding kind of document, though. It was short and lacked substance, basically stating what I'd already said: Wanda was a resident and pet-sitter at Brigadoon, and she had delegated to me her authority to care for some owners' animals this weekend. I also handed over one of my pet-sitting business cards.

"Which units?" barked the bitch, handing back the letter.

I wasn't about to tell her. Sure, I was a visitor with

limited reason to be there. But her attempts at intimidation didn't exactly provide unquestionable credentials for her presence. What if she, too, was a stranger to Brigadoon and simply wanted to know which residents were away, for nefarious reasons of her own?

"Sorry," I said as pleasantly as I could muster. "I'm not at liberty to say."

"That's unacceptable," she shouted so loudly that the walls around us seemed to tremble. Could she be causing an earthquake? This was, after all, Southern California.

But, no, someone turned a corner from what I assumed was the elevator corridor, shoving a mini shopping cart along the brown textured carpeting. It most likely caused the vibration, not Ms. Obnoxious's loud voice. The person holding the handle was a man, maybe mid-forties, with a receding hairline and bulky build. The metal cart held several large sacks. He'd obviously heard the woman's bellow, since he barreled down the hallway toward us.

"Everything all right, Margaret?" he asked as he drew near.

"Not at all, James," she responded. "Wanda Villareal supposedly gave this woman"—she shot her evil eyes toward me—"keys and permission to come in to take care of pets this weekend." She spat out the word "pets" as if she referred to the vilest of animal excretions instead of some innocent creatures who might deposit them.

Which gave me an indication of why she was so nasty.

He glanced quizzically toward me beneath brown brows that dipped sharply at the sides.

"Hi." I put perkiness into my tone. Would he be an ally or an enemy? And why, in this perfectly innocuous situation, should I even have to worry about such things? "I'm Kendra Ballantyne, pet-sitter." I handed him a card, too.

"Good to meet you, Kendra." His smile seemed welcoming, and I relaxed a little. "Wanda has mentioned you. I'm James Jerome. I live down the hall." He gestured in front of him. "Wanda watched my guinea pigs recently, when I went out of town."

Beside me, I saw the woman he'd identified as Margaret shudder a lot more than the hallway had. "Guinea pigs," she repeated with utter scorn. "Pretty soon I'll get enough support from our association board and other residents to ban rodents from our lovely condominiums. What if your creatures ever get out of your unit?" Her face screwed up into such a creepy look of contempt that I considered taking my cell phone from my purse and snapping a picture. I could use it to scare off hawks from my clients' homes to ensure that no small pet was swept away.

A nearby door opened, and a man and woman walked into the hall.

"If you had your way, Margaret Shiler," James said with equal disdain, "you'd have all pets banned from our complex. Pets have been allowed since Brigadoon opened seven years ago. There are rules, and all responsible pet owners follow them. If you didn't like how things were here, you shouldn't have bought a unit."

"Except for allowing animals"—again, that contemptuous tone—"this place is utterly charming. That's why I ran for the board, so I can help fix what's broken here. That damned, antiquated pets-permitted policy—I'll be lobbying even more strongly against it, starting at our next board meeting." She let her eyes bore into mine once more. "And if that bothers your dear friend Wanda, tough luck. The woman is obviously not acting in the association's best interests. Look at how she hands over keys and her responsibility to a total stranger."

Meaning me. I opened my mouth to protest but was immediately interrupted.

"What's going on, Margaret?" This from the woman who'd emerged through the now-closed door. She was tall and slender, with grooves beside her mouth that suggested she scowled a lot.

"We have an unwelcome visitor." Margaret proceeded to introduce me and state my reason for being there.

"She's very welcome," contradicted James, earning a small smile of relief from me. At least I had someone here who wasn't ready to toss me out of one of the nearby windows.

"Ruth is considering running for the next opening on the condo association board," said the other man, who joined us. He gestured toward the woman who had asked about me, presumably Ruth. He had a large, upswept mane of salt-and-pepper hair above squinting blue eyes. "She feels nearly as strongly about pets around here as you do, Margaret."

"That's excellent news, Ruth. And, Teddy, with your background in public relations, I'm sure you can get her elected." For the first time, Margaret acted semi-human and approached Ruth, giving her a small but stiff hug. "Together, we'll fix what's wrong with Brigadoon!"

I half expected an invisible orchestra to start playing

the music indicating the end of act one of whatever drama we were acting out. I glanced at James, who scowled his obvious anger.

"There's nothing wrong with Brigadoon," he said coldly. "And I'm glad you've all given me this heads-up. I'll fight the election of any resident who wants to ban pets. A lot of us love animals. That's one reason many of us chose to buy units here. Nice to meet you, Kendra." He stalked down the hall, pushing his shopping cart in front of him.

Leaving me with the evil three.

Well, hell. Hating me was their problem. I had a reason to be there, and I knew I didn't look like a burglar. I'm in my mid-thirties, reasonably presentable, wearing casual clothes today, sure, but my shoulder-length brown hair was nice enough, and I always wore makeup to enhance the best features of my ordinary but relatively okay face. I was sure I didn't scare them.

Even so, I sighed, then said, "I'm sorry to hear there's such a controversy here, but I've just come to take care of the animals I was assigned." And if I could do anything to help their owners chuck these nasty characters and their hatred of pets out of there, I'd consider it. "Please excuse me."

As I started to turn toward one of the wreathed units—its number was on my list—a scream issued from behind me, causing me to cringe.

It was Margaret. "There's that damned cat again!" she shouted.

I turned once more, and saw a streak of light yellow fur disappear down at the end of the hall. I guessed it was a small ginger cat—no, kitten, considering the size.

I inhaled sharply. Wanda had warned me about a certain little kitty—an indoor, apartment sort not intended to roam outside at all, especially at Brigadoon, which had rules against such activities. Wanda had taken on its care this week. Which made me its weekend guardian.

"That isn't Lady Cuddles, is it?" I asked, glancing again at Margaret. Would someone who clearly hated animals as much as she did even know a cat's name?

When she glared at me and nodded angrily, I cried, "Oh, no!"

Ignoring Margaret and her equally nasty neighbors, I hurried down the hallway in the direction the kitty had dashed.

Chapter Two

LADY CUDDLES WAS every bit as elusive as Wanda had warned. Fortunately, James Jerome assisted me after he saw the kitten run by him. We finally cornered her at the far end of some additional twists in the hall. She'd found a decorative ficus plant and leaped into its upper leaves. As I reached to remove her, she hissed and extended her claws. Her blue metal ID tag, a cute little kitten face attached to a white mesh collar, sparkled as she moved, reflecting the sunlight streaming in through the nearest window.

"Hi, Lady Cuddles," I said soothingly. "We don't know each other, but I'm here to take you home."

"Here." James took off his cotton shirt and handed it to me. "Wrap this around your hands when you reach for her. I have some guinea pig food in my pockets, but it's all vegetarian, and I don't think it'll tempt a cat."

I noticed he didn't offer to attempt to pluck Lady Cuddles off the plant. But the kitten was my responsibility, so I couldn't complain. I did use his shirt as protection, though, as I reached out and retrieved the clearly unhappy little feline from her precarious perch. I expected she'd try harder to claw me in an attempt to get away. Instead, she became absolutely docile in my hands.

"Good girl," I praised, as I hugged her against my chest—clad in a sweatshirt on this Saturday in January, rather than one of the nicer garments I wore on days I both pet-sat and practiced law. I'd be heading to my law office later, but no client meetings were scheduled, so dressing down was de rigueur.

"Mrrrow," responded Lady Cuddles, rubbing her small, fuzzy face against me, her eyes closed in what appeared to be ecstasy.

She definitely lived up to the cuddly part of her name. I hugged her closer, won over by her sweet change of mood.

I unwrapped James's shirt from my hands and handed it back. "Thanks," I said. "And thanks, also, for sticking up for pets' rights against Margaret and friends. Do you really think they could outlaw residents' keeping animals here?" That would be awful for Wanda, who had become chief pet-sitter at the complex since moving in a few months ago. Many condo owners were in the film industry— surprise! Burbank is an adjunct of the Hollywood area— and they often traveled for meetings and movie shoots. That kept my fellow PSCSC member nice and busy, along with clients she'd had before she moved there.

"Not if I can help it," James replied grimly. "A lot of us own pets and, far as I know, we all care for them responsibly. Not too much noise, or droppings not picked up, or anything like that. Margaret'll face a lot of opposition if she tries to change anything. We'd all rather get rid of her than our beloved animals."

"But those other people—"

"The Bertinettis?"

I hadn't heard their last name before. "Ruth and Teddy?"

James nodded, then shrugged. His expression was mildly bemused. "I don't know them well. They moved in about six months ago, and I don't think they have any pets. But the idea of their moving here and wanting to make major changes like that . . ." He scowled. "They can go right back to wherever they came from, if that's their attitude. And I'll do all I can to keep any of them from any position of authority here."

Lady Cuddles wiggled in my arms. "I'd better get her back home," I told James. "I'll let Wanda know everything that went on here this afternoon. She'll probably be in touch with you to help work out a plan to protect pet ownership. If you don't hear from her first, please contact her."

"Thanks, Kendra. I'm glad to have met you." He seemed to really see me for the first time. Did I detect a glimmer of interest? Probably, since his gaze headed toward my left hand, which clutched Lady Cuddles. I wore no ring.

But my emotions were definitely involved with someone else. Someone really outstanding.

I made sure my smile in return was remote. "I'll be interested to hear, from Wanda, what happens around here."

As I suspected, I had to guess at how Lady Cuddles wound up where she'd been. A window in her owners' unit was raised so slightly that I couldn't imagine one of

James's guinea pigs slipping through, let alone a kitten. Of course, a few guinea pigs grow big, so that might not be an appropriate analogy. In any event, Lady Cuddles must be basically boneless to have gotten through there. The window opened onto a balcony several feet from the balcony of the adjoining unit. The building's outer wall was stucco, not entirely smooth but not easy to get kitty claws into for edging along it. Had Lady Cuddles leaped?

I might never know, but I did see a window open next door. Still, how would she have gotten out of that unit and into the hall?

I asked her, before all this surmising made my brain ache. She looked at me with her baby blue eyes, her pointed little ears at attention and her small white whiskers twitching. She was so adorable that I had to hug her again.

I have to admit I'm more of a dog person than a cat lover. My own furkid is a tricolor Cavalier King Charles spaniel named Lexie. The felines I've pet-sat for have been varied in looks and temperament, and tend to be more standoffish than cuddly.

But I really liked Lady Cuddles. Which made me worry about her all the more as I attempted to lock all windows, check every vent, and close off all other potential avenues of escape. Sure, I worried about my liability in the event one of my charges got loose and disappeared, or worse. But I had my clients sign contracts. I wasn't sure Wanda did the same. My insurance should cover both me and my company, Critter TLC, LLC, in the awful event of Lady Cuddles having an exit strategy I couldn't conceive of.

But it was concern, not only potential costs, that

made me double- and triple-check on Lady Cuddles between visits to the rest of the additional Brigadoon units where I tended to other pets on Wanda's behalf.

I didn't need to stop in at Wanda's apartment, though, to care for her pup, Basil, a Cavalier like my Lexie, but of the Blenheim—auburn and white—coloration. Basil was beloved enough to be invited along on the humans' weekend outing.

I returned to Lady Cuddles's abode a final time before I left the Brigadoon complex altogether that day. She was still there, thank heavens. And I was doubly blessed by not running into Margaret Shiler or the Bertinettis again before my departure.

In my car, a blue Ford Escape hybrid, I used my hands-free device to call Wanda as I drove away. I hoped I'd just get her voice mail. I wasn't one for wanting to interrupt a romantic tryst, especially since the male involved was an even dearer friend of mine than the female one.

But Wanda picked up on the second ring. "Hi, Kendra. Everything okay?"

I filled her in on the best parts of my visit to Brigadoon first: how the pets were getting along without her—basically fine.

Then I told her about my run-in with Margaret and her pet-despising buddies. I finished with my concerns about Lady Cuddles. "I did my darnedest to find and close off other possible ways for her to get out, but if you have any suggestions, just let me know and I'll go back."

"Oh, Kendra, I'm so sorry you had to deal with all that." I heard a male mumble somewhere in the background. "Darryl says hi, and thanks, and it's time to hang up." Wanda laughed, then grew serious again. "I don't know what else to tell you about Lady Cuddles's escape routes. And I really, really appreciate this, Kendra. Please do feel free to call if there's anything else I should know." Another mutter from Darryl, and she finished, "As long as it's really important."

"Tell Darryl he owes me, too," I said with a laugh of my own. "Give him a hug for me, and Basil, too." I ended the call.

I went next to visit a longtime client, Stromboli, who also lived in Burbank. Stromboli was a good-natured shepherd mix, and I always enjoyed sitting for him. I especially liked the fact that he was the next-door neighbor of my good friend Maribelle Openheim and her energetic terrier mix, Meph—short for Mephistopheles. Maribelle and I had become buddies after I'd chided her about leaving Meph neglected in his yard while I watched Stromboli. She'd been going through a difficult time in her life, but she'd pulled through fine and now treated Meph like the pampered family member he should be.

Maribelle wasn't home this afternoon, though, so I spent a significant amount of time playing with Stromboli after feeding him.

I decided to head next to North Hollywood, not far from Burbank. There, I stopped at a modest house and used a key to get in. I went immediately to the living room and looked into the huge double-sided aquarium that occupied its center.

"Hi, Py," I crooned to the beautiful ball python that resided inside. Pythagoras was a stunning glossy blue, patterned all over with beautiful magenta swirls. He'd gotten a little larger than when I'd first met him some time ago, but he remained utterly tame.

At least I thought so. I didn't take him from his tank much now when his owner, Milt Abadim, wasn't around—although when I'd first cared for him, I had carried him around with me now and then.

Today, I did the standard cleanup and care that Milt liked me to do. Unfortunately, that involved feeding Py a mouse. Fortunately, Py was used to eating frozen rodents that Milt bought in bulk. I defrosted one first, then made certain that the microwaved mouse wasn't too hot for Py to handle.

I placed it in his habitat, watched Py happily slither toward it, then turned away. I didn't enjoy watching. But a while later, when I turned back, there was a bulge in Py that hadn't been there before.

"See you tomorrow," I told him, then left.

More stops, to see pups who required two visits a day, including a couple at Brigadoon, plus a last check to ensure that Lady Cuddles was where she belonged.

Finally, my pet-sitting ended. Time to go pick up my own adored pup, Lexie, who'd been pampered for the day at Darryl's place, Doggy Indulgence Day Resort.

I LOVE DOGGY Indulgence. It's even open on weekends, mostly to accommodate customers who work in the entertainment industry, so I'd happily brought Lexie there on this Saturday while I was tending to other pets at their homes.

Even more important, Lexie likes it, too. She plays with other pups there when she wants to, sleeps in the area filled with people furniture when she doesn't.

She always dashes over, from wherever she is, to greet me.

That day, I walked into the facility filled with pups, interspersed with staff members. I headed for the desk at the front of the mostly open main room, but didn't see Lexie at first.

I didn't see her at second, either.

Puzzled, I approached the nearest staff member. Unfortunately, it was Kiki, the employee I liked least. The blue-eyed bombshell was a wannabe actress—who in L.A. isn't? The good thing about her was that she was great with dogs, gushing over them as if she adored them all.

The bad thing about her was that she was awful with people.

"Hi," I said, pasting on a perky smile. "Where's Lexie?"

She shrugged skinny shoulders beneath her lacy shirt. "Oh, I'm sure she's around somewhere." Her glance over my shoulder suggested she really didn't give a damn. Had she stopped caring for her canine charges? If so, why was she still employed?

"Yes, but where?" I asked slowly, as if talking to someone who didn't understand the language.

"Ask Darryl. Or his dear Wanda. Your friend, isn't she?" Kiki started to walk away. "It was so nice of you to introduce them."

"They're not here," I reminded her through gritted teeth.

"What a surprise," she tossed back. "That means we can't talk to either of them."

Every muscle within me tensed up. Oh, how I wished Darryl was there!

Of course, if he was there, Kiki wouldn't dare be this offensive to a client.

I blocked her path. "Let's find Lexie, right now," I said as calmly as I could. Inside, I was really worried. It wasn't like Lexie to ignore me this way.

"Oops," Kiki said, "I think I'm needed in the kitchen." She slithered away from me even slicker than Py did, and headed for that part of Doggy Indulgence.

What was that all about?

Speculation about Kiki's feelings for Darryl suddenly shot through me. Did she have a crush on him? Was his tryst with another woman—whom he had met thanks to me—making Kiki even crazier than usual?

But she hadn't seemed that attached to him before. She'd even teased me about the ID of Darryl's new main squeeze when he'd first taken up with Wanda.

Who knew what stick had slid up Kiki's spine now?

And most important, where was Lexie?

I hurried to one of the other attendants, an older lady named Lila who wore a Doggy Indulgence green knit shirt like the one Darryl usually wore. Her ample curves made it look substantially different from the way it looked on Darryl's skinny bod. I asked, "Have you seen—?"

"Lexie? Sure, Kendra. She was in the kitchen last time I saw her. And . . . well, I heard that scene with Kiki. She's . . . well, it's not my business, but I think she needs a talking-to by Darryl when he gets back. She's been acting really weird, like her hormones are out of kilter or whatever."

"Whatever." I hurried to the kitchen, but it was empty of anyone—dog or person—other than Kiki, who stood staring out the window over the sink. She seemed aware of me when I walked in, and glanced up, giving me a nasty, yet somehow smug, glare.

Did she know where Lexie was?

Had she harmed her?

My panic increased. "Where's Lexie?" I demanded again.

"Like I said, she's around somewhere," Kiki said. "Maybe she interfered with some other dog and got snapped at." She smiled remotely, barely budging the smoothness of her overly made-up face.

I felt certain that cryptic remark was intended to tell me something, but I had no time to figure out what it meant. I hurried back to the main room. "Lexie!" I shouted.

A few of the other dogs—a Yorkie, a Lab mix, and a pit bull—dashed over as if to let me know of something amiss.

"Where is she?" I asked them.

But none of them answered.

Neither did any of the human attendants.

"Lexie!" I wailed. "Where are you?"

Chapter Three

To MY RELIEF, I heard an answering bark. But from where? I stared all around the pine-patterned linoleum floor from one large playroom zone to the next. No Lexie. I inhaled deeply, as if I could scent her over the usual disinfectant smell. But as much as I adore dogs, I don't share their acuity of senses.

I called her again, listening carefully for her location.

Sure enough, the smart pup barked back once more. From the direction of Darryl's office? That seemed odd. I knew he kept it locked when he wasn't around.

But there were multiple reasons why it might not be locked. He'd forgotten. He'd given someone a key. He'd hidden a key that someone had found.

Or someone with no right to be there had broken in.

At least I no longer felt like following my first instinct, which had ordered me to call the guy most important in my life at the moment—Dante DeFrancisco. The megamillionaire was powerful as well as sexy, but there wasn't a damned thing he could have done to fix this for me, even if I'd wanted him to.

Except be there for me . . . Only, he was out of town.

"Over there!" Lila pointed unnecessarily in the direction I was heading. I seemed to have turned into the Pied Piper, in fact, since canines and staff members all were following me.

I got to the door of the office that jutted into one side of the playroom and tried it. The knob turned. And as I pushed the door open, Lexie leaped out. She danced on her hind legs as we were finally reunited. I knelt to throw my arms around her and let her lick my face. Other doggies joined us on the floor, and I petted as many as possible, then laughingly stood up.

I glanced at the beaming human faces around us.

"Anyone have any idea how she got in there?" I asked with a smile intended to be disarming and relieved, not accusatory. But no one admitted to knowing anything.

I saw Kiki near the big front desk, greeting an owner who'd come in to retrieve his pet. That was part of her job. But she was definitely not expressing the joy and relief that the other staff members showered over Lexie and me.

When she shot a gaze in our direction, she did smile, at least. Only . . . from that distance, it seemed more snide than joyous.

Had she done this on purpose to make me squirm, in retaliation for whatever harm I'd allegedly done her by bringing Darryl and Wanda together? Or had she just snapped altogether?

Just in case, I'd have to watch out for Kiki.

A LITTLE WHILE later, Lexie and I were in my Escape, heading home. I had her blocked in the backseat for her safety, but I glanced often into the rearview mirror, reassuring myself that she was there and okay.

It hadn't really been a big deal, after all. All along, Lexie had been where she was supposed to be—kinda. But I still felt utterly frazzled.

"I don't suppose you'd explain, in Barklish, exactly how you wound up in the office, would you?" I asked when we stopped at a red light. "Like, who opened the door, why you headed in there, and who shut you inside?"

My Cavalier just sat there looking cute, keeping it all to herself.

"Was it Kiki, on purpose, with a key she'd stolen somehow?" I sounded as if I was playing a game of Clue.

Still no response from Lexie, so I gave up.

We soon headed up the narrow, twisty road in the Hollywood Hills that led to the lovely mini chateau I'd bought several years back when I was a high-paid associate at a major law firm. I adore that place.

Lexie and I live in the apartment over the garage. I'd been renting out the main house for a while, ever since I lost my lucrative job because of being unjustly accused of an ethics violation. I'd cleared myself, but by then I was supporting Lexie and me by pet-sitting. And once

I got my law license back, I kept up my new career and also became a partner at a small elder-law firm started by another escapee from my former employer, a senior attorney named Borden Yurick. I brought in some pet-law cases of my own, too. But I didn't make as much money.

Even so, I loved what I did now—most of it. Because my friends, acquaintances, and I have the unfortunate habit of being in the wrong place at the wrong time, I'd also found myself in the middle of a lot of murder investigations, sometimes as the accused. And it seemed like an inordinate number of people I knew also became suspects in murders. Having been there myself once—twice, actually—I invariably assisted them. Even Dante, whom I'd recently helped to clear from a nasty situation that had partly resulted from his secret past . . .

But being a murder magnet wasn't an avocation I'd chosen. If it never happened again, I'd be more than happy.

I stopped the Escape at the gate in the wrought-iron fence enclosing my property and pushed the button on the visor that opened it. As I drove in, I saw my tenant, Russ Preesinger, on the walkway that crossed the well-mowed lawn between the main house and the driveway. With him was his sweet Irish setter, Beggar—short for Begorrah.

Russ's daughter, Rachel, is my employee and assistant at Critter TLC, LLC. She is also a hostess on *Animal Auditions*, a TV reality show I'd helped to create, which was produced by Dante. It was between seasons now, though the next one was well into its planning stage.

At this moment, Rachel was on rounds visiting the Critter TLC, LLC, clients that I'd assigned to her for the day.

I parked in my spot beside the garage. The inside spaces were for my tenants. When I opened the driver's side door, Lexie leaped over the seat and dashed out, running toward Beggar.

I followed, but much more slowly. The two dogs started cavorting in a game of canine tag.

"Hi, Russ," I called.

Russ, a Hollywood location scout, was usually on the road, so I saw him infrequently. He had dark reddish hair, similar in shade to his setter's, and was a good-looking guy. At the moment, he was clad in a knit shirt as green as his eyes and snug blue jeans, and he looked up from studying some papers in his hands. "Kendra! Good to see you."

"Do you have some pictures there of film locations?" I asked, nodding toward the pages.

He looked abashed as those paper-filled hands of his suddenly drooped to his sides. "No," he said. "It's—I've been wanting to talk to you, Kendra."

My heart had been happy about this day's homecoming, as always. But now it shriveled and slowed. Those words, and that tone, boded something bad, I was sure.

I pointed toward the steps beside the garage that led up to my apartment. "Should I sit down?"

His laugh didn't sound especially jovial. "Not necessarily. But . . . well, I'm thinking of ending my lease here."

Talk about my heart sinking. The Preesingers were my best tenants. Of course, they were only the second ones I'd had here. And I still remained friends with their predecessor, Charlotte LaVerne, a noted reality show star and advisor on *Animal Auditions*.

"Mad at the landlady for some reason?" Joking was better than crying.

"Not at all." He reached over and squeezed my upper arm. "You know better. We both—Rachel and I—love you." I knew he meant that platonically. He and I had never meshed that way. "But my job is changing somewhat, and I'm going to be in town more. I figured this is a good time for me to buy a house here in L.A. I'll certainly help you look for another tenant, if you'd like."

Would I like that? Maybe. I certainly couldn't keep my beloved mansion without having a tenant to help with the mortgage, even though I'd recently refinanced it at a lower interest rate.

Yet I wished I could afford to move into the main house again. My home-sweet-garage was certainly adequate, but I hadn't originally bought the place with living in the maid's quarters in mind.

I wasn't going to achieve moving into the mansion by juggling part-time lawyering and pet-sitting, though.

And though Dante would undoubtedly buy the place if I asked, and let me live there, I didn't want to be obligated to him that way. It would smack too much of a serious commitment—something I doubted I was ready for.

"Sure," I said brightly. "Get the word out to your friends in the film industry about this place becoming available . . . any idea when?"

"It'll be a while, I'm sure." His green eyes filled with soulfulness. "I'll want to find the right place for

Rachel and me first, and then it'll take time to close the transaction and move."

Of course Rachel would be moving, too. I really liked the young lady. I'd gotten to know her well, and found her a bright and caring pet-sitting assistant, as well as a somewhat traditional Hollywood wannabe who was now developing her own small niche as a reality show hostess. Both of those vocations were partly thanks to me. But I wouldn't hold that, or anything else, over her. Or her dad.

"It's been great living here, Kendra," Russ said. "And we'll definitely stay in close touch."

"Of course." I stepped forward and gave him a hug.

Then I called Lexie. I wanted to go inside my apartment and mull all this over. Maybe have a glass of wine to cry into.

But as we got to the top of the stairs and I put my key into the lock, my cell phone rang. I pulled it out of my purse as Lexie sat on the doorstep, eagerly waiting to be let inside.

It was Wanda calling. I propped my phone under my chin as I finished opening the door. "Hi," I said. "How—"

She interrupted immediately, sounding frantic. "Kendra, I don't know what's going on at Brigadoon, but I think you instigated a firestorm."

Chapter Four

"WHAT DO YOU mean?" I asked. I hadn't instigated anything at Brigadoon besides a hunt for an elusive kitten. I stepped into my apartment, checked to see that Lexie was there, too, then closed the door behind me.

"I've gotten phone messages from both Margaret Shiler—the bitch—and James Jerome. Margaret's all pissed off that I gave a stranger—you—free access to our condos and blames it on the fact that Brigadoon allows pets. She'd already started campaigning against our liberal pet policy, and now she thinks she has an issue to hang it on. You didn't steal anything, did you?"

This last was said lightly, but it wasn't such a good thing that I was still standing in my small entry, since my foot ached after I stamped the tile. Limping slightly, I walked into my compact living room and sat on one end of my beige sectional sofa.

"No," I finally said, "I haven't added thieving to my

multiple vocations. Although I might consider assault—like aiming a good swift kick at Margaret's door when I'm there tomorrow morning." Especially if she was standing there. If my foot stopped aching. "You might have warned me about her, like you did about Lady Cuddles's elusiveness."

"I was hoping you wouldn't run into her. Fortunately, I don't see her often. But she seems to be getting worse."

Another thought occurred to me. "I assume you still want me to take care of the animals there tomorrow."

For Darryl's sake, and hers, I hoped they weren't ending their weekend abruptly and heading back on Sunday.

I also hoped I'd avoid seeing Margaret and her pet-hating pals, the Bertinettis, on my upcoming visits.

"Of course. James's message was a warning about Margaret and the others, so I'll call him back and see if he'll be around tomorrow. Maybe he can hang with you and head off any claims that you're uninvited and up to no good."

"That would be great," I said in relief. "He seemed a nice enough fellow."

"Did he introduce you to his guinea pigs?" Wanda asked.

"No, but I'd love to meet them. Go ahead and check with him, and if it's okay, let me have his phone number. I'll coordinate my comings and goings there with him."

"Sounds good." I heard the inevitable murmur from the background. "Darryl says you should stop making trouble."

"Fine with me," I responded. "And why don't you go shut him up with a big kiss?"

"Soon as I return James's call."

I laughed as I hung up. I made a quick dinner for Lexie and me—hers, a gourmet combo of special kibble interspersed with luscious-looking canned beef canine food, and mine a less exciting frozen dinner, along with a small, pre-made salad. When we were both done, it was time to head outside for her evening constitutional.

The new year had begun only a few days ago, and it got dark early now. I turned on the yard lights, then put Lexie's leash on her. We'd take a short walk, and then I'd let her burn up any excess energy by romping in the yard.

As I followed her down the steps, my cell phone rang again. I'd stuffed it into my jeans pocket, and had to move the tail of my hoodie out of the way to get to it.

When I looked at the caller ID, I couldn't keep the grin off my face.

Dante.

"Hi," I said.

"Hi, back. How's L.A. tonight?"

He was on a business trip to Denver, attending the grand opening of yet another HotPets pet supply store, the most successful such chain in the country. The world. Maybe the universe, if people on other planets had pets.

"It got cold here today," I said. "Sweatshirts and light jackets all around. How's Denver?"

"If I'd worn just a sweatshirt or light jacket, I'd probably be standing outside the store encased in ice."

I laughed. "How did the opening go?"

"Crowded. The freebies didn't hurt."

"I bet."

"And you? How was your pet-sitting?"

"Very interesting. I'll tell you about it when you get back."

"Which gives me a reason to make it as fast as possible." I heard the teasing note in his tone. But he wasn't scheduled to return for another few days.

"Sounds good to me," I said. "How's Wagner?" Wagner was Dante's German shepherd, who'd stayed at home during his master's recent travels. No, I didn't pet-sit for him. Dante's personal assistant at his Malibu house was at Wagner's bark and call.

"He's fine. Do you and Lexie want to see him the evening I get back?" That was shorthand for, "Do you want to spend the night?"

"We'd love to." I glanced down at my Cavalier, who was patiently waiting at my feet. "Right now, though, Lexie needs her evening walk. So . . ."

"Good night, Kendra," Dante said softly. "I miss you."

"Ditto," I whispered hoarsely, wondering if he was going to end this conversation with the L word. But he didn't, and I certainly didn't.

But I'd told him so before. And I was feeling it more every day, with or without his being around. I was even considering the possibility of forever.

With my history of unhappy relationships, was I simply deluding myself?

BY THE TIME I got to Brigadoon the next day, Margaret and her cronies had been busy. I saw some signs in the lobby of the back building, after James let me in. I still had the keys Wanda had given to me, but I was glad to be under James's auspices as I did the morning's pet-sitting rounds.

"I'm really offended by that," I said.

I pointed to a colorful poster on the door to the stairway that said, "Hate the smell? The noise? The unsanitary conditions? Come to the next meeting of the Brigadoon Board of Directors to hear a proposal to restrict pet ownership."

In the center was a photo of pet feces—most likely a dog's, since it took up the entire center of a stair. A genuine picture, or staged? Probably didn't matter to those here who hated pets.

"You're not the only one," James said. "As a board member, I get all kinds of e-mail correspondence from our residents, and people are up in arms about this argument." He wore a gold-colored sweatshirt on this chilly January day that seemed to bulk him up even more than the clothing he'd worn yesterday. It had a pair of cute and perky guinea pigs in its center. "I've contacted all the people I know here who have pets. I want to be sure they come to this meeting, too. It promises to get ugly."

Fortunately, it would be on the upcoming Thursday. Wanda would be home. Far as I knew, she wasn't on this board. She remained active on our pet-sitter organization's, though, and helped to manage it, so she probably didn't have time to deal with squabbles among condo residents.

But I felt certain she'd want to be at this meeting—especially if she intended to keep up her pet-sitting practice at Brigadoon.

My first visit that day was to the unit belonging to Trudy and Jamiel Gustin—of course. They were the people who owned the cunning and slippery little Lady Cuddles.

Fortunately, said ginger kitty was right where she belonged. She greeted me at the door, let me pick her up, and started purring in my arms. I cleaned her litter box, fed her, played with her a bit since she seemed amenable. I walked the perimeter of the apartment and checked all windows, vents, and other potential avenues that might allow her to get outside.

Then, breathing a sigh of relief, I headed into the hall, where James waited for me, talking on his cell phone. "Hey!" he cried, pointing at a ginger streak fleeing down the hallway.

The small scamp had slid past me as I'd exited the door!

This time, I caught up with her soon after I rounded the first corner—mostly because she wasn't alone in the corridor. Margaret Shiler stood there speaking with her pet-hating ally Teddy Bertinetti, and both had their arms crossed belligerently as they stared at the innocent-appearing kitty.

"What's that creature doing out here?" Margaret demanded. "And why are you back, Ms. Ballantyne? Didn't I make it clear yesterday that intruders aren't welcome?" Today, she had traded her knit top for a sweatshirt, too—and she must just have had it made. It had the same feces photo in the center, with a big red line through it.

"She's my guest today," said James, coming up behind me. "And that kitten's an escape artist. She got out of the Gustins' place accidentally, and we're about to take her home. Let's go, Kendra." He paused as I scooped up a fortunately unprotesting Lady Cuddles.

"Oh, by the way—I've been in contact with the other board members and a lot of residents, too. Don't think you'll have an easy fight on your hands. We're all clear that the right to keep pets is grandfathered in. It was in the rules from the time this condo complex was built. You won't be able to change that."

"Oh, but we can try." Teddy ran a hand through his upswept graying hair and shot a look I couldn't interpret at Margaret.

"In any event, we'll get the rules amended to be a lot more restrictive while we're fighting the rest of it out." Margaret seemed mightily pleased with herself, especially when Teddy aimed a conspiratorial smile at her.

"Let's talk about it, shall we?" said Teddy. They were standing outside his unit, which had a wreath on its door that was made of dried-out plants. He motioned to Margaret to follow. "Ruth's inside, too, and she'll be anxious to help." He reached into his jeans pocket and pulled out a key. After an unsuccessful attempt to open the door, he located another key in his pocket and this time got the door open.

I was absolutely glad of a couple of things as I trotted Lady Cuddles back to her abode. Number one: I didn't live at Brigadoon.

Number two: I'd hate to be in the fight Wanda was certain to have later in the week.

I HAD ONE more round of visits to Brigadoon on Monday morning, since Wanda and Darryl were due back a little later. I wasn't certain what James's job was, but he wasn't available. I held my breath as much as possible on my rounds, but fortunately didn't see Margaret or the Bertinettis.

And, hallelujah! Lady Cuddles didn't exercise her amazing escape abilities.

When I was finished, I went home to pick up Lexie. My next stop was at Doggy Indulgence to hand keys back to Wanda. Plus, I'd leave Lexie. I figured half a day there was better than none—especially now that Darryl would be back. I'd worry less about Kiki's odd behavior of apparently hiding Lexie from me.

As soon as I entered Doggy Indulgence, Wanda exited Darryl's office and thanked me. She was a petite person who favored flowing, gauzy tops, even when the weather grew chillier. Today's was soft blue.

"I take it you haven't been home yet," I said to her as Darryl joined us by the big front desk. Lexie was already cavorting with some of her canine friends, including her Cavalier friend, Basil.

"No, but I've gotten even more of an earful from James. We're in the middle of a war, I'm afraid. And as always, the ones who could suffer most are the innocents—the animals this time, if the pet lovers don't unite and fight off this stupidity." As sweet as Wanda had always struck me, her expression had turned utterly angry and unyielding.

"You could always just sell your condo," Darryl said softly. "Not put yourself through all this." My lanky, long-term friend was regarding his significant other with obvious concern.

When Wanda aimed her gaze up into his, I could see the love radiating there, and I figured she had a standing invitation to move into Darryl's Studio City house not far from here. Sweet. Yet I felt another reaction, too. Envy?

No, more like fear. I could be in a similar situation with Dante, if I wanted to go to the next level. Maybe. Maybe not.

In any event, I left them looking at each other. I left Lexie playing with Basil.

I also left Kiki, who'd finally appeared, glowering at all of us until I caught her gaze. Then, she turned her expression into absolute innocence.

I simply nodded a greeting—and a warning—to her, and departed.

THE NEXT FEW days were relatively painless. I did my regular pet-sitting rounds mornings and evenings, with my assistant Rachel's help.

She acknowledged that she and her father were looking for a new place, and reassured me that it wouldn't change anything between us.

Except that she wouldn't be as easily accessible for meetings mornings and evenings, when I was at home. But we would work something out.

I hoped.

My days passed smoothly at my law firm, Yurick & Associates.

I talked to Dante at least once a day. Sometimes more.

I missed him.

Finally, it was Thursday evening. I thought about calling Wanda to send along my moral support, but decided I'd wait to hear from her about the condo board meeting.

Which I did, at about ten o'clock. "It was awful, Kendra," she exclaimed as I sat on my living room sofa with my phone to my ear. "The pet lovers outnumber the haters, but the people who want to change the rules are a terrible bunch. Loud. Angry. They were especially upset that we dared to take down their awful posters of pet feces. I'm so afraid of what might happen to our ability to keep pets, especially if we get a board vacancy any time soon. That bitch Ruth Bertinetti has made it clear she's running for the next seat. Whenever that is, I'll need to find someone on our side to oppose her. And—" Her sudden stop was so dramatic that I waited eagerly to hear the rest. "We want to hire your legal services, Kendra. Those of us who intend to keep the pet policy as it is. I'll talk over the particulars with you, if you're interested."

"Sure," I said. "Of course I can't guarantee results." Nor could I guarantee to myself that I'd enjoy this new matter much. Not with emotions running so high. But at least I'd be representing the right side.

I had a court appearance on an elder-law situation the next day, a Friday, so I couldn't get together with Wanda and her compatriots then. We decided to hold the first law conference with pro-pet people as an unofficial gathering in her condo on Sunday, and set up a time.

"Give Basil a big hug for me," I said as we got ready to hang up. "And Darryl, too, of course. By the way, are Lady Cuddles's owners back in town yet?"

"Not for another week."

"Then . . . have you had better luck keeping her at home than I had?"

"So far. Keep your fingers crossed for me."

As it turned out, I'm not sure that having all of my fingers crossed on Wanda's behalf would have worked to prevent what happened.

That Friday night, I was happily preparing to go to the airport to pick up Dante—yes, he could have had a chauffeur or other employee do it, but I'd wanted to see him first thing—when . . .

I got a call from Wanda.

"Kendra!" she wailed as I answered.

"What's wrong?"

"It's so awful . . . Lady Cuddles wasn't in her apartment when I got there, so I started looking around for her. I knocked on the nearest doors, and the one to Margaret Shiler's unit opened when I touched it. I thought I heard a mew, so I went in and . . . Oh, Kendra, I found Lady Cuddles, but Margaret was at home, too. On the floor. And she's dead!"

Chapter Five

OKAY, IT COULD have been a heart attack. Something simple. Natural.

But, murder magnet that I am, I felt certain it was something a lot more insidious.

"What happened to her?" I asked Wanda, leaning on my living room wall while Lexie observed me intently, her sweet head cocked so one long ear neared the carpeted floor.

"I'm not sure, but she's all bloody." Wanda's voice shook. "I called 911 and Darryl before phoning you."

"Good call. Do you—" I hesitated to ask. "Would you like me to come there to be with you?" Before she could answer, I interjected, "Problem is, though, that I'm on my way to pick up Dante at the airport." I wasn't about to abandon him there, or even arrange an alternate form of transportation. I'd promised to be there for him, and that was what I'd do.

Afterward, though . . . Well, my preference would

have been spending the whole night with Dante. But if I could somehow help a friend with my presence . . .

"Oh, yes, Kendra, please come here. I don't know what's going to happen when the police arrive, but you have lots of experience with such things."

I definitely did, much to my dismay. "Tell you what," I said. "I'll call you after I get Dante, and you can let me know for sure if it makes sense for me to come."

DANTE'S FLIGHT WAS right on time. Of course it would be. No one would dare to delay Dante DeFrancisco— even when he flew in a commercial airliner instead of his private jet. First class, naturally.

In any event, I waited at a fast food restaurant for his call. I'd left Lexie at home, alone. One way or another, I'd wind up back at my digs that night. Preferably with Dante. His assistant would still be caring for Wagner, so one more night away from home should be okay. I hoped.

When my cell phone rang, I immediately answered it. "I've landed," he said. "Can't wait to see you. I checked a bag, so I'll call you again once I have it in hand."

Ten minutes later, I heard from him. Five minutes after that, I drove my Escape up to the area outside baggage claim for the airline Dante had taken, and pulled over when I saw him standing there.

I parked fast, pushed the button to open the rear compartment so he could throw his luggage in, then darted from the car. In moments, I was in his arms. Damn, but his embrace felt welcome! It was as if we'd been separated for months instead of a week.

I really had it bad for this guy.

"I missed you, Kendra." He gave me one heck of a passionate kiss. I returned it and raised him one. Although he'd been stabbed several months ago because of a murder situation we'd been involved in, he'd healed well and always encouraged me to hug him hard.

But standing there necking all night wasn't advisable, especially since the airport police would want me to move on.

"Hold that thought," I said, and he smiled before heading for the Escape's passenger seat.

It was all I could do to drive instead of staring at this gorgeous example of maleness. Dante's hair was dark and wavy, and his smile drew sexual shudders from me all over. And the way his dark eyes smoldered . . . well, I knew he, too, hoped we'd spend the night together.

Only . . .

"You won't believe what happened tonight."

"Another murder?" he responded immediately, and not exactly with enthusiasm.

"How did you guess?"

"Your voice takes on a certain excited tone when you get involved in something like that."

"I'm not involved, but—"

"Then why did you bring it up?" Uncharacteristically, he sounded a tad irritated. Was it because his own imagined night of passion had fizzled into a puff of murderous smoke? I certainly hoped that night had only been delayed.

Or maybe his painful memories of the last murder had stabbed at the surface of his mind.

In any event, I briefly explained the gist of Wanda's

call to me. Then I filled him in on my less-than-pleasant experiences with the victim, Margaret Shiler.

"I told Wanda I'd call her after I picked you up, so she could tell me what was going on, and if she wanted me to come there. If so, I'll be glad to drop you off at your place first"—although it would be way out of the way, and time-consuming—"but I'd love your company and insight." And presence. And the possibility of still having a few glorious hours of making up for lost travel time. If we were still on speaking terms, of course.

"Go ahead and call her, then we'll see."

I reached Wanda immediately. "It's awful here, Kendra," she said softly. "Darryl's come and he's really great, but some of the other residents, especially those nasty Bertinettis, have told the detectives about how I was arguing with Margaret. And since I was the one to find her . . . Oh, by the way, I kept Lady Cuddles in Margaret's unit rather than taking her home, since I didn't want to move anything pending the murder investigation. That was right, wasn't it?"

I assured her that it was. "How did she get there?"

"I've no idea how she escaped her apartment this time, but I assume she got into Margaret's because the door was ajar."

"Have you been interviewed by any detectives?" I asked her.

"Detective Candace Melamed of the Burbank Police Department talked to me. She acted so . . . well, accusatory. As if I had something to do with Margaret's death."

I'd had sufficient run-ins with police detectives to empathize a lot with Wanda.

"So . . . Well, I've picked up Dante. Do—"

"Then you're free to come here now? Please, Kendra. It would make me feel so much better."

I aimed an inquisitive glance toward Dante. His sensuous lips were now curled up into a sardonic smile. "Go to it, babe," he said, shaking his head wryly. "I'll come along for extra moral support. Or immoral, as the case may be."

BRIGADOON WAS IN an absolute uproar.

"You sure they'll even let you in?" Dante asked as we waited outside the security gate after calling Wanda to let her know of our arrival.

"No, but—There." The gate opened before us, and I drove in. I parked near the entrance in the first space I found, since most other areas were filled with cop cars with flashing lights. Then there were the media vans with their satellite dishes on top. Was my longtime media contact and sometimes friend Corina Carey among them? I had no idea.

I also had no ID that would easily get me to Wanda's. I'd occasionally acted as an apprentice private investigator when looking into murders in which my friends were involved—or in which I was—but that had worked out best when I was dating a P.I. My old flame Jeff Hubbard and I had reached a parting of romantic ways a while back, after he had thought me capable of some pretty ugly stuff during an investigation that concerned him. We were still friends, but I wasn't exactly his apprentice—or anything else—anymore.

Without something more than my wish to visit a friend, I suspected it wouldn't be easy to get through

this throng of cops and condo residents, but I gamely
called Wanda nonetheless.

"Oh, you can come up, Kendra," she informed me. "I
told everybody that my lawyer was on the way."

"But—" I began.

"I didn't say you were representing me in this case,"
she said hurriedly. "I know you're not a criminal lawyer. And I'm hoping I don't need a criminal lawyer.
But—"

Lots of buts were being belted out around here. "I'll
try playing the lawyer card and seeing how far it gets
me," I told her. "And Dante. He's now my assistant." I
looked up at his handsome face, and he had the grace
to wink at me. I grinned.

After explaining several times who we were, we
managed to get to Wanda's unit. It had the same con-
figuration as several I'd visited while caring for pets last
weekend, but Wanda had made it her own with gauzy
draperies at the windows that resembled the tops she
favored, in colors that coordinated with the sofa and
chairs.

I immediately bent down and hugged Basil. The
poor Cavalier was clearly confused by all the people
and noise. At least Wanda's place was on a different
floor from Margaret's unit—the second. Same building, though.

Darryl was there, too. My long, lanky friend had a
thunderous expression on his face. He was usually so
mild-mannered that it would have startled me if I didn't
know the reason behind it.

He loved Wanda. Wanda was involved in a murder
case because she had discovered the body. Plus, she'd
been in a pet-related verbal altercation with the victim.

Ergo, she could be in trouble. And Darryl didn't want to see her there.

"Please get her out of this, Kendra," Darryl said to me first thing. "Fast."

"I can't make any promises," I said. "You know that. But I'll give her any help I can."

"Good. Thanks." His tone had gone from sharp to bleak.

I opened my mouth to ask what he was thinking when a loud knock sounded on the apartment door. Wanda looked through the peephole, then pulled the door open.

"Hi," she said sorrowfully to the throng of people who stood there. "Come on in." There were probably too many, but a few obeyed her request. "These are some of our residents," she explained to me, and started rattling off names I wouldn't remember.

But before she got very far, Ruth Bertinetti burst through the crowd to face Wanda. "I know you had a bone to pick with Margaret about her wanting to fix the antiquated pet policy here," she said. "But you didn't need to kill her, you bitch!"

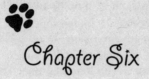

Chapter Six

I HEARD BASIL barking his contradiction from behind a closed door. For an instant, his voice was the only sound in the room.

Then Dante said, in a tone dripping ice, "Time for you to leave, lady."

Ruth shot him a look that started out scornful, then turned uneasy as she noticed the fury on his face. And an angry-looking Dante is a scary thing, even when he is dressed casually and not in a situation where he is clearly in charge.

I knew that. I had, on occasion, been on the receiving end.

"I didn't kill her," Wanda wailed. Darryl put his arm protectively around her, and she seemed to recoup her resilience. "You have a hell of a lot of nerve accusing me, Ruth, just because we're on opposite sides of an important issue around here."

"Well, poor Margaret argued directly with you about it." Ruth Bertinetti was a tall woman, and she seemed to attempt to gain height with her anger, standing straighter with her hands on her hips.

"If I kill people that I argue with," Wanda said coldly, "then I'd suggest you watch your back."

Ruth appeared shocked by that rejoinder. So was I, in fact. Wanda had always seemed like a fairly reasonable person.

But emotions can make people say strange things. I felt certain that no matter what ill feelings there'd been between Wanda and Margaret, my pet-sitting pal wouldn't have killed Margaret.

Even so, some of the residents who'd come into the unit murmured to one another uneasily. A few sidled toward the exit. Some shot irritated looks in the direction of Basil's unyielding barks in support of his owner.

Wanda apparently realized the impression she might have made. Her face was as green as the pale, flowing top she wore, a shade lighter than Darryl's Doggy Indulgence shirt, as she attempted to improve it with a smile. "You know I'm just joking," she said to no one in particular.

"Of course you are," Darryl stated staunchly. "And you've every reason to get angry about such unfounded accusations. Right, Kendra?"

His gaze bored into me over his wire-rims, as if he was attempting to control my response. I didn't quite see my easygoing best bud in that look, but I of course understood why he was so upset.

The woman he loved had been accused of murder.

And even could have done it . . . although I didn't

think she had. Dante, too, acknowledged how upset Darryl obviously was. He stood beside me and stared back at Darryl with a look not yet menacing but that suggested it could get threatening if my friend didn't back off a bit.

The crowd nearing the door stopped suddenly, the stream of people parting. I saw why in a second. A couple of uniformed Burbank cops were swimming upstream into their midst.

When they got inside, the older, chubbier one demanded, "What are you doing here, everyone? You were told to stay in your own apartments until our investigation here is through. Have you all been interviewed?"

From the responses, it sounded as if most hadn't been.

"We were all friends of Margaret's, Officer," Ruth Bertinetti said softly, as if in explanation. "We thought it appropriate to show some unity on her behalf."

If these folks were all friends of Margaret's, and therefore against the possibility that pets' rights would be maintained at Brigadoon, then Wanda's ability to keep Basil here and maintain her pet-sitting operation were definitely in danger.

But that still didn't mean she'd have cut down the most vocal opponent of pets in desperation. Did it?

Besides, I counted the members of the crowd. There were only twelve people, though they felt like more in such close quarters. Even so, that meant that only a maximum of a dozen apartments containing occupants who were potentially pro-Margaret were represented here. And although he'd remained silent, Teddy Bertinetti was among them.

"Go back where you were told to stay," said the other

cop, who looked younger but sounded more authoritative. Everyone except the Bertinettis bailed out of Wanda's unit.

Teddy Bertinetti finally found his voice. "Whether you killed Margaret or not, we're going to carry on with what she started. And for now, unless you get your mutt to be quiet, we're going to tell the remaining board members to fine you."

"But we won't do it," said a voice from the doorway. James Jerome edged into the room, saw the cops, and stopped. "I was on my way back to my unit when I heard the anti-pet people grumbling as they left here, and thought I should offer my support. It's no wonder that Basil's been barking, with all the commotion around here. No fines for you or for him."

"Go on to your apartment, sir," said the more officious officer.

"Okay, but don't worry, Wanda," James called over his shoulder. "Pets still rule here at Brigadoon."

Wanda's apartment wasn't in the mainstream of Brigadoon, yet it seemed like a whole lot of people were seeking her out—including these cops.

I saw why they were there a minute later, after I'd gone to comfort Basil and returned to the living room with him in my arms.

A woman in a dark suit stood there. A local police detective?

She confirmed it in an instant. "I'm Detective Candace Melamed of the Burbank Police Department," she said, slipping a badge from her pocket. She was the one Wanda had mentioned before. "Please identify yourselves and state what you're doing here."

"These are my friends, Detective," Wanda said

defensively. "Darryl Nestler is my boyfriend, Kendra Ballantyne is a lawyer and a friend, and Dante DeFrancisco is—"

"The owner of HotPets? Very good to meet you, sir." The detective suddenly looked impressed, but only for a second. She was a woman of moderate height, with glasses and a slick, short haircut. "But I'm afraid you're possibly interfering in a police investigation. Do you own a unit here?"

"Just visiting," Dante said mildly. "Offering moral support to our friend Wanda. It's a terrible thing she's gone through—finding the body of an apparent murder victim that way."

"Are you her attorney?" the detective asked me.

"I'm not currently representing her," I replied. "Is the situation such that she requires counsel?" Okay, I was sounding like a lawyer—intentionally. Not that I was dressed like one this evening. I'd donned an outfit intended to seduce Dante—snug black sweater over attractive charcoal slacks—and, since the January evening was chilly, I'd tossed a zippered sweatshirt over it. A shocking pink one.

"That is entirely up to her." Detective Melamed's blue-eyed gaze narrowing cunningly. "She's not being taken into custody at the moment, if that's what you're asking. Whether she'll be deemed a person of interest in this case hasn't yet been decided."

Translation: Wanda could indeed be considered a suspect, if not at the moment, then imminently— maybe.

"Well, then, I'm cautioning her not to answer any more questions than she already has, not without her attorney present. Since my specialty is not criminal law, I'll refer her to someone who can help her."

"But I didn't do anything!" Wanda wailed yet again.

"That doesn't always stop the police from suspecting someone perfectly innocent," I cautioned, earning another glare from Detective Melamed.

"Please leave these premises," she insisted, "all of you except Ms. Villareal."

Wanda immediately turned and clung to Darryl. "I need for him to be with me," she cried. I noticed some scratches on her arm as her gauzy sleeves slid up. Lady Cuddles's work?

The detective eyed Darryl up and down, then turned to Dante and me. "That will be all right for now," she said, "if Mr. DeFrancisco and Ms.—Valentine, was it?—leave."

"Ballantyne," I corrected, believing she had intentionally mangled my name. "And yes, we'll go as long as Darryl can stay. But once again, Wanda—"

"Yes, I won't answer any more questions until I have a lawyer with me. Do you know someone I can hire?"

"I do indeed," I said.

AS DANTE AND I headed for my Escape in the outer area of the condo parking lot, we ignored all media cries for attention. No Corina Carey, my main media contact, so ignoring them was easy. When the January sun rose later, the temperature would warm, but for now it remained chilly for California. I zipped up my sweatshirt again.

Fortunately, since it was very early morning, the parking lot was well lighted. Pulling my cell phone from my purse, I called my good friend Esther Ickes, a lawyer whose expertise included criminal law. In fact, I recommended Esther to all my friends who needed criminal counsel.

She'd been there to help me when I'd been in that awful situation myself.

"Another one, Kendra?" she asked immediately. "If I gave you a commission on all your referrals, you might get as rich as your guy friend—not that my clients pay that well, you understand. I assume Dante's still in your life?"

I glanced beside me and beamed briefly. "For now. Anyway, I'll give Wanda your contact information. And—well, as always, thanks, Esther."

I quickly called Wanda and gave her Esther's info.

"She's the one you always recommend?" she asked.

"Absolutely. She's great."

"Good. I'll call her right away."

We reached my Escape and I pressed the button on my key ring to unlock the doors. But as we started to get inside, Darryl came dashing up.

"Is Wanda okay?" I inquired anxiously.

My long, lanky friend drooped dejectedly. "She changed her mind. Decided she'd be better off alone for now, facing this, than having me around worrying about her."

"Oh," I said. "I'm so sorry about all this, Darryl." What I meant, of course, was that I regretted that my good friends were in the middle of such a mess.

But Darryl seemed to take it a different way. "I figured you would be. But gee, Kendra, couldn't you have, just this once . . . ? Never mind."

I stood utterly still as I saw Dante edge around the back of the Escape to watch us. "Do you think I somehow brought this on Wanda? You know better."

He didn't meet my eyes, but instead stared at the ground through his wire-rims. "It's not that. Not really. But—"

"But what?"

"But everyone you know who's not murdered becomes a suspect in a killing. Even I was somewhat of a suspect once—enough that I had to hire one of your lawyer friends."

That had been Martin Skull, another good criminal lawyer of my acquaintance. But fortunately the police vibes against Darryl hadn't reverberated very deeply.

"I don't understand it, either," I told my longtime best bud sadly. "You know that. And I'm going to do everything I can to ensure that Wanda is cleared of all suspicion. I promise. And you also know that, as awful as it's been for me to be a murder magnet, I've always been able to determine, and acquire evidence against, the genuinely guilty party."

An expression I interpreted as anguish distorted dear Darryl's face. His puppy-dog eyes looked utterly sad as he said, "You said that like a lawyer, Kendra."

"I *am* a lawyer."

"I know. It's okay. Sorry I said anything." He pivoted on his heel and walked off.

I simply stood there for a minute, watching him move farther away—and not just in distance.

Only when Dante took me into his arms did I realize that I had tears in my eyes.

I INSISTED ON driving my car anyway. It gave me something to concentrate on as I attempted to adjust my mood to something less than miserable.

After all, the man I might actually love was still at my side, in the passenger seat. And he'd been a suspect in a couple of my murder situations lately, one more so than the other—the one that had resulted in his being stabbed.

"I know it's late, but will you take me to my house tonight, Kendra?" he asked as I pulled onto one of the major Burbank streets.

"Sure," I said, attempting to sound perky.

"And will you stay there with me?"

"Sure," I said again, this time definitely more enthusiastically. "As long as we can stop at my place to pick up Lexie." Which we did.

The drive to Dante's Malibu house did, in fact, help to lift my mood. He spoke lightly of the latest HotPets to open, the one in Colorado.

"We held the usual parade of pets, where we encourage people who live around the new store to bring in whatever kind of animal they love best. We had mostly dogs, of course, but you'd enjoy the fact that a couple of people brought their potbellied pigs. And there, ferrets are legal as pets, so we had a bunch of them, too—in cages."

I'd of course told Dante of my own experiences with ferrets when the first tenants at my home had kept them as pets even though that was illegal in California. At that time, I was trying to keep my record spotless since I was attempting to get my law license back after those spurious allegations of ethics violations. And those cute but criminal ferrets had also been involved in a murder . . .

I started to relax as we neared Malibu. Dante's home was high in the mountains overlooking the Pacific. Despite the darkness along the twisting road that led to his abode, I easily found the opening in the tall hedge that edged his lot, and punched in the code on the mounted key pad to open the gate. Then I drove up the driveway to the circular part at the entry to his lovely stone mansion.

"Just park here for tonight," he said. He got his suitcase from the back of the Escape as I let the leashed Lexie wander around a little to take care of her final eliminations for the night.

When we went inside, Wagner, Dante's sweet and smart German shepherd, was there to greet us. Lexie and he were good buddies, and they immediately exchanged sniffs and wags.

I smiled and yawned as I watched them, then let Dante lead me upstairs.

To his bedroom.

And, yes, I did have some articles there for my nighttime ablutions. As well as a change of clothes. Which had freaked me out when Dante had first suggested it. But, hey, it made sense since I came here often.

Dante and I were soon ensconced in his delightfully decorated bedroom, with its firm, comfortable bed that had a regal, red plush headboard. The dogs were on special beds, too—from HotPets, of course—at the side of the room.

Sure, I was exhausted. But before Dante crawled under the covers with me, I couldn't help glimpsing his bare, sexy bod, including the slight scar from his stabbing . . . and, well, I woke up just enough to indulge.

And then I slept like the proverbial log, nestled in Dante's protective embrace. Somehow, his presence helped to ward off my sadness about Wanda's situation and Darryl's reaction—at least long enough to let me doze deeply.

The dogs' stirring woke us in the morning. I immediately stood, ready—prime pet-sitter that I am—to take them outside.

"Just open the door," Dante said drowsily. "Alfonse will put them out."

"Sure." I guess I wasn't awake enough to immediately think of that. Then again, I didn't have a full-time personal assistant staying in my small apartment. "But I'd better get dressed. I've got my morning pet-sitting rounds to start on." And they were many miles away, in the San Fernando Valley.

"Why don't you just move in here, Kendra?" Dante asked softly.

Though halfway out of bed, I stopped moving. "Can't," I said airily, as if my heart hadn't stopped. "Like I said, I have pet-sitting to do."

"But if you were—"

"And lawyering. My office is in Encino. This is just too far a commute." I kept my tone both light and firm. Moving in together was just too much of a commitment—wasn't it?

Besides, what I was saying was the truth. Even if I decided to go the next step with Dante—a big if—I wasn't about to give up all that was important to me, like my double career. And this was L.A., land of lots of traffic. I didn't want to get sucked into an awful commute.

But the next thought that passed through my mind was the fact that my tenants, the Preesingers, were soon moving out. What if Dante took over my house payments as rent . . . and we both moved in there?

Nah. I simply wasn't ready for that. I didn't even bring it up, although it kept sloshing through my mind as I showered.

When I returned to the bedroom, the dogs were back. And Dante was on a cell phone. *My* cell phone.

"It's Darryl," he said, handing the phone to me. I gathered that it had rung while still buried in my purse. Seemed a bit forward for Dante to have dug for it, but surely our relationship had gotten that far, at least.

"Hi, Darryl," I said eagerly. Had he reconsidered the way we left off yesterday, decided to call me so we could kiss and make up?

"I thought you'd want to know," he said in a sad voice. "The cops have called Wanda. They want her to come to the Burbank police station today for further questioning. She's called the lawyer you recommended." He paused. "That's all. 'Bye, Kendra."

And then he hung up.

Chapter Seven

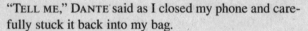

"TELL ME," DANTE said as I closed my phone and carefully stuck it back into my bag.

I attempted to keep my voice calm as I said, "Darryl just thought I should know that Wanda's being questioned further today about Margaret's murder."

"And he blamed you for it again." It wasn't a question emanating from Dante's frowning mouth, but a statement.

"Not overtly. He's too kind for that. But I'm sure it's what he was thinking." Still in a terry bathrobe I'd left there, I headed for Dante's huge closet, where I'd find stuff to change into for the day. It was across the bedroom, which was a good thing, since I didn't want him to see me in tears again over this awful turn of events.

I was suddenly in his strong arms. "This is just one situation too many, Kendra," he said softly. "I know it hurts you to have Darryl acting this way, overtly or not. And I know you've promised to help. Let *me* help *you*.

Please. I'd like to see you stay out of this, so you don't get hurt in other ways, too. I'll get Brody involved. You know he's good at investigations."

Brody Avilla was a longtime friend of Dante's. They'd been in covert government operations together years back, a fact which, unsurprisingly, they'd both hidden. I'd learned about it while investigating—yes, another murder.

"He's a star now," I reminded Dante unnecessarily. "Plus he's busy getting ready for the next season of *Animal Auditions*." He had replaced its murdered judge last season—and I had been involved with solving that homicide as well.

"I'll help any way you say," Dante said. He held my damp face in his big, warm hands, and his magnificent mahogany eyes bore deeply into mine. "I'll even hire Jeff Hubbard to investigate."

Which was a huge concession and sacrifice. Since Jeff was my ex–significant other, no love was lost between the two men.

"Just, please, Kendra, don't get involved with this one."

"Too late," I said as lightly as I could, reaching into my robe's pocket for a tissue which I used to dry my face. "You know I'm involved, Dante. I really appreciate your offer. And I really wish this murder magnet stuff would stop. But it hasn't yet. And you can help me just by being a shoulder for me to lean on if I need it. Okay?"

"Well—"

I leaned forward and gave him one long, hot kiss on his incredibly sexy lips.

"You win," he eventually said as our embrace eased

a little. "But just be careful, Kendra. And keep me up on everything you're doing, so I can help, if possible."

"I will," I whispered. "And thanks."

We finished dressing and adjourned to the kitchen to eat the light breakfast that Alfonse had prepared for us. Alfonse, as always, stayed in the background—a fiftyish guy dressed in casual clothes, definitely more a personal assistant than a butler, but always deferential.

The dogs dined at the same time—again, thanks to Alfonse's ministrations.

"Hey," Dante said as he slathered raspberry jam on thick wheat toast, "I know how I can tempt you to join me tomorrow."

"How's that?" I inquired with interest.

"Lauren Vancouver is helping with a pet adoption event in your area—the Valley—tomorrow afternoon. I promised to be there with some HotPets stuff as prizes. Care to attend?"

I'd met Lauren Vancouver during a legal issue she'd had recently. She ran HotRescues, the pet rescue organization funded by—who else?—Dante.

"That sounds like fun," I said, taking a sip of deliciously rich coffee. "Count me in."

LEXIE AND I left Dante's digs soon afterward, hustling to the San Fernando Valley so we could start our pet-sitting schedule for that Saturday. Fortunately, since it wasn't a weekday, traffic was relatively light.

On the way, along twisty Malibu Canyon Road, I called Wanda. She was due to drop in at the Burbank Police Department that day, but I didn't know what time. She wouldn't answer her phone there, but I could leave a message making it clear I cared what happened to her—Darryl's innuendos notwithstanding. Not that I'd mention them to poor Wanda.

But she did answer. "Oh, Kendra, I'm so nervous. I already like your friend Esther, by the way. She called and got the cops to agree that we didn't have to come in till this afternoon. She's visiting my place first so she can see what Brigadoon condos are like, which might help her represent me."

"I agree." I wished I could be at that conclave, too. But that could make what was said susceptible to discovery, since I wasn't actually representing Wanda, and I would jeopardize attorney-client privilege.

"I've finished my morning rounds of pet-sitting," Wanda continued. "That adorable, dratted Lady Cuddles did it again, by the way. I had to chase her down at a balcony on the other side of her family's building. At least she didn't scratch me this time."

"Wish we knew what's on her mind when she wanders. In fact, I wish there was an equivalent of Barklish, the language I'd like to use to communicate with canines—for cats. Kittylish, Meowlish, whatever. It would sure help us figure out what really happened to Margaret, since you found Lady Cuddles in her unit."

"Yes," Wanda replied with a sigh. "The poor kitty seemed curious, and freaked out, too. She must have seen exactly what happened. There were little bloody paw prints in the kitchen, where I found Margaret's body."

"She was stabbed, then?" I realized that I hadn't even asked before how Margaret had met her demise.

"Skewered," Wanda said, and suddenly sounded as if she were gagging. "She had a grill outside on her balcony, and I gathered she liked to make kabobs. The spit . . ."

"I get it," I said, not wanting to hear any more. The picture in my imagination was awful enough. "And Lady Cuddles was right there?"

"At some point, though when I found her, she was elsewhere in the apartment. Fortunately, she hadn't gotten out then—for more reasons than one. With all her Houdini-like escapes, I'm glad she has an ID tag on her little collar, but yesterday she wasn't wearing a collar. I went to the nearest HotPets when I had a chance, and bought her a new collar and name tag."

"Of course it was HotPets," I said with a smile. I wondered, though, what had happened to that cute little kitty ID tag I'd noticed on her.

"Where else?"

I'd reached the Valley end of the road and aimed my Escape onto the Ventura Freeway, heading south, according to the sign. Actually, it was east, but that particular freeway was labeled oddly.

"Gotta run, Kendra," Wanda said. "My landline just rang. Esther must be at the gate."

"Let me know what happens," I told her.

"I sure will."

My next call was to my now-buddy Detective Ned Noralles of the LAPD. The great-looking African American cop certainly wouldn't be investigating this homicide case in the separate small city of Burbank, but he'd been involved in a lot of the other murders I'd solved—sometimes irritating the heck out of him. He'd also assisted me in dealing with cops in other jurisdictions, when necessary now and then.

Best of all, I'd recently helped to clear him and his sister from being possible murder suspects, so we were now sort of friends.

"Hi, Ned," I said as he answered immediately. "Guess what."

"Another one?" I heard the groan he didn't stick into his voice.

"Unfortunately." I described the situation, then said, "My friend Wanda found the body. I think the Burbank cops suspect her. Could you check into it? If you'd let me know anything you're permitted to say under police protocol that could help her—or could help me find out who really did it—I'd definitely appreciate it."

"And I'd appreciate it if you'd butt out for a change, but I'm not even going to ask this time, Kendra. I know better."

"Thanks, Ned." I hung up.

I held a one-sided conversation with Lexie as we drove to our first pet-sitting destination of the day, the northern Valley, where Beauty, the lovely golden retriever, lived. "It may be a better situation than I'm anticipating," I told my Cavalier, "but if the Burbank cops want Wanda to come in for interrogation, they must genuinely suspect her. I'd better figure out which other people might have had it in for Margaret."

I glanced in the rearview mirror. Lexie sat on the Escape's backseat, cocking her head as she listened. I smiled.

"I'll drop you off after my rounds this morning," I told her. "Then I'll visit Brigadoon while Wanda's gone. Maybe James Jerome will be willing to chat with me, right?"

Lexie's tongue slipped out of her mouth in an affirmative pant.

● ● ●

OF COURSE I didn't hurry while handling my pet-sitting responsibilities. Animals whose owners are out of town need extra attention and adoration. I spent time with each baby, getting Lexie's assistance where possible by her playing with my canine charges. I left her locked in my Escape, parked in a safe, observable place in the shade. At least January in L.A. is comfortably cool.

Back in my car, I jotted everything I did into the journal I keep. I'm also a listaphile. A listaholic. While I sat there in Lexie's company, I also jotted down a list of questions I wanted to get answered about Margaret Shiler: who she was and why she died.

When I was finally finished with the morning's sitting, I drove Lexie home and called James Jerome.

Fortunately, he was home. Even more fortunately, he was willing to talk to me.

I headed back to Brigadoon—ignoring the little voice in my brain that kept reminding me that Dante might be a bit peeved. He knew I was leaping into yet another murder investigation without availing myself of any of the ideas he had offered to pay for to keep me safely out of it. I appreciated his concern. Even understood it, after his having been stabbed.

But despite what I'd told him, I wasn't about to inform him each time I made a move.

Sure, I'd rather give up my murder magnet status as soon as possible. As if I could control it!

James pushed whatever buttons were necessary to get me through the Brigadoon gate, since I no longer had a key card because I wasn't pet-sitting on Wanda's behalf. I went back to the area where I'd first met Margaret, mostly because James's unit was on the same floor where Margaret and I had argued. Unsurprisingly, his third-floor apartment looked much like the rest I'd seen. The biggest difference was that he had several large cages containing the cutest guinea pigs I'd ever seen. Of course, I hadn't pet-sat for that particular kind of pig before, only potbellies. And guinea pigs are absolutely more rodentlike. These were fluffy and rotund, and had the most adorable little floppy ears. And twitchy little noses surrounded by whiskers.

James had half a dozen of them, all in shades of black and brown, and most with white stripes.

After I'd oohed and aahed over his cavy children— that was an alternate name for guinea pigs, he told me—he got me a glass of diet soda and we sat at his kitchen table to talk.

Unlike most of the units I'd seen at Brigadoon, which tended to be decorated as if their owners were attempting to outdo each other in decor, James stuck to utilitarian furnishings. His fridge was old, white, and battered. His table and chairs could have been rescued from his childhood. The sofa I'd seen in his living room, where some of his cavy cages were kept, had big sags in its cushions. Maybe James had spent all his funds to acquire the unit and hadn't had anything left for attractive furniture, or maybe his pets were really his only priority.

"What would you like me to tell you, Kendra?" he asked. Since we were indoors, he wore a T-shirt instead of the sweatshirt I'd seen him in before; it, too, had representations of guinea pigs in its center. He was a large enough guy that he quite filled the shirt. His droopy brows made him seem almost maudlin, but I doubted he mourned Margaret. "I honestly didn't know Margaret very well," he confirmed, "and what I knew about her, I didn't like. Not"—he held up his pudgy hands—"that I disliked her enough to kill her, you understand."

"I figured." Not that he'd admit it to me if he had. I had to keep him on my list for now as I investigated on Wanda's behalf, but I hoped it wasn't him. "But I'd like to help Wanda," I said, "and I want to hear anything useful you might know about Margaret and her friends. And if you know of any enemies she might have had."

"Not really." He knitted his fuzzy brows nearly together. "Of course there are a lot of us who are pro-pet here and didn't like Margaret's attitude. I'll give you a list of others, but I don't see any of them hating her enough to hurt her. A few of us have gotten together to talk about what happened to her, though, and we've some suspicions of our own."

"Such as . . . ?"

"Well, a couple of people mentioned that she had an ex-husband she'd been arguing with. His name's Paulino—Paulino Shiler."

I pulled a notepad from my large purse and jotted that down. No need to act anything but real in front of James. He knew the reason for my inquiries.

"Any idea why they argued?"

He shrugged hefty shoulders. "Who wouldn't, with Margaret?"

"Good point. So, do you know anyone else who might have disliked her?"

"Dislike might be too strong a word, but there's a guy a lot of people around here hire to remodel their units who's got a dispute going with her for payment, I think. Name's Rutley Harris. Margaret started a campaign to keep him from working for anyone else around here. Claimed he didn't finish on time and did a lousy job."

Something like that could provide a motive for murder—especially if this Rutley guy's lucrative gig of remodels around there was jeopardized. I noted his name as well.

"Those are all the people I'm aware of now," James said, "but I'll continue to ask around, let you know if I hear of anyone else. I like Wanda, and her pet-sitting around here has won the hearts of those of us who love our animals."

"Thanks, James. Before I leave, can I take another peek at your guinea pigs?"

"Absolutely!" His grin was huge.

And I was certain that Wanda had a contingent of supporters here who'd help figure out who'd offed Margaret.

Now, if I could only solve the situation soon . . .

I wished that I dared to let Darryl know what I was up to. But there was no guarantee I'd figure it out.

And our cherished friendship might be jeopardized in any event.

I got James to accompany me through the Brigadoon hallways before I left. "Seen Lady Cuddles anywhere around here today?" I asked.

"That cute cat? No. Is she loose again?"

"I hope not." We walked past the door to her abode. No sign of her.

Which was a good thing. I felt fairly sure she wouldn't tell me what she'd seen the night Margaret died, even if I ran into her.

Too bad. I needed all the help I could get.

Chapter Eight

I CALLED DANTE later in the day, just to say hello. Only, he didn't answer his cell phone. I left a message, feeling a smidgen hopeful about getting together that evening. It was, after all, Saturday night, traditional date night. Not that we were dating traditionally. Even so, I wouldn't have minded spending some time with him.

Didn't happen. He returned my call eventually—nearly eleven that night, when I'd already showered and was preparing for bed, Lexie lolling on the floor at my feet. Too early for Dante to have gotten in from a date with someone else—wasn't it?

And why was I acting like a swooning, sorrowful teen with a crush? At least I kept it inside.

Besides, he was the one in this sorta relationship who kept asserting his feelings for me.

But did he mean what he said?

And I was agonizing too much over this as he was talking.

"So you'll just meet me there, right, Kendra?"

Oops. I hadn't exactly been listening. "Where is it, again?" Like, what were you talking about?

"The small park at the corner of Moorpark and Laurel Canyon." At least his tone remained neutral. "Lauren is bringing some of the dogs and cats from HotRescues that she hopes to rehome."

Oh, yeah. The pet adoption event I'd promised to attend tomorrow.

"Sure, I'll meet you there. What time?"

This time he sounded a bit peeved. "Nine a.m. is when I'll arrive, but as I said, I know you'll be later than that because of your pet-sitting."

"Right. I'll get there as soon as I can." I paused, then said softly, "Good night, Dante. See you tomorrow."

"Yeah," he said, his tone again calm and, perhaps, a touch sad. "I'll be thinking of you, and wishing we were together like last night."

Me, too. But I didn't ask him why we weren't, why he didn't even return my call till so late.

Not that we had any right to keep tabs on each other, of course.

I didn't sleep well that night. Lexie lay in bed with me, a privilege I didn't always give her. But as much as we snuggled, I still missed Dante's arms and lips and sexy bod. And how he used them all.

I felt somewhat groggy when I woke in the morning, so I showered again. Wanted to be wide awake to take care of my pet-sitting charges, of course. They deserved my absolute attention.

I visited the dogs first, as I often did, since they were most likely to be waiting for someone to take them outside to accomplish their morning duties. That meant visits to Beauty, Stromboli, and a couple more. Too early on a Sunday to check in on Stromboli's neighbors, my friend Maribelle Openheim and her pup, Meph. Next I took on the kitties, which once more meant Abra and Cadabra, Harold Reddingham's elusive cats. He was one of my best customers, and had just left town again.

His Siamese and tabby felines didn't greet me at the door of his North Hollywood home that day. Sometimes they did, and often they didn't. But their elusiveness on this Sunday reminded me of Lady Cuddles. Was Wanda's mind on her pet-sitting enough to keep track of all her charges, including this escape-artist kitten?

And what had Lady Cuddles actually seen the day Margaret Shiler was killed? A lot, most likely. She'd had blood on her little paws, according to Wanda. Had the cops checked its DNA? And had it all oozed from Margaret? Some could have come from Wanda's scratches, which might be why she remained a suspect.

One more stop before heading to the pet adoption affair. I went to Milt Abadim's home to check in on amazing Py, the python. All was well there, and I fortunately didn't owe him a mouse that morning.

Finally, I was free enough to head toward the Studio City pet adoption event—and meet up with Dante.

The area was already full of people when I arrived, all of them meandering around the many enclosures containing dogs and cats who needed homes. The canines and felines were separated, and the kitties mostly remained in cages, poor things—although the crates were roomy and attractive enough to have come from HotPets. But the pet rescuers undoubtedly understood the escape artist nature of cats. Their enclosures had to have ceilings so they wouldn't climb out and flee.

Not so the dogs, though. They were mostly confined in open-air pens, although in some instances they were leashed and strolled about the environs with happy volunteers who extolled their adoption-ready virtues to all people wandering around.

I immediately recognized Efram Kiley, the twenty-something muscular man who'd sued HotRescues, its director, Lauren, and even its deep pockets, Dante, a while back. He'd claimed that his dog had been rehomed by the organization without an adequate attempt to find its owner. Thing was, Lauren had believed that the Jack Russell terrier mix had been abused in its prior home—Efram's. I had, of course, come up with an ADR solution—which most attorneys thought of as alternative dispute resolution, but for me was animal dispute resolution. Efram received an exorbitant settlement, funded by Dante, as long as he also volunteered a lot at HotRescues—thus ensuring that he learned not to be abusive to animals.

Efram was apparently following through with his commitment. Today, he was shepherding a German shepherd mix among the potential adoption crowd.

I smiled, happy I'd been able to help. I scanned the rest of the throng, and my gaze landed on a long table where Lauren Vancouver sat, speaking with someone across from her. Behind her stood Dante, surrounded by boxes and apparently putting together the bags of stuff to give away to adopters, courtesy of HotPets. Which meant *him*.

I hurried in that direction. The person sitting across the table from Lauren was an older lady who cradled what appeared to be a shih tzu mix in her arms—small, fluffy, but with a slightly longer nose than normal for a purebred of the breed.

"I'll take little Harvey, here, to the vet tomorrow to check his health," the lady was saying. "I'll bring him back to you if there are any problems." But the way she hugged the little guy suggested she never wanted to let go, which made me grin sappily.

"Fine," Lauren told her. "We have a vet on call, and all our animals are screened and well cared for, but if you find any problems, we'd much rather know about them than not. In fact, we'll be in touch anyway. We'll want to follow up on how Harvey and you get along."

Which also hummed along my heartstrings.

But I recognized this reminder for what it was. At these adoption events, there was only a limited ability to check out a possible adopter. Forms were filled out, but people could lie.

It wasn't done by all shelters, but Dante had described what he required of HotRescues. Lauren or a staff member would visit to ensure that the home environment described was in fact a reality. And that the new owner cared for the animal at least adequately. Better yet, lovingly.

I didn't know Lauren well, despite having represented her in a lawsuit. She was an attractive lady, probably mid-forties. She had green eyes and wore her dark hair clipped short in a becoming bob. The only thing I disliked about her was that she was thinner than me.

The lady rose from her chair. Dante darted around Lauren to hand her what appeared to be a brand-new leash and a large bag with the HotPets logo on it that brimmed with goodies.

"Enjoy your new pet," he said. "Thanks a lot for giving him a home. And take good care of him." He came around the table and looked little Harvey in his big, brown eyes. "And you, fellow—you take good care of your new mama."

The older woman laughed, snapped on the leash, and put her new baby, prancing, onto the grassy ground.

Dante then looked directly at me. I knew he'd noticed me before. Not that he'd done anything differently, but . . . well, I guess I was starting to have a sixth sense where he was concerned. I couldn't read his mind, of course—darn it. Or maybe it was simply wishful thinking on my part that I did feel a connection with the guy.

Even if he frustrated the heck out of me with his frequent lack of disclosure. Like what had he really been up to last night?

"Hi, Kendra," he said in a voice so soft and sexy that I wished like heck we'd been alone. "Glad you could make it."

"Me, too." I was in his arms in a moment, and the recipient of a wonderful but quick little kiss. We were, after all, in public.

I then gave my greetings to Lauren, who was smiling sassily. "Good to see you, Kendra," she said. "But don't expect any kisses from me."

"Glad to hear it," I responded.

"Walk with me, though. I want to see if I can find a particular person and dog who stopped here before. You wearing your lawyer hat?"

I reached up to my hatless head and ran fingers through my hair. "Always," I said. "Right on top of my pet-sitting one."

She laughed, and motioned one of the volunteers who hovered near the table to take her place. "I'll be around," she told the young woman. "Find me as soon as the next person interested in adopting comes over."

We walked through the throng of people, prospective pets, and everyone else meandering in the park.

"I take it that Efram Kiley's doing what he's supposed to?" I made it a question, even though I'd already seen the guy.

"I think so, although . . ." Her voice trailed off, and then she said, "There they are." She pointed to our right and dashed in that direction. I could only follow, though I wasn't especially happy to leave Dante's side. But, hey, the park wasn't very large. I'd see him again soon.

The person to whom Lauren brought me was a kinda homely woman walking an adorable French bulldog on a leash. The dog appeared to be purebred, and the lady's own puggish nose and round cheeks reminded me that people were often said to choose pets that resembled them.

"Here's the lawyer I told you about," Lauren told the lady. "But no guarantees she'll agree to represent you. I'd better get back to the HotRescues table." She left us alone—if you could consider being together in a crowd this size being alone.

"What seems to be the problem?" I asked, wondering if I should simply walk away.

But the woman looked so forlorn that I had to at least listen to her.

"It's about Pierre, here," she said. "I bought him from a breeder with a great reputation a few months ago. She made me sign a contract, but I didn't think much about it. I know that's standard when you buy a dog with the credentials Pierre has. But . . . well, she's now insisting on enforcing some stuff in it that isn't in his best interests. Or mine. And I don't know what to do. Can you help me?"

A potentially interesting dilemma. But this wasn't the time or place to decide. I reached into my big bag and pulled out my business cards. I plucked a lawyer one from the pile and handed it to her. "Call me this week, and you can come to my office to discuss it. And your name is . . . ?"

"Joan Fieldmann." She looked at my card. "Thank you so much, Ms. Ballantyne. I'll definitely be in touch."

I hadn't committed myself to anything but a meeting. But I had a sneaking suspicion that I'd just had my first brief conversation with a new client.

I HUNG OUT in the park a while longer, watching with fascination and delight as several more orphaned pups found new homes—thanks, sometimes, to Lauren's strolling around and extolling not only the doggies' virtues, but how well the new potential owner seemed to fit with the canine he or she was assessing.

"She's really something," I said to Dante as I put some samples of dog foods into one of his HotPets bags. Yes, I'd allowed him to recruit me for the assignment.

He nodded. "She does a good job." He looked down at me. "I missed you last night."

Then where were you earlier? Hell, no reason I couldn't inquire. "I spent a quiet evening at home with Lexie. We missed Wagner and you, too. I'd hoped to hear from you earlier." I looked straight into those deep, dark eyes of his and asked, "Where were you?"

He laughed. "You could have asked before. I had a feeling you were tiptoeing around it. And in case you're wondering, I was, in fact, with another woman."

I froze, my insides suddenly squeezed with such anguish that I could have sunk to the solid ground. Or screamed.

Instead, I shrugged. "Okay." But that word didn't sound as offhand as I'd intended.

"Her name is Flossie Murray. Remember her?"

I relaxed so fast that I nearly did fall to my knees. Better yet, throw myself into his arms.

"The manager of the Long Beach HotPets, right?" She'd once been married to a man who'd been a judge on the pet reality show I'd gotten involved with, *Animal Auditions*—and who also had been murdered.

He nodded. "She's been doing such a good job that I'm bringing her into the office for a more responsible position. We're both busy enough that finding the right time to talk about it meant some odd hours, but everything is settled now."

"That's great!" I said brightly, not really caring if my relief was obvious.

He smiled, then grew serious. "Just in case you're wondering, there's no other woman on my agenda for any kind of romantic relationship, Kendra. You're the one for me, even if you don't accept that yet."

I swallowed, unsure what to say . . . and I was saved by the bell. My cell phone's, that is.

"I'm—sorry. Just a second." I looked deeply into his eyes as I answered, and got way lost in them. So much that I stumbled over my hello, and didn't really pay attention to the caller ID.

"Hi, Kendra, it's Wanda," said a familiar yet strained

voice. "I did okay at the police station today, I think. Esther said to say hi. And Darryl—well, could Dante and you meet us for dinner tonight, after we're both done pet-sitting? I'd like to keep you informed about what's going on."

Chapter Nine

I DIDN'T GET the sense, from Wanda's invitation, that she'd been cleared of suspicion. Her voice had sounded somewhat sad and resigned, and not especially relieved.

Which meant, for her sake and my own—hopefully to strengthen my fraying friendship with Darryl—I needed to keep my nose in this nasty situation. With luck, I'd find the real killer, in case the cops continued to look in the wrong direction, toward Wanda.

I soon left Dante in the park with Lauren and the others, after getting his agreement to meet for dinner. The adoption fair would soon be over, and he had promised to help return the pets who hadn't found a new home to Lauren's excellent shelter. It was a good environment, and no-kill, of course, but could never top getting a dog or cat a loving family of its own.

I had several suspects to contact, thanks to James Jerome. I doubted, on this Sunday, that I'd be able to reach the condo's contractor especially fast, so I instead opted to attempt to locate Margaret's ex-husband for a quick conversation.

All I knew about him was that his name was Paulino Shiler. And there I was in my car without handy access to a computer. Yes, Dante had an excellent smart phone, but I hadn't graduated yet from cell phone to one of those miraculous gadgets that lets you access the world with your fingertips.

I could call Althea Alton, the amazing computer whiz at Hubbard Security, but this was, after all, a Sunday, and she probably was playing with her grandkids instead of her keyboard. Besides, that might mean I'd need to get special dispensation from her boss, Jeff Hubbard, my former lover. So what if Dante had suggested hiring Jeff to do the investigation I was now getting embroiled in? It could become awkward.

No, it was better, for now, that I not head in that direction.

If I instead headed home to work on my computer, I might run out of time for any follow-up conversation with Mr. Shiler, in the event I found him. So . . .

I pulled into a shopping center parking lot and stopped. One interesting avenue came to mind. I pressed in the number for my sometimes friend and always interesting media contact, Corina Carey. We'd scratched each other's backs often in murder investigations. I had a feeling she would have the info I needed right at her fingertips.

"Hi, Kendra," she said as she answered, indicating my name had come up on her caller ID. Hers had come up on mine as well. Our acquaintanceship had evolved into something I'd never have anticipated when we first met. Why would I have assumed I'd become near-buddies with a brash tabloid-type reporter?

"Hi, Corina." We went through the formalities—me, asking about her cute puli, ZsaZsa, and her asking about Lexie . . . and whether I was still seeing Dante. I sidestepped the latter inquiry and asked, "Are you looking into the Margaret Shiler murder at the Brigadoon condo complex?"

"I wasn't at first, but I am now. It sounds interesting, though no one of particular notoriety seems to be involved . . . true?"

"That's right, but I happen to be helping a fellow pet-sitter there, so I'm sort of involved. Do you know anything about any of the suspects?"

She paused, and I assumed she checked either her computer or smart phone. "I gather that your friend is Wanda Villareal?"

"Yes," I said. "And I'm sure she's innocent, which means—"

"Well, the next obvious suspect would be the ex-husband."

I nearly cheered, since he was the one I was calling about. "Maybe. In fact, I was hoping to have a talk with him. Do you have any contact info for him?"

"Sure do—but it comes with a price."

"Keeping you informed, and giving you an exclusive if I come up with anything interesting." I said all that in a singsong chant, retrieving it from my memory bank as among Corina's most usual conditions.

"You got it." She gave me Paulino Shiler's phone number and address, and I jotted them in one of the notebooks I carried in my car.

"Any idea what he does for a living?"

Another pause. "It appears that he and his ex were accountants for competing major firms. Maybe that's why they split up."

"Or they joined competitors after they split," I surmised.

"Maybe. That's something else you can find out and let me know about. Oh, and, Kendra?"

"Yes?" I waited for the next axe to fall.

"Keep me in the loop, especially if you come up with any other suspects. And you can be sure I'll be in touch with you often. By the way, have you heard of any witnesses I might be able to interview?"

"How does a small escape-artist kitten sound to you?"

She laughed. "That's more up your alley cat than mine. But if it meows anything of interest to you, let me know."

My next call, unsurprisingly, was to Paulino Shiler. Since he was such an obvious suspect, I wasn't sure I'd reach him very easily. The cops could have been questioning him around the same time they interrogated Wanda.

But a man answered immediately after the first ring. "Hello?"

"Hello, Mr. Shiler," I said. I'd already come up with a cover story. "My name is Kendra Ballantyne. I'm a lawyer representing some of the residents of the Brigadoon Condominium Association." Wanda had talked of hiring me in some capacity, after all, even if it hadn't occurred yet. "By the way, I'm sorry to hear of your loss—your ex-wife, Margaret, was the woman who died there, wasn't she?"

"Yeah, and no need to send any sympathy my way.

We didn't exactly end things amicably. What can I do for you?"

"I wonder if I could come and talk to you. My clients are determined to make sure they can still keep pets there, and even with Ms. Shiler gone, there is a contingent of residents opposing them. I'm hoping you can shed some light on why Ms. Shiler moved there, and why she took a position that was so contrary to the current policies. Since she was so vocal, and so strong in her recruitment of others to her point of view, I might be able to use any reasons you can give me to help maintain our position."

Which didn't make a hell of a lot of sense, but I hoped it sounded somewhat rational.

"Sure, I can tell you about that. Tell you what. I was just heading out the door. You can meet me at the dog park off Mulholland Drive, in Studio City."

I SPOTTED THE guy who had to be Paulino Shiler almost immediately, since he had described his boxer-mix pups. He was running right along with them, his short hair a similar shade of light brown, his eyes squinting into the chilly January sun.

Too bad I didn't have Lexie with me, with all the other canines involved in dashing around inside the vast fenced-in area—there were at least a dozen of them, all being observed by their owners. If I told Lexie I'd come without her, she'd pout for a week. Not. She was a Cavalier. She'd forgive me in a minute.

I closed the gate behind me and just stood there, watching Paulino till he glanced in my direction. He headed toward me, his dogs trailing behind.

"Ms. Ballantyne?" He was moderate height, in work-out clothes, and thinner than his ex-wife had been. He wore a backpack, which he removed to extract treats and toys for his dogs, then shoved some treats into his pocket.

I found the fact that he owned dogs interesting, given his ex's dislike of pets. Had he gotten them after their breakup, or had his having dogs been one of their bones of contention?

Okay, I'm a lawyer. I'm not exactly known for my subtlety. I asked him as we headed toward one of the few benches in the park.

"Margaret pretended to like the dog I had when we met," Paulino said, putting the backpack on the ground beside him, "but as soon as we were married, she started imposing restrictions. No dog in the bedroom, first. Eventually, she wanted him confined to the kitchen or the yard. I, on the other hand, would have insisted that she stay in the kitchen or yard instead." He grinned, revealing uneven teeth. "So tell me again why you wanted to talk to me. I'm not sure what I can say that would help the people in that condo association fight off the people with the same mind-set that Margaret had about pets."

"Actually," I told him, "a good friend of mine who was opposing her position is one of the suspects in her death. I'm just looking for people with other motives."

"Like her ex-husband?" He smiled and shook his head. "You're barking up the wrong tree with me." His dogs had bounded off to play with a couple of others in the busy park, but they now came back to nuzzle him for more treats. Reaching into his pocket, he complied.

"How long ago were you divorced?" I asked him.

"About a year. Irreconcilable differences, and all that. And before you ask, yes, if I were the kind of guy who wanted revenge for stuff, I'd have had a motive to kill her. We're both accountants, met at one of the big firms downtown. When we split, she found another job. She tried hard to bring as many of my company's clients along as she could—especially ones whose accounts I managed. Even succeeded with a couple. I'd come to despise Margaret. But all that happened many months ago. If I'd decided to kill her, I'd have done it then, not now."

Maybe, I thought as I said my farewells. He rose and maneuvered his pack onto his back. I patted his two pups and left the dog park.

But he could have waited till now for his revenge, so his role would not have been as obvious.

I ATTEMPTED TO stay utterly upbeat at our . . . group dinner. Double date? Whatever it was, there were two couples, all four people potentially torn apart by the death of someone barely known to only two of us.

But it was up to me to set the atmosphere, and I chose pleasant optimism. After all, I had jumped in and started my own inquiries into who might have killed Margaret Shiler.

So what if I hadn't been successful yet? The murder had occurred only a few days earlier, and the couple of leads I'd been following were still very fresh.

But considering my company at the Mexican restaurant where we'd met, I didn't dare simply start talking too positively about how I was going to solve the case.

We sat in a booth toward the back of the busy

establishment. The server brought tortilla chips, salsa, and the margaritas we'd ordered. I'd chosen mango-flavored, and it was deliciously sweet and sour with its hint of lime.

Wanda was clearly depressed and scared, though she maintained a courageous demeanor. She had chosen a drab brown gauzy top that evening, which said scads about how she was feeling. Her margarita was the standard kind—no experimentation, no particular sweetness added.

Darryl drank nothing alcoholic. My lanky friend looked equally morose, sipping on his cola as if he were drinking pure lemon juice. He sat directly across the table from me, and the few smiles he aimed my way seemed forced.

Then there was Dante, beside me. He'd ordered an imported Mexican beer and seemed to savor it as much as the salsa.

The two men would immediately be at odds—with me and with each other—if I brought up my efforts to help Wanda. Darryl would expect it, since I'd promised him I'd try. Dante, although he'd known I wasn't following his orders, might be irritated about it and would definitely be unhappy that I wasn't conveying chapter and verse of my investigation to him so he could help in his way—and, perhaps, protect me.

The wait staff had done their duty until our dinners were ready. No interruptions were anticipated for at least a few minutes.

"So," I said, prepared to attack the thousand-pound gorilla sitting somewhere beside us at this small table. "How did things go at the Burbank Police Department today, Wanda?"

Even though she had suggested this dinner, Wanda glanced at me with horror in her eyes, as if she really hadn't expected me to prod that sleeping gorilla with a pointed stick. "I . . . I'm not really sure."

"They told her not to leave town and all those stupid clichéd cop phrases." Darryl's voice was low, his gaze behind his glasses sad.

"No big surprise," I countered lightly. "Not from stupid, clichéd cops. Okay, I take that back. For all I know, they could be brilliant cops who just happen to have started off in the wrong direction. But that'll change."

"You're going to change it?" Darryl challenged. He took a swig of his soft drink as if he now regretted it didn't have more punch.

"I'm going to try." My voice was soft, and I didn't look beside me, toward Dante. "I can't guarantee anything. You know that. But I'm definitely working on it."

"You are?" Dante's voice was soft, too—but much more ominous than mine. "You haven't discussed it with me, though you said you would."

I looked at him. "Oops. Sorry. But you knew I'd be busy with it, whether or not I kept you up-to-date. I haven't learned enough to develop much of a plan so far, but when I do, and if I need backup from you or Brody or anyone else you suggested, like Jeff Hubbard, I promise I'll ask."

I watched the warring emotions behind the expression on Dante's face. He'd felt concerned enough to suggest Jeff in the first place, and I knew that couldn't have been easy for him. But at the moment, Dante had no reason to worry about my possible interest in any other man.

Our dinners were served just then. I'd ordered relatively lightly, a small taco salad. Even so, I hadn't much appetite.

Neither, it appeared, did anyone else. We all requested *bolsos perros*—my probably inaccurate translation of doggy bags—when we got ready to go.

Dante, the sweet megamillionaire, treated us.

Outside the door, we stopped, then got out of the way as another flood of hungry people slipped into the restaurant.

I looked at Wanda, who stood beside Darryl. He had his arm around her. "We'll figure this out," I said. "Somehow. Please keep me in the loop if there are any other interrogations, or whatever. You can tell Esther I'm eager to help." I looked at Darryl. "You know I'll do all I can."

"Yes, I know, but if only she wasn't—" He stopped talking, and I saw his gaze had fallen to Dante, beside me, who undoubtedly was glaring.

"I wish she wasn't involved, too, Darryl." I wondered whether it would feel less hurtful if he came right out and blamed me—but didn't really want to find out. I knew that his attitude wasn't really rational, that it resulted from his fear and pain. Too bad he'd decided, consciously or not, to pass the pain around. I turned and walked to my car—glad that Dante was behind me.

Chapter Ten

HE STAYED BEHIND me, too. We'd driven separately, and he followed me home in his car—so I of course invited him to stay. Very polite of me . . . hah! My emotions were low, and I hoped he'd help pump them up with some mind-blowing sex. All night.

Instead, after driving through the security gate and parking his high-end Mercedes behind my Escape, he walked me up the stairs to the door of my home-sweet-garage, his arm around my shoulders. Our kiss was hot—but it meant good night.

"I'd love to come in," he said, "but I'd better get home. I have a conference call early in the morning, one I'll need to be wide awake for. I'd better not start the night with any distractions, since I might forget to leave."

I laughed and kissed him back, hearing Lexie sniffing at the door from inside.

"You'll be okay here?" he asked.

I wondered what he'd do if I said no, but there wasn't any reason to lie. "I'll be fine. But . . . well, I'd be finer if you came in for a while."

"Tomorrow night I'm all yours. If you want me."

Good question. Did I want him?

For tomorrow night? Of course. But my mind veered in a much wider direction, and I narrowed it back on course.

"Sounds great. Can Wagner come, too?"

"Count on it."

I used my key to open the door, then punched in the code to turn off the security system Jeff Hubbard had installed for me, as Lexie leaped around my legs. Dante stood there for a moment, obviously assuring himself that I was indeed okay, then said, "See you tomorrow, Kendra." Another kiss—abbreviated yet explosively hot—and then he was gone.

Tomorrow was Monday. I'd pet-sit in the morning and late in the day, as always. In between, I'd engage in my law practice. And the entire time, I'd be anticipating my evening—with Dante.

Now, though, I'd spend the end of this day alone with Lexie. Once Dante was gone, his car outside and the gate closed behind him, I turned on the yard lights and Lexie and I bounded down the steps for her last constitutional of the night. I saw the outdoor lights go on at the main house, and soon Beggar joined Lexie on the lawn, frolicking with obvious enjoyment.

Russ and Rachel came out the front door, and I headed up the walkway to join them. I felt my shoulders brace in anticipation of whatever they had to say. Had they already located a house to buy?

Fortunately—for me—they hadn't. "How are you,

Kendra?" Russ asked, looking somewhat anxiously into my face. He apparently had headed out of the house in a hurry, since his cotton shirt was unbuttoned. At least it was long-sleeved, since the January air was chilly, and he did wear a white T-shirt beneath. I sensed he was worried about me. Did he expect me to have a meltdown because he and his daughter were leaving someday?

"I'm fine," I said. "Any success in finding a new home?"

"Not yet. But . . . well, we love this neighborhood." He looked down into his daughter's eyes. My waiflike pet-sitting assistant smiled up at him encouragingly. "We've been looking in this area, but I think you have the nicest house around."

Uh-oh. Was this leading up to his wanting to make an offer to buy me out? That would solve my issues about not being able to afford the place without a tenant. But I wouldn't consider giving it up. Unless I absolutely had to. I still loved this property, even if the bank maintained a major financial interest in it.

"The thing is, Kendra," Rachel finally said, turning to me, "we don't want to leave you in the lurch. If you want us to buy you out of this place, we'll try to do it. But—"

I hurried over to hug her, then Russ. "Please don't worry about me," I said. "I had tenants before you got here, and I'll find someone else, if necessary, when you leave. But it's really sweet of you to think about it."

Russ looked relieved. "I was serious about loving this area. We're holding out till we find a house around here that we like enough to buy—one where we'll still remain neighbors."

"Perfect," I said. Then, since Lexie and Beggar had ended their romp and now sat at our feet, I said good night.

When I got back inside, I realized I was too jazzed to think about going to bed. It wasn't really very late—only nine o'clock. I decided to follow up on the issue that had been manipulating my mind that day. That way, I wouldn't have to think too hard—now—about looking around for new tenants soon.

Nor about how much I appreciated the way I'd gotten close to my current ones. And how I'd miss having them this close, even if they wound up staying nearby.

I went into the living room and sat on the sectional sofa, turning on the TV to one of the shows where civilians are hired by cops to psych out crooks—pretending to be particularly perceptive or even clairvoyant. I kept it on mute as I pressed a familiar number into my cell phone.

"Kendra," said Esther Ickes's raspy little-old-lady voice into my ear, "I was hoping to hear from you."

"You can always call me. How are things?"

"Meaning Wanda Villareal's defense?"

"Well, that, too. You know I'm always interested in how you're doing, what you're up to besides defending my friends in murder cases."

She laughed. "You keep me pretty busy, Kendra."

"Unfortunately."

"It's fortunate for me, though," Esther said, as I started absently patting Lexie, who lay on my lap. "Especially since you always figure out who really committed the crimes my clients are accused of—and it isn't them."

"This time, too. I mean, Wanda's innocent . . . isn't she?"

"I certainly think so. I consider the case against her to be really weak. She had a difference of opinion with the victim, one they both were public about, but that doesn't mean Wanda would kill over it. She's a smart enough lady to back off, even move to another condominium complex where she could pet-sit, without resorting to murder."

"Exactly," I said.

"The only evidence they seem to have against her is that the cat she found there—Lady Cuddles, I think—had blood on her paws, and some of it was Wanda's. Of course the cat did scratch her a little when she initially tried to take it from the apartment, but then she decided to leave it there."

That answered one question I'd had. The cops had, indeed, tested the DNA found on the little cat's paws. Amazing, considering the huge backlog in the official DNA testing system, that they'd already gotten results. Or maybe they were still simply guessing.

"That doesn't make her a killer," I stated. "Just so you know, I'm starting to look into other potential suspects, and—"

"I was sure you would, dear. Thanks. And feel free to run any ideas by me."

"Well, I did go see Margaret's ex-husband, Paulino Shiler, today. He's on my list, but I didn't find him a particularly good suspect. And I've been told about someone else Margaret was arguing with—a contractor who did remodeling in some of the condos. His name is Rutley Harris, and I figured I'd track him down tomorrow or the next day."

"Yes, Wanda mentioned him as a possibility. One other place you could look, if you're so inclined, is at a couple of the other members of the condo association's board of directors. And they could lead you to some of the other people siding with Margaret on the pet issue—and those against her. Although I still find that too insubstantial a motive for murder."

"People kill for all kinds of dumb reasons," I reminded Esther—unnecessarily, since defending people in criminal matters was the major part of her practice. "And murder because of a threat to a family member isn't necessarily an insubstantial motive. Pets are relatives people choose, after all."

"You're right, dear. I can really identify with that now. Did I tell you that I've adopted a kitten? Her name is Sacha, and I had to laugh when Wanda started telling me about Lady Cuddles and her escapades around the condo complex—besides hanging around the murder site. My little Sacha isn't quite that elusive, but I do find her in the oddest places in my home, like in cabinets beside my sink and in shoeboxes in my closet. She's gray with light stripes rather like a tiger's."

"She sounds wonderful," I said warmly. "You'll have to introduce me to her one of these days."

"Gladly."

"And I'll follow up on those ideas of yours to help clear Wanda."

"I'm sure that you already thought of finding other people at the condominium complex to interview, Kendra. There's nothing especially unique in that."

"I appreciate all suggestions. Let me know if you think of anything else."

When we had said our good-byes and hung up, I made a quick call to James Jerome. "I'd love to get together with you again soon," I told him. "I've been following up on the people you suggested, but maybe you could point out more people who were Margaret's friends and enemies around the complex. Wanda's solidly in the cops' radar right now, and I'd love to get her out, if possible."

"There's an emergency board meeting on Tuesday evening," he told me, "and all residents are invited to attend. I can get you in as a guest. It would be a great way to introduce you to more people on both sides."

"I'll be there!"

Chapter Eleven

I COULD HAVE spent all of Monday drooling in anticipation of the delightful evening to come . . . with Dante.

But first I had pet-sitting to do. And all of my charges took priority over my own emotional—and physical—expectations.

I brought Lexie along with me first thing, and we visited all of my standard morning animals—Abra and Cadabra, the cats; Stromboli, Beauty, and some other adorable dogs; and, of course, Py the python. Where appropriate, Lexie came inside with me to assist in pet care and play.

Then we headed toward Doggy Indulgence. As always, I wanted to indulge my Lexie while I did my legal work.

Plus, I wanted to see Darryl. If possible, face him alone in his office. See how he was doing.

Determine whether I could further mend our fragile relationship.

As we went inside, Lexie immediately dashed off to play with some of her Indulgence pup pals. Kiki was the one to sign her in. She glared at me, but didn't say anything especially nasty.

Maybe she was waiting for her boss to do that, since Darryl came over to me after ending a conversation with another pet owner.

"Could we talk for a minute in your office?" I asked.

He seemed somewhat reluctant, but he shrugged his narrow shoulders beneath his orange—today—Doggy Indulgence knit shirt and said, "Sure."

Inside, with the door shut, I took one of the seats facing his messy desk. His window on his world, the day care facility, was behind him, and the mostly sound-proof glass kept out the noise.

It was just him and me.

"Darryl," I began, "I—"

He started speaking at the same time. "I've been acting like an ass, Kendra." His head drooped before he raised it again to look at me sadly through his wire-rimmed glasses. "I apologize. I know you can't help being a murder magnet, and you certainly didn't wish this on Wanda—or me, for that matter."

"So what's the 'but'?" I urged him on. Foolishly? Maybe. But since we'd started to try to clear the unhealthy air between us, I figured we'd better try to finish it, too.

"*But* . . . I've been blaming you in my mind because I'm just so frustrated. Have you ever loved someone so much that you'd do anything to protect them?" His tone was anguished. So was his look.

Even worse were his words. I'd had relationships before, and every one of them had ended badly.

Now, I was involved with a man who had it

all—wealth, power, sexiness, and, yes, sweetness. Would I do anything to shelter Dante?

I knew he would for me. He'd even tried to force protection on me the last time I'd looked into a murder, but at least then he'd known some nasty secrets about the guy who was killed, plus his enemies—and Dante himself was the major murder suspect. Now he was doing it again as I leaped into attempting to fix things for Wanda. Sweet, sure, but also a bit too controlling.

Or caring. He'd once lost a woman he'd loved in a car accident. He mentioned it the first few times without follow-up, but I'd eventually managed to extract some additional details. It happened just after he'd opened his first HotPets stores. She was a rep for a major pet food manufacturer. He'd fallen for her—hard. Her death occurred on a slick freeway during an early-season Los Angeles rain. An accident, and that was that. End of story—and he didn't really want to talk about it.

I suspected he was being so overprotective of me now because his wound reminded him of his loss, and life's fragility. Never mind that he'd formerly enjoyed a potentially toxic government job. That was then, and this was now.

As sweet as his caring was, I'd remind him—often— that I could take care of myself. Would I do anything to protect him, like Darryl asked? I'd certainly managed to blame myself a bit after Dante got stabbed . . .

"How much I've cared for anyone isn't the point, Darryl. You obviously feel that way about Wanda, and that's a wonderful thing. She's my friend, too. And I'll do everything in my power to help her out of this mess—even though I didn't really get her into it. You know that, don't you?"

He was staring at me. For a horrible instant, I thought he might contradict me and claim I'd not only chosen to be a murder magnet, but I'd also wished suspect status on many of my friends, including Wanda. Instead, he nodded. "I do know that, Kendra. I'm sorry for even considering otherwise. Can we still be friends?"

In a second, I was on his side of his desk, hugging the long, lanky, lovable guy. "Friends," I said soggily in agreement. I backed away. "Now I'm on my way to my law office. I plan to follow up on at least one suspect from there. And tomorrow night, I'll go to the special condo association meeting to see what I can learn there. And—"

Darryl held up his hands and laughed. "Whoa, Kendra. I know you've been successful in solving all those murders, but—"

"But it really matters this time, Darryl. Not that it hadn't with the others—especially when I was accused." And when Dante was accused. But enumerating suspects here seemed inappropriate. "You know I can't make any promises about clearing Wanda, but I'm sure as hell going to try."

"Thanks, Kendra," he said softly as I headed for the office door. "Either way, I'll owe you."

"All I want from you, Darryl, is your friendship."

"Count on it," he said.

But I couldn't help wondering what would happen if helping Wanda was my first failure.

"HI, KENDRA," EFFERVESCED Mignon, the bubbly receptionist at my law firm. Her auburn curls bobbed as she spoke while seated at a small desk in the area that had once been the hosting area of a restaurant. "You had a few calls this morning. The callers all asked to be sent to your voice mail."

"Thanks." We conversed for a few lively minutes about her weekend, and I sipped on a cup of coffee I'd picked up along my way. Mignon had just started dating a new guy, and was really jazzed.

"And how about you?" she piped after extolling the exciting virtues—or sinfulness—of her new guy. "Are you still seeing Dante DeFrancisco?"

Word got around everywhere—especially places where I spent lots of valuable time. Like here.

"Yeah, Kendra," said Elaine Aames, a senior-aged attorney who'd just walked into the reception area with Gigi, a Blue and Gold Macaw, perched on her shoulder. "How's Dante?"

I noticed the silver-haired founder of our law firm, Yurick & Associates, standing behind her in what had once been an aisle between booths in this former restaurant building. "What about you, Borden?" I said somewhat ruefully. "Are you going to ask about Dante, too?"

"Not me," he said in his high-pitched voice. "I'm not going to ask . . . but I'll listen to your answer."

Which made me consider wringing a neck or three. But, hey, Dante was definitely newsworthy, so it wasn't surprising he'd be the subject of gossip around here— and everywhere else. But I preferred privacy.

Not that I'd get it. "Dante's fine," I said rather smugly. "I spent some time with him yesterday at a pet adoption event, and we're getting together for dinner tonight. Any more questions?"

If they wanted to know how he was in bed, they were at least discreet enough not to ask.

"Nope, but I think it's really cool that you're seeing him," Mignon chirped.

"So do I," I said.

As Borden and Elaine headed into the conference room that was once a bar, I went down the aisle past attorneys' offices along the outer wall of the single-story building. Cubicles for secretaries and paralegals abutted on the inside. My office was a comfy corner one, and my litigation style of collecting files everywhere made it feel even cozier.

I sat down in my ergonomically correct chair behind my cluttered desk and noted that the light was indeed blinking on my office phone, indicating messages.

There were four. The first was from Corina Carey. Surprise! But I owed the tabloid reporter, since she had given me contact info for Margaret Shiler's former husband. I called her back immediately.

"Why didn't you call me on my cell?" I asked.

"I did, earlier today, but you didn't answer. You might have been doing your pet-sitting, but it was late enough I figured you could be at your office."

I wasn't certain why I'd missed her, but I gave her a rundown now of the little I'd learned from Paulino Shiler.

"So who else are you interviewing now?" she asked.

"Off the record?"

"Of course . . . for now. But if you give me anything interesting, I'll want to run with it."

"Right. Well, a couple of possibilities. I'm going to try to contact a contractor Margaret was arguing with. And tomorrow night's a newly scheduled meeting of the condo association. I've been invited to attend."

"Now, that could be damned interesting," Corina said. "Keep me informed."

I wondered if she'd attempt to show up there. Guess I'd find out tomorrow night.

Two other calls were from clients referred to me by Borden, both with some elder-law issues I was working on. I returned those immediately, too.

And the fourth? It was from the lady I'd met at the pet adoption fair, Joan Fieldmann, who had a bone to pick with her French bulldog Pierre's breeder.

I reached her right away. "I'm really upset, Kendra," she said. "I purposely chose a really good-quality pure-bred pup, one who could compete in dog shows. And he's so sweet, definitely my baby now."

"He's adorable." I agreed. I'd met him at the pet adoption event.

"The thing is," she continued, "the breeder had me sign a contract—that's not unusual. But she kept so much control over my Pierre . . . I've shown Pierre once, at a show where that woman was present. I enjoyed it, want to do more, even though Pierre didn't do as well as I'd hoped. Well, the breeder—Elmira—didn't like how I handled him, and now she wants to take over everything. Maybe even take my Pierre back if I don't let her be the one to show him."

"Is that allowed by your contract?" I asked.

"So she says. But Pierre's mine now. I want to be the one to show him. To decide where and when he should compete and, in between, keep him home with me. I don't want her intruding or having him travel without me."

"Tell you what," I said. "Bring Pierre and your contract to my office tomorrow. I'll look over the documentation, and we'll figure out where to go from there."

We determined a mutually agreeable time—early afternoon, so as not to conflict with my pet-sitting or my attending the condo association meeting.

"Thank you so much, Kendra," she said. "I'll look forward to your helping me out of this mess."

"No guarantees," I told her. But I was hoping for a nice, pleasant, and enjoyable bout of animal dispute resolution—assuming the other side would be reasonable.

And lawyers all know how big an *if* that can be.

Chapter Twelve

AFTER JOAN'S PHONE call, I drafted a response to a motion in one of the elder-law cases I'd taken on for Borden and his senior buddies. I also looked over some interrogatory answers I'd received in response to questions I'd sent out in another case. I reviewed a couple of additional files, both in anticipation of upcoming court appearances—argument of a motion in one, and the possibility of a trial in the other. Yes, the Yurick law firm kept me busy.

But not so busy that I ignored the other matter making me nuts.

I made one phone call relating to Margaret Shiler's murder. Fortunately, it turned out to be fruitful.

Which meant I left the office a little earlier than I otherwise would have for my late-day pet-sitting.

I headed to the area where the person who answered the phone at Harris Commercial Construction said the man in charge, Rutley, would be. Of course I lied a little to get the information. I'd indicated that I was a supplier of construction materials, and Rutley Harris had left me a message to meet him at his current job site with some quotes on costs. Only, dumb little me, I'd lost the address.

Harris was working in Simi Valley, a distance northwest from my Encino office. I'd have to hurry there and back to avoid keeping my animal charges waiting too long.

Turned out he was upgrading another condo complex. Fortunately, enough work was being done there that I had no trouble sneaking through the partially ajar gate in the fence surrounding the place. No trouble, either, locating Harris, since his van had his company's name painted on the sides. It was parked just outside a building with doors left wide open.

I wasn't sure which guy he was, though, since the unit being remodeled that day was occupied by half a dozen workers, all dressed equally grungily. Couldn't tell the company owner from his employees.

So I asked. Rutley Harris turned out to be the shortest of the crew, but his Harris Commercial Construction T-shirt's contours suggested he was substantially strong. His dark hair was long, his jaw thick, his expression indecent when I'd barely said hello. In fact, I gathered that Harris always attempted to ooze slimy sexiness.

I wondered uneasily if, this once, I should have let Dante know what I was up to this afternoon. No doubt he'd have thought so.

"Hi," I said to Harris. "Could I speak with you?"

"Sure can, babe." His leering assessment of me plus his suggestive tone made my skin crawl.

We went out onto the balcony of the condo unit

being worked on. It was still noisy, with power saws slicing away at boards propped across wooden saw-horses. But at least I was in less danger of inhaling the sawdust fluttering everywhere. And I was within plain sight of the other workers, in case I wound up in an altercation with Rutley.

I'd considered my approach on my way there. How I might hide what I was really asking, and why. I pondered mentioning a nonexistent remodeling project I was considering at my house. Or questions about who'd designed the changes made at the Brigadoon condos.

Instead, I immediately decided that directness was the best way of eliciting any useful responses.

"My name is Kendra Ballantyne," I told him. "I'm a lawyer, among other things, and I'm looking into what happened to Margaret Shiler. I understand that you recently remodeled her unit and a few others at the Brigadoon condominiums in Burbank."

The good-looking face that had suggested steaminess a few seconds before suddenly turned scrunched-up and nasty. "That's right," he replied curtly. "Bitch kept complaining about my work. Said I was taking too long to finish remodeling all those condos, especially hers. But if she'd chosen building materials that were easy to find without having to order them from China or wherever, everything would have gone a lot faster. Plus, she started claiming things were done wrong, insisted I redo them. My specialty is building nice wooden shelving and installing decorative floors, and she even complained about that."

"Sorry things were so rocky there," I said sympathetically, wanting to throw him off guard, if possible, before I hinted at any accusations.

"It didn't help that—Hey, look, I admit I didn't like the bitch. Especially after she came on to me."

Aha! Another reason for him to hate her . . . or vice versa. Either way, an even more impressive motive for murder was now out in the open.

"But if what you're asking," he continued, "is whether I hated her enough to kill her, the answer's no. I've run into women like her before."

Ones lusting after him? Considering the way he looked at any female near him, I figured he assumed he elicited sexual interest, real or imaginary, from nearly every woman he came across. Ugh!

He wasn't done explaining himself. "I'm used to dealing with ladies who seem to think I'm eager to get into their pants, then get themselves into a snit when I don't take them on that way. I don't kill them. Though maybe they'd consider offing themselves if I didn't show them any interest."

The egotistical idiot! "Oh, I doubt that," I said, eyeing him up and down and pasting a disgusted sneer on my face. "Anyway, you disliked Margaret Shiler, she'd come on to you—or so you'd believed in your imagination, at least—you'd rejected her, and you didn't kill her. Is that it in a nutshell?"

His turn to aim a sneer at me. "Thing was, I didn't reject her till after we'd had one hell of a night together. She was actually okay in bed. But she wanted more, and I didn't. Most of her complaints started after I made it clear we were over with that. So, I don't know how she died, but the cops should consider suicide as a possibility, depending."

I'd heard the murder weapon was a barbecue skewer,

though there had been no official public acknowledgment. But if it was, suicide was surely unlikely.

"Far as I know," I said, "they're not seriously considering suicide, but we'll see. In any event, I'm not ruling you out as a suspect, Mr. Harris, and I'd imagine the cops aren't either. Have they questioned you yet?"

"No." He sounded suddenly fearful. "Do you think they will?"

"Count on it." *You egotistical bastard*, I added in my mind. I wondered why he'd be so concerned about an official interrogation.

I wasn't sure he'd killed Margaret, but neither had I ruled him out.

And I was eager to hear what the cops might otherwise have on full-of-himself Rutley Harris.

JUST IN CASE Harris was an overlooked suspect, I called Esther Ickes on my way back toward North Hollywood and my first pet-sitting rounds of late in the day.

She answered her phone immediately. "Hi, Kendra. Tell me something good to help get my client off."

Which I did, kinda. "I honestly don't think Harris did it, though I can't be certain. But there's some reason he's eager to avoid the cops—which means it would make a lot of sense for you to mention him to them. Whatever it is might not have a connection to Burbank, where Margaret was murdered, but cops talk to each other." I related the gist of my conversation to my criminal attorney friend—including how icky the guy was, in a sexually suggestive way. And his claimed liaison with a later-spurned Margaret.

"Interesting," Esther said, drawing the word out speculatively. "Thanks, Kendra. I'll let you know what happens."

"Have you heard about the Brigadoon Condo Association meeting tomorrow night?" I asked.

"Yes. Wanda and I will be there."

"Great!" I said. "Me, too. James Jerome told me about it and invited me. Should be an interesting session. For Wanda's sake, I hope the pro-pet contingent turns out in droves. We'll have to watch them all, see if anyone gives away their happiness that Margaret's not still around to head the opposition."

"Although," Esther said dryly as I slowed for a yellow light, "the anti-pets might also have had a motive to kill her: turn her into their martyr, as long as they make it look like someone pro-pet did her in."

"Hmmm." I was now stopped at the red light, watching opposing traffic zoom through the wide intersection. "Good point. We just have to hope that someone there simply stands up and admits killing Margaret for whichever reason fits."

"In your dreams," Esther said.

"But not tonight's," I told her without elaborating.

My dreams tonight would be filled with Dante, since I intended to spend my time in bed and in his arms.

DANTE'S ARRIVAL WITH Wagner was fairly late in the evening, which was fine with me, considering my need to rest a bit and get my second—third? fourth?—wind after my busy day including pet-sitting duties.

I was waiting with some wine in my living room,

where I'd started watching TV news. I moved the bottle when Dante came in with a pizza, since he also brought Wagner, and the exuberant German shepherd, despite being well trained, could easily knock the bottle off my coffee table with a modest leap or wag of his tail. Lexie could, too, of course, but she'd remained pretty mellow till our company arrived.

"Mmmm." I peeked into the pizza box. "Extra cheese, mushrooms, and pepperoni—my favorites."

We sat there and ate and drank, then took the dogs outside for their end-of-evening constitutional.

They even got to romp for a few minutes with Beggar, who was also out in the yard. Rachel was there, too—and we chatted about nothing in particular.

Which was a good thing. I hadn't told Dante yet about my dilemma involving my tenants' search for a new home. I needed to decide what I wanted to do before I talked to him about it. I actually was considering, sort of seriously, his offer made some time ago to buy my property and let me lease it back from him. But I wasn't certain what would happen to our relationship if we added landlord-tenant to our current status as business associates in *Animal Auditions*, plus avid, caring lovers in our leisure time.

"Good night," I finally said to Rachel and Beggar, and led Dante, Wagner, and Lexie back up the steps to my abode.

Dante knew me well enough to know I hadn't sat back on my buns and ignored my latest murder investigation. "Have you learned anything else I should know about Margaret Shiler's death?" he asked once we were again ensconced with wine and pups on the sofa.

I snuggled up against him and told him the results of my latest inquiries. "I didn't like that guy Rutley Harris at all," I said with a quick shudder.

"And you went to see him by yourself, without even telling me, because . . . ?"

"Because I'm a big girl, and it was the middle of the day, and lots of other people were around. But"—I put our glasses down on the table beside one another, and gave Dante a big kiss—"I appreciate your concern."

"And I don't appreciate your taking risks—but I know you'll do whatever you want anyway. Just be careful." He returned the kiss, and then it was my turn again, and . . .

Well, no need to go into any detail about the rest of the night. Suffice it to say that it was delightful.

And when Dante drowsily said, "Good night, Kendra. I love you," I had to say virtually the same words in return.

Nope, our relationship was absolutely too wonderful to muddy it with my resenting his concern about my physical well-being, whatever the reason. In fact, I was coming to appreciate it—even though I wasn't ready to tell him everything on my mind, like what I intended to do to find Margaret's killer.

Or my concern about my living arrangements in the near future.

I might keep Dante apprised about my investigation. With his background, he might offer advice I'd be willing to take. But I wasn't sure I'd feel the same way if he shoved too many suggestions at me about where I should live.

Whatever I determined about the house, I'd let Dante know when I was ready.

Chapter Thirteen

DANTE LEFT EARLY the next day. He needed to take Wagner home, then get to his HotPets corporate headquarters in Beverly Hills for a battery of meetings he had planned.

I'd been to his offices only a couple of times and hadn't stayed long, but they were every bit as impressive as I'd anticipated this pet products tycoon's quarters would be. I had a standing invitation to visit but had my own extensive business to conduct that day.

I felt bereft when I saw his Mercedes pull out of my driveway, which was silly. I'd see him again soon. I was getting much too addicted to his presence.

But it wasn't an addiction I hoped to withdraw from anytime in the near future.

"Time for us to get ready, too, Lexie," I told my prancing pup, and soon we were off, ready for me to dig in to the day's pet-sitting.

When I'd spent lots of time with my animal

charges—Lexie along with me whenever possible, and safely ensconced in the car when it wasn't—it was time to take her once more to Doggy Indulgence. I now felt more comfortable taking my dear dog back there. Even with Kiki and her odd behavior—which seemed to have sort of stopped, despite her evil glares toward me now and then when Darryl wasn't watching—I knew Lexie loved it there and would be well treated. I didn't think she'd disappear again. I hadn't made a big deal of the last time with Darryl, since our friendship was somewhat strained then, but now that it might be on the mend, I wouldn't hesitate to tell him about less-than-stellar treatment by any of his staff.

Darryl was greeting doggy guests and their own-ers, and I gave him a big hug as I headed out the door. "Will you be at the condo association meeting tomor-row night?" I asked. "Wanda and Esther will be there, and me, too."

"Wouldn't miss it." He smiled somewhat. "Then maybe I can make suggestions about people who might be worth your looking into to clear Wanda."

"You bet," I said, then left.

My lawyering that day was relatively painless. I looked forward to the meeting I'd scheduled that afternoon—the one involving pet law, and the lady chafing under the collar imposed by the contract she'd signed with her dog's breeder.

Joan Fieldmann arrived right on time, and she had brought her adorable French bulldog, Pierre, with her.

"What a cutie," gushed Mignon when she phoned to let me know that my visitors were there. I popped down the hall to greet them, then showed them to my office.

Joan wore a colorful print dress that drew attention

away from the fact that her face vaguely resembled Pierre's puggish features. She carried a briefcase in the hand not holding Pierre's bright blue leash. I hadn't asked her profession previously, and now she told me she was a sales representative for a major home cleaning products manufacturer. She visited grocery chains and discount stores to discuss how her company's products were being displayed and to encourage store managers to promote them, especially when her employer offered special prices that could be passed along to consumers.

She settled into a chair facing my somewhat orga-nized desk. Pierre occupied the other chair, looking every bit as if he knew the purpose of this meeting.

"So," I said, "have you brought along that infamous contract?"

She had, and I left my office for a minute to make a copy. Then I scanned the document. It contained the kinds of clauses Joan had described. I'd look them over in greater depth later, but I hated how onerous the docu-ment appeared.

Joan confirmed that she had, indeed, signed it. So, apparently, had Elmira Irving—owner of MirVilous Kennels and breeder of French bulldogs.

"I'd fallen in love with Pierre," Joan said, slinking her hand over toward her pup, who licked it. "I paid more than I'd anticipated, but he was worth it. And I so looked forward to showing him, letting him demon-strate to the world how beautiful he is."

"Did Ms. Irving go over the contract clauses with you?"

"A little. Elmira said it was standard stuff she put into all the agreements she used when placing one of her show-quality puppies into another home."

"Did she explain her expectations about showing Pierre?"

"Not really. She made a point of discussing Pierre's lineage and past champions in his family tree. Said he had a lot of potential, too, and that he should be shown to see how he did. But nothing more specific."

"Here's what we'll do," I told her. "Let me read this in more depth, then we'll talk again, by phone. We can discuss how you can initiate a conversation with Elmira. See if she has an attorney involved, and, if not, you might suggest she get one, assuming you don't want to follow all the terms of the agreement and she still insists on it. I hope we can reach a compromise without going to court, but that could be a last resort."

"Whatever you say, Kendra," Joan said. "I just want what's best for my Pierre. Being a show dog? Sure, I love the idea—as long as I can be the one to show him."

I HAD TO leave my law office early to be able to spend sufficient late-day time with my pet-sitting charges. My evening was spoken for, thanks to the Brigadoon Condominium Association's special meeting.

I picked Lexie up early from Doggy Indulgence and left her at home, since I didn't think she was invited to the gathering—not when a major topic would involve whether pets would continue to be permitted in the place. "Sorry, girl," I told her, and gave her an extra treat as I left.

I grabbed a fast-food dinner on the way. Everyone in my immediate party would meet me at the complex, so we were on our own for our evening meals.

Soon as I got to Brigadoon's gate, I called James Jerome on the official condo intercom. "Glad you're here, Kendra." He buzzed me in.

After I parked, I called Wanda on my cell phone. Darryl was with her, and they were heading toward the apartment where the session would be held—one of the larger ones in a side building at the complex's west end.

As I exited my car, I received a call—Dante. "Where are you?" I asked.

"Right outside the gate."

I called James and got Dante buzzed in as well. I waited for him in the parking lot. He was dressed in business casual, with a blue shirt tucked into dark slacks, and he looked wonderful. But when didn't he?

I was glad I hadn't taken time to dress down after my short day at the office. I didn't want to overwhelm this group with my lawyerly aura, but since I hadn't gone to court today, my outfit wasn't especially dressy, either—a floral blouse, khaki slacks, and a brown jacket.

Dante and I kissed sort of chastely, since we weren't exactly alone, but that appetizer made me consider what the rest of a meal of Dante might involve . . . later? Well, next time, anyway. I was certain, from the heated glimmer in his gorgeous dark eyes, that there would be a next time soon. We walked toward the meeting.

A lot of people were heading the same way we were. Was everyone here in on the argument about pets? Or did most want their curiosity satisfied about what was going on—and whether it had anything to do with Margaret's murder?

The unit where the condo association met that night was on the ground floor. Someone had propped the building's big front door open, and the crowd piled in. Most were clad casually, but a few wore suits and other dressier stuff, as if dressed to impress others.

I neither saw nor heard any pets, probably a good thing. Better that their fates be discussed without any of them being able to create unacceptable diversions—and thereby possibly prop up the pet-haters' positions.

James waited at the door. As usual, his shirt featured guinea pigs, but the rodent on the pocket of his white knit shirt was fairly small this time. "Glad you could make it, Kendra." His droopy eyebrows raised high when I introduced him to Dante. "Glad to meet you." His tone made it clear he meant it. Yes, HotPets carried guinea pig products.

We walked in, and I soon spotted Wanda and Darryl, who were saving us some folding chairs in the sizable living room.

"How are you?" I asked as Dante and I sat down, looking mostly at Wanda but intending to include Darryl in my inquiry.

"Okay, I guess. I'm just hoping we learn something here."

"Something you can follow up on," Darryl added. "I know how good you are at figuring things out, Kendra."

"I'll definitely do my best."

Dante, on my other side, squeezed my hand. I read that message to be that he, in turn, would be there for me. My smile grew larger, and I turned toward him.

"I have to go up there." James pointed toward the front of the crowd where half a dozen chairs were facing the rest. Presumably, that was where the board members would sit.

Would one chair, Margaret's, remain empty? Or had someone already been appointed to take her seat? Or would they not have designated a place where she might otherwise have been?

Turned out my first guess was correct. Five board members took their seats, leaving one on the end of the row vacant.

James stood first to address everyone. The Bertinettis had found seats in the first row, and though I couldn't see their expressions from behind them, I saw James's brows elevate as he noticed them. I assumed their expressions weren't pretty.

"Hi, everyone," James began in a raised voice, then repeated it even louder when the hubbub of conversation failed to hush. "Hi! Everyone! Welcome!" Suddenly, the group fell silent. "As you probably all know, I'm James Jerome."

He introduced the four other board members: Julie, John, Sheldon, and Rick. As each one's name was called, he or she stood and waved, then all resumed their seats.

"This special meeting," James continued, "is to make sure that everyone who lives in the Burbank Brigadoon complex is aware of what happened to one of our members, Margaret Shiler." Murmurs started among the audience members, and James lifted his pudgy hands. "Yes, I'm sure most of you know at least some of it. Poor Margaret . . . she was killed by someone who, so far, hasn't been identified or arrested. But I'm sure the police are working on it. Hopefully, there'll be news about it soon. Meantime, the board wants to be sure that association members take appropriate security measures so that nothing happens to anyone else around here. Make sure all doors are locked properly, use alarm systems if you wish, don't go out walking alone, especially at night—that kind of thing. We just don't know what kind of intruder might have done that to poor Margaret."

Suddenly, Teddy and Ruth Bertinetti were standing. "That's a crock of shit, James," shouted Teddy. He was dressed all in black, as if in mourning, except for the upswept silver of his hair. "You know that Margaret was killed because she had started to make waves around Brigadoon. And we—Ruth and I—are going to ensure that she didn't die in vain."

"That's right," said his tall, thin wife. She was clad in yellow, but still managed to appear somber. "We're going to continue her fight against the dirty, untrained pets around this place. Right, everyone?"

A goodly group of people in the corner where the Bertinettis had been seated rose around them and started chanting, "Yes, yes, yes."

Which caused terribly pained looks to appear on the faces of James and his fellow board members. Apparently, all the current members favored the complex's pet policies.

The only woman—Julie—rose and put her arms up as if to direct the band of shouters into silence. They actually did stop and watch her. "We'll all miss Margaret." I felt certain she exaggerated intentionally, judging by her scrunched expression. "Those of us on the board acknowledge that her opinions might have been different from ours. But you all need to realize—and let me remind you—that the Brigadoon Condominium Association has always allowed pets here. What sometimes changes are the rules governing how they are trained and handled in the respective units. But we simply can't change—"

"Of course you can change anything by vote," Ruth insisted. "The majority governs."

"But I think you'll find that the majority of people who live here are happy with our pet policy and rules," James said, standing beside Julie.

"Not if we can help it," Teddy said.

"But the rules work," Julie interjected. "Sure, there are occasional incidents with animals, but when anything like that happens, we can impose fines or other consequences. Everything about pets around here works well. It's all under control. Honestly, people."

Which was exactly when I noticed a little ginger streak dash behind the board members' chairs.

"Lady Cuddles!" I whispered in horror—at the same time that Wanda looked over at me and said the same.

Chapter Fourteen

WANDA WENT ONE way. I went the other.

By the time we got anywhere near Lady Cuddles, she'd climbed up a curtain in the condo unit's bedroom and onto the top of a tall dresser. She looked down at us quizzically with her adorable kitten face, as if she wondered what all our fuss was about.

Wanda is a petite person, way shorter than me, but even I couldn't quite reach that high. We stood there dumbly for an extra second, wondering how to get the feline down from her perch. Fortunately, our respective guys had followed. Darryl was there first and able to reach up to retrieve the kitty, and Dante was right behind him, smiling.

Only then did I take in the room's decor—pretty nice. The bed's headboard matched the dresser, which matched the vanity table, which matched the nightstands at either side of the bed. The pillows appeared both pretty and comfy, and the satin-covered duvet was divine.

"Whose place is this?" I asked Wanda as I retrieved the kitty from Darryl.

"It's Julie Tradeau's, and her husband, Ivan's. He's in the film industry and she's a hairstylist to the stars, so they have money."

"And their position on pets?"

"They have a cat of their own," Wanda said. At the same time, I heard an irritated meow from the vicinity of the bed, and a black head emerged from under it. "That's Smouser. He's a little shy."

"Cute," I responded as Dante bent to give the kitty a reassuring pat. "Look, I think it's important for you to stay at this meeting, without Lady Cuddles. I'll take her home. Are her owners back yet?"

"Not till next weekend."

"Well, I'll try to figure out how she escaped this time, but as far as your fellow condo folks are concerned, blame it on me. It'll be better for you in the long run if it doesn't appear that one little kitten has found the way to bend the pet rules—even though she apparently has. Or that you were careless, which I'm sure you weren't." I hoped. "Just say I was filling in for you and somehow mustn't have gotten things closed up well enough at Lady Cuddles's place."

"Oh, Kendra, thank you!" Wanda gave me a big hug, gentle enough not to squish the cute little kitten I still held. She also reached into her pocket and extracted a bunch of keys, from which she pulled one. It had a tag on it with the number of the unit where Lady Cuddles lived.

All four of us—five, if you counted the kitten—went back into the living room of the apartment, but the feline and I kept going toward the door. I was pleased to see, as I exited the unit, that Dante was still with me.

"Interesting timing," he noted as we hustled down the hall. He bent slightly to make it clear he was addressing the kitty. "Did someone tell you how to make such a dramatic entrance—and when? It really wasn't in your best interests to do so, though—not if you want to keep living here at Brigadoon."

I chuckled, then handled Dante the key as we reached the right unit's door. That door was clearly closed; there was no gap through which Lady Cuddles could have made her escape.

Inside, we looked around. Best I could figure, her means of escape was a really tiny opening in a bedroom window that overlooked the balcony. I was surprised that Wanda, knowing Lady Cuddles's amazing abilities of escaping, would have left it ajar even a crack. I'd let her know what we'd found and not so subtly suggest that she be more careful.

At least Lady Cuddles had a name tag on her collar, the one Wanda said she'd picked up at HotPets. Not that I'd tell Dante, but it wasn't nearly as nice as the one she had before, with the cute representation of a kitty on one side. I still wondered how she'd lost it. I'd discuss that with Wanda sometime.

I closed the window, let Dante back me up in scanning the entire place for other ways Lady Cuddles could slip out, then locked the clearly unhappy little ball of ginger fur inside her home.

By the time we got back to the unit housing the meeting, the group was starting to break up. I received nasty glares from a few of the people filing out. I assumed Wanda had done as I'd suggested and blamed the kitty's escape on me.

Dante and I squeezed in and approached the front of

the room, where Wanda and Darryl stood talking to the board members.

"How did the rest of the meeting go?" I asked, not sure I wanted to hear the answer.

"The anti-pet people were really vocal about that kitten," James said, sounding discouraged. "And how even good rules could get broken."

"Did you really leave a door open?" board member Julie asked me accusingly.

"Er . . . I accidentally forgot to fully close one window," I responded, looking tellingly toward Wanda, who flushed. "Unfortunately, that was enough for Lady Cuddles's escape."

"I've done that before," Wanda said, "but not since we discovered how elusive Lady Cuddles is." Her remark was obviously intended to tell me she hadn't done it this time, either. But if not her, and if the unit's owners weren't around, who was guilty?

"That damned cat had perfect timing, didn't it?" This was said snidely by Ruth Bertinetti, who'd come up behind us. "It certainly made our point. Pets simply don't belong in a busy condominium complex like this."

"Right. They could get hurt," said her husband, who had joined her.

"If any animal is hurt around here," I said coldly, "we'll know who to question about it."

"Oh, we'd never hurt an animal." Ms. Bertinetti put her skinny hands up as if warding off even the thought. "We just don't want them bothering us."

"Right. Well, if you'd just leave them alone, they'd leave you alone, too." Wanda snapped this before I could aim a warning look her way. At least Darryl knew the score. The arm around her shoulder squeezed her in concern.

"Not really," said Teddy with a sneer. "Dogs bark with no provocation."

I considered describing in detail what caused dogs to bark—including mistrust of a nasty human—but forbore. We weren't going to change this man's mind about anything. Nor his wife's.

I could only hope, for Wanda's sake, that the majority of the rest of the condo association's members were more rational about the role of pets in people's lives . . . and around here.

SEVERAL PET AFICIONADOS banded together for a brief, pessimistic recap in James's apartment.

Julie Tradeau started speaking, sitting on the sofa in the midst of the other board members. "That was really awful, especially when Lady Cuddles . . ." She aimed a sour glance at me that she immediately erased from her face. "But anyway, Wanda said you'd be willing to act as our lawyer, Kendra. Help those of us who want to keep the status quo about pets find a way to fight off the anti-pet gang. I'd thought that with Margaret gone, they'd stop making so much noise, but I guess they're rallying behind her position instead."

"Looks that way," James said glumly, regarding his fuzzy guinea pigs as they sat still in one of their cages at the side of his living room. "And, yes, Kendra, if there's anything you can do to advise us, we'd really be grateful."

"Tell you what," I said. "It's getting late now, but if

some or all of you would be willing to visit me at my law office soon, we can talk about the possibilities."

"Tomorrow?" Wanda asked eagerly. She glanced toward the others. John, Sheldon, Julie, Rick, and James nodded.

"How's two o'clock?" I suggested. Everyone agreed.

Dante and I left a short while later. "You can't come to my place tonight?" I asked sadly as we stood in the parking lot beside my car. After the ordeal of the condo association meeting, I'd have loved his company.

And his body.

"Sorry, but Alfonse has the night off, so I need to get home to Wagner. I've also got an early morning meeting. And—"

"I get it." I tried not to let my regrets show too readily. "Maybe another night. Soon."

"You got it." He took me into his arms. Nearby, a car pulled out of a parking space. We ignored it and kissed. Then Dante said, "Meantime, what do you have planned tomorrow for your snooping—I mean investigation—into Margaret Shiler's murder?"

"Not sure yet. Maybe I'll check with my friend Althea, see if she can find anything on that construction guy, Rutley Harris. I like him for the murder—only because he's a jerk, not necessarily because I came up with any evidence on him."

"Tell you what," Dante said. His dark eyes bored into mine beneath the parking lot lights, and I was immediately lost in them. He could have told me anything, and I'd have bought it just then. "I'll talk to Brody tonight. Have him run a check on this Rutley Harris and get back to you with the results." I'd no doubt he'd report them to Dante first, but that was okay. "Anyone else you'd like for him to look at?"

I pondered for a short moment. "How about those Bertinettis? They were on Margaret's side, and they're not very nice people. It wouldn't hurt to look for anything in their backgrounds that might indicate they could be killers. And maybe even James Jerome. He seems like a good guy, but he clearly didn't like Margaret—with good reason."

"I'll throw in the other board members, for good measure," Dante told me.

"Sounds good."

"So Brody will be in touch with you tomorrow."

What about you? I wanted to ask. Well, hell. I could always call him. And if there was some reason he didn't want to talk to me, he wouldn't have to answer.

"And I'll talk to you, too, Kendra," he said softly. His kiss punctuated that promise so adamantly that I no longer had any doubts. "Think of me while you're in bed tonight."

"You do the same." I'd attempted to make my tone absolutely light, but there was a longing and huskiness I hadn't intended.

"Count on it." He opened my Escape's door and ushered me inside.

Of course I complied. How could I do otherwise? In bed, by myself except for Lexie, I let my mind meander to thoughts of Dante, and how I'd like him there with me.

Which of course didn't allow me to fall asleep.

So, lying there, too comfy and half lonely, I pondered Dante's offer to have Brody Avila check into anyone I considered a possible suspect in the murder of Margaret Shiler. My habit, for a long time, had been to have Althea Alton, that fantastic employee of Jeff's, work her computer magic, which I felt certain included hacking—not that I'd ever tell. In any event, she was a wonder at coming up with absolutely everything I needed.

Brody had been around nearly as long as I'd known Dante—which was only a matter of months. Even so, I'd known of him before. Who hadn't? He was a film star of some note, and had been in an acclaimed cinematic remake of the old *Rin Tin Tin* TV shows, among other movies.

With Dante's assistance, we'd gotten Brody to act as a judge on the *Animal Auditions* reality TV show that we were both affiliated with.

But I'd only recently learned that Dante and Brody had previously worked together in some pretty secret government stuff, way back.

It did make me feel certain, though, that if Brody checked into more info for me, online or otherwise, he'd do great. As well as Althea? Maybe. But I could certainly see what he accomplished, and if I wasn't satisfied, I'd call on my regular computer expert.

And . . .

Okay, I finally managed to make myself sleep. A good thing. I'd a sufficiently busy day planned for tomorrow that I couldn't leave myself in a position to nod off during the day.

I admit I had to drag myself out of bed, though, after my alarm went off and Lexie insisted it was, indeed, time to get up. I decided I needed a Darryl fix of friendship, now that we were talking to each other again, so

I determined I would take Lexie to Doggy Indulgence first thing, before I started my pet-sitting.

Guess I shouldn't have been surprised when Darryl wasn't there yet. Wanda would need some extra TLC after the last few difficult days, and Darryl would undoubtedly stay close to her as much as possible to provide it.

When I walked in, the place was already busy with lots of active pups, and Lexie immediately joined them. Lots of employees, too, to take care of them. Games were already going on in the different areas designated for multiple kinds of fun. Barks and growls and laughter filled the air, and doggies slid along the pine-like linoleum floor as they chased balls and played other kinds of games.

I waved to one of the nice employees, Lila, as she went by in pursuit of a pup, but she didn't stop. Unfortunately, Kiki was the one who edged up to ensure that I signed my doggy in sufficiently for her day of indulgence.

"So, have you fixed things for your friend Wanda yet?" Kiki asked, her tone snide as she regarded me with blue eyes whose friendliness was as false as the blondness of her hair.

"Working on it," I said, not even bothering to smile back. I'd never liked this lady, but I didn't understand why she'd become even more difficult lately.

I still wondered whether she'd decided to have a crush on Darryl, now that he was no longer available.

Now might be a time to attempt to figure it out. . . .

"But I'll bet you'd be happier if she was arrested and convicted, right, Kiki?"

Those blue eyes widened, and this time their expression of surprise seemed real. "I . . . What makes you think I have any interest in that damned murder?"

And before I could get her to explain her odd reaction, she turned her back and joined in the nearest canine ball game.

Which made me wonder, as I said my farewell to Lexie and headed out to my car, what interest she actually had in Wanda.

I'M NOT EXACTLY the most patient person in the universe. Even so, I took my time getting through my morning pet-sitting visits, since that was only fair to my many charges.

I also managed not to pick up the phone as soon as I sat down at my desk in my law office.

But I was dying to say good morning to Dante.

And find out if he had in fact enlisted Brody to do some online research.

I hadn't erased the contractor Rutley Harris from my suspect list in Margaret's murder, after all. I wanted to know as much about him as was available before I fully made up my mind.

And—

Well, hell. It didn't show utter impatience if I called someone else altogether . . . did it?

Who cared?

I called a number that had become familiar lately—Detective Ned Noralles, of the LAPD.

"Hi, Ned," I said brightly when he answered.

"The answer is no, Kendra."

"And the question is . . . ?"

"Have I pushed the Burbank PD to tell everything

they know, or think they know, in the murder at that condominium that you're interested in."

"Oh."

"But I do have a call in to one of their detectives who's an acquaintance. If I learn anything, I'll let you know."

"Thanks, Ned," I said. "By the way, how are Nita, Porker, and Sty Guy?" I'd become buddies with his sister and their pet potbellied pigs recently, too.

"They're fine. And I've a standing order to say hi from them whenever I talk to you. So, hi. And 'bye. Talk to you soon, Kendra."

My cell phone suddenly went silent, and I was left staring at my messy desk.

Wishing I had a contact as helpful as Ned at the Burbank PD.

Chapter Fifteen

MY ENSUING DISCUSSION with Brody was almost as disappointing.

"I just got the request from Dante, Kendra," he said, sounding half amused—which had just the opposite effect on me. "Give me some time."

I almost blurted that my friend Althea would probably have deep and dirty info on everybody on my list by now, but that wasn't exactly true. Althea was damned good at dealing with stuff on the computer. Fast, too. But she was still human. Plus, her work from Jeff always came first.

And these days, her help always came with a catch—like sharing a meal with my former lover.

"Okay, Brody," I said with a sigh. "I didn't mean to be too pushy, but some of the people on your list who live at the Brigadoon condos and opposed Margaret's pet-hating ways are coming to see me this afternoon. They may want to hire my legal services to ensure that

Margaret's views aren't adopted by the association. I figured I'd ask some pointed questions while they're here. See if any flinch when I talk about how Margaret died. Background info on who to push might come in handy."

"I've got a meeting later this morning with your buddies Corbin and Shareen Hayhurst and Charley Sherman about the next season of *Animal Auditions*." Corbin and Shareen were my law clients whose legal issues had helped lead to the establishment of our animal reality show. Charley Sherman, too, was a former law client now affiliated with *Animal Auditions*—and a longtime animal trainer for Hennessey Studios. "I assume you're still happy with me being a judge."

"Ecstatic," I said. "And you're right. That comes first. But anything you can get to me, as soon as you're able, would be absolutely welcome. About *Animal Auditions*, too, by the way. I'm sure I'll get a recap, but your opinion would be great."

"You got it," he said, and hung up.

Leaving me staring at my office walls and the small, messy credenza flanked by oak file cabinets at the other side of the room.

My reverie was interrupted by an incoming phone call. "Kendra Ballantyne," I said automatically into the receiver.

"Ms. Ballantyne, this is Cornelius Eldt. I'm an attorney representing Elmira Irving."

The client's name sounded vaguely familiar, but I couldn't place it.

"Please remind me who she is," I said.

"She owns MirVilous Kennels and raises French bulldogs. Your client Joan Fieldmann apparently called and asked if she'd have her counsel contact you about a contract dispute they're having."

"Oh, yes. That's right, Mr. Eldt. But now that we've introduced ourselves, please just call me Kendra."

I expected a similarly friendly gesture from him, but didn't get it. On the other hand, maybe he didn't like the name Cornelius.

"Right, Kendra. Now, here's the situation." He proceeded to relate the contract's requirements of showing Pierre from his client's perspective.

"I haven't fully read the contract," I told him, "but perhaps we could meet in a couple of days, clients included, and discuss whether things are as dire as Ms. Fieldmann believes."

"That should work." We agreed on a tentative time, at my office, subject to our respective clients' okays.

I called Joan immediately to report. "I didn't get a sense of how easily we might work out a mutually beneficial solution," I said, not mentioning that I wasn't necessarily on a complete first-name basis with opposition counsel. That might not bode well in our favor.

"I'm not surprised," she said. "I don't think Elmira's the type to compromise."

"We'll see." In my experience, most people could be convinced to work something out—if it turned out to be strongly in their economic favor. But this didn't seem like the kind of situation that could be solved throwing money at it, even if Joan had some to toss in Elmira's direction and was willing to do so.

I soon got down to some of my elder-law stuff. Had a nice, if quick, lunch with boss Borden and senior attorney Elaine. I felt slightly overdressed, since their clothing was more casual than business today. But I had an official meeting scheduled for later, so I'd worn a nice blouse and gray skirt, over which I could stick a coordinating jacket when the time came.

When we got back to the office, I went through my so far sparse notes about the Brigadoon pet situation.

I was ready and jazzed when my new potential clients arrived. I met them at the former restaurant's entry when Mignon buzzed, then chirped, to let me know they were there. I'd reserved the firm's bar conference room since they were a substantial crowd. Wanda was there, and she'd brought Darryl, too. Then there were James Jerome, Julie Tradeau, and the three other surviving board members. They introduced me to a few other players who apparently weren't on the board but didn't want the rules regarding pets at Brigadoon to change. In all, there were a dozen of us who gathered around the table in the center of the room.

Wanda was the one to start. "Thanks for meeting with us, Kendra." My petite friend wore a gold gauzy top today, trimmed with green piping.

I noticed that Darryl held her hand under the table. He must have come straight from Doggy Indulgence, since he was in one of his usual green knit shirts with the logo on the pocket. I noticed some white dog hair on its shoulder and had to keep from pointing it out, though I smiled about it.

"You're very welcome," I responded to Wanda. "How can I be of assistance?"

"Well," said James, "we need your help making sure things at Brigadoon don't change with respect to our pets." This was one of the few times I'd seen him in a shirt without guinea pigs depicted on it. He must have assumed this was going to be a formal law meeting, like in court, since he wore a blue suit. He'd even slicked his hair back from his forehead.

"You'll need to tell us, Kendra," said Julie, "if we can hire you as the condo association board or if we have to do it as individuals. We do constitute the entire board at the moment, but we have a vacancy. We know there'll be a fight when we hold the election to fill it—those who supported Margaret's position on pets, and the rest of our residents, including us."

"Depends on what you want my advice on." I leaned earnestly on the table. "If, as a board, you have questions on how the association's governing documents should be enforced, or how they can be amended if someone initiates a change, then I would represent the board. But then you couldn't include Wanda or the others here who aren't currently on the board, or you would risk waiving attorney-client privilege. If you all, instead, want a legal opinion about how to deal individually with a fight over pets, then it wouldn't be the board who'd hire me. The distinction's a bit obscure, so I'll want to consider the question further. In either event, if you hire me, I'll want to review the association's articles of incorporation, bylaws, and rules and regulations before I can give you definitive advice."

"Which would you suggest, Kendra?" James asked anxiously.

"It may be a matter of waiting to see what happens," I said. "When will you hold an election to fill the vacant seat?"

"Our bylaws say a special election should be held within sixty days after a vacancy occurs," Julie responded.

"Then at the moment, the current board, as constituted,

remains in charge. You can keep things going as they are now. Pets will continue to be allowed to live there, assuming your governing documents permit it—which I've gathered, even before reading them, they do. Your current rules about how owners are to ensure their pets don't constitute a nuisance will stay in effect, and you should be sure to follow them as exactly as possible in the meantime. I'd imagine you'll have one heck of a contentious campaign to fill that seat, but keep things as calm and uncontroversial as possible. And if the candidate you choose to run is someone who's pro-pets, and that person wins, you'll just have to see what the other side does."

"They won't stop fighting," Wanda surmised.

"No way," James agreed.

"We'll know better how to counter them when we see what they do," I said. "And . . . well, it'll be a whole different ball game if their candidate wins. But you'll still be in the majority. I'd imagine your meetings won't be fun at all, though."

"That's an understatement," Darryl muttered, his first comment since our meeting began.

I exchanged sympathetic glances with him. "In the meantime," I went on, "I can look at your governing documents. You can act as a board to hire my firm to review them. I wouldn't suggest taking any steps to strengthen them in your favor right now, or you'll be courting a lawsuit."

"Darn!" James exclaimed. "I'd thought about doing that."

"Which is why I warned you. Anyway, let me know who should be my main contact—James, or Julie, or someone else on the board—for now."

"James is fine," said Julie, and everyone in the room appeared to agree.

"Then James, please get me a set of the governing documents. I can either read them now, assuming there'll be a problem, or wait to see what happens and save you the expense of my legal fees if things don't go as badly as you think."

"Read them," Julie said.

"Definitely," James agreed.

The meeting adjourned soon afterward. Wanda and Darryl lingered after the rest had left.

"What do you think, Kendra?" Wanda asked anxiously.

"Looks as if you've got some stalwart folks on your side who really want to ensure that Brigadoon's pet policies don't change," I said.

"Right," she agreed. "But I'm nervous about that special election thing. I'm pretty sure Ruth Bertinetti will run for Margaret's seat, and you already know what she's like."

I shuddered in sympathy. "What about you?" I asked her, as Darryl closed his eyes in apparent agony. He knew what I meant. "Are you going to run for the empty seat?"

"I'm thinking about it," Wanda said slowly. She, too, glanced at Darryl, obviously knowing his dubiousness over the possibility.

"You'd make a great Brigadoon board member," I told her. "But, as you know from your work with our pet-sitters' club, that kind of thing's a lot of effort. And you'd be right in the middle of the pet dispute."

"I already am," she said dryly. "And . . . well, I'm

afraid I'm still under suspicion about Margaret's death. I don't know that I should take on anything like a campaign like this till it's resolved."

I didn't disagree. But I also wondered if suspicion was being cast on Wanda to keep her preoccupied and not wholly centered on the pet issue. If so, was the actual killer involved, or one or more of the anti-pet folks?

"You may be right," I said. "By the way, how's Lady Cuddles today? Home in her apartment, as she should be?"

Wanda's gaze suddenly grew anxious. "She was before. And I certainly hope she still is."

"Me, too."

They left soon afterward. I was worried about Wanda, and Darryl, too. And their relatively new relationship. They were both clearly upset by this whole situation. And its outcome was absolutely unclear.

So was Wanda's position as a possible murder suspect.

Well, I hoped to help out with both.

Before I left the office to start my pet-sitting, I called Brody Avilla.

"I'll have at least an initial report for you tomorrow, Kendra. I promise."

"That's great," I said. After the meeting today, I'd hoped to have some other possible suspects for him to look into—pro-pet people who might have hated Margaret.

But of those who'd come to my office, most had stayed fairly quiet.

That meant my original suspects, those on the board, had the best likelihood of wanting to do away with their pet-hating counterpart. Them, Margaret's ex-husband, Paulino Shiler, and that contractor Rutley Harris.

I hoped that the info Brody gave me on them tomorrow would tell me exactly who the killer could be.

Chapter Sixteen

No Dante that night at my place. Nor did I go to his. He had another early morning meeting to mull over, and I had pet-sitting duties first thing.

We talked, at least. He expressed concern over what I was up to. He said he'd talked to Brody, too. No surprise. But he'd spoken with his longtime friend after I had, and he assured me that Brody would report some interesting information to me . . . tomorrow.

So, Lexie and I headed for bed.

And, yeah, I thought about Dante. Probably even dreamed of him, though my conscious mind wouldn't admit it when I woke.

The next day, I took Lexie again to Doggy Indulgence—partly to check on Darryl. She accompanied me on part of my pet-sitting route first, though. Getting to Doggy Indulgence too early could mean I'd miss seeing my old friend again.

He was, indeed, there when Lexie and I strolled in

just before I prepared to head for my office. He stood near the front desk, engaged in conversation with Kiki.

I hated to interrupt them—mostly because I didn't want another confrontation, or even a dirty look, from the bleached-blond actress wannabe who was so good with animals but so awful with people. I admit I was getting even cattier where she was concerned, and she seemed to get nastier the longer I knew her.

Even so, as Lexie lunged toward the main room's zone where other dogs were already engaged in supervised feigned fights over toys, I approached. And heard, even though their voices were muted, that Kiki and Darryl were arguing.

"But you know I can do it," she said. "You used to be so receptive to my ideas. Before . . ."

Her voice trailed off, and I could only imagine the ending of what she'd begun. Before what? Before the first of the year?

Before he'd become involved with Wanda?

That could imply Kiki had some kind of crush on Darryl. I hadn't seen it *before*, but maybe it arose only after he became unattainable.

I decided to rescue him, though I was certain my long, lanky friend could take care of himself.

"Good morning," I said brightly.

The look Darryl leveled on me didn't seem especially relieved. In fact, he looked a little annoyed. "Hi, Kendra. Excuse us for a minute, will you?" I thought he was talking to Kiki at first, but then I realized he was still looking at me.

Not only didn't he want me to save him from a difficult conversation, but he wanted me to butt out.

I attempted not to allow my feelings to be hurt. And

my curiosity not to be stoked—too much. "No problem. I just wanted to say hi. Lexie's here for the day, so I'll see you later." I started to leave. Slowly.

Even as I heard the conversation again heat up behind me. I thought I heard Darryl utter the words, "Like I was saying, things are different now."

Kiki's response: "After all I've done for you . . . well, things are about to change, unless—"

But my shuffling had already gotten me too near the door to hear more. I turned and took one more look toward where Lexie played. I darted a stealthy glance toward Darryl and Kiki, and saw them staring each other down.

Then I was gone.

I HAD A court day coming up soon in an elder-law case, so I started to prepare for it after reaching my office. I'd checked with Mignon when I came in. She'd fielded no calls for me.

Nor did my phone ring as I sat there occasionally staring at it, willing Brody to finally finish his research and let me know what he'd found.

"Hey, Kendra," my dear friend and boss Borden Yurick eventually said from my doorway. His usual colorful aloha shirt that day had a blue background. "I haven't seen you all day. Just wanted to be sure you're here and okay."

"Yes and yes," I said with a smile. "And you?"

"Yes, and hungry. Up for lunch again today?"

"Why not?" But as I grabbed my purse from a drawer and stood to leave, my phone rang. "Mind waiting for a second while I see who this is?" If it was Brody, I'd have to beg off lunch.

As it turned out, I still missed lunch, even though it wasn't the guy researching possible suspects for me.

"Kendra, this is Julie Tradeau, from the Brigadoon board. I'm . . . well, I'd really like to talk to you about this pet situation. And Margaret. Plus, I want to show you something. Can you come to my place this afternoon?"

MY CURIOSITY SWIRLING, I arrived at Brigadoon less than an hour later. I had walked with Borden to a nearby sandwich place, but got mine to go. That way, I at least had a little time to spend with my sweet, grandfatherly mentor.

I ate in the car, so when I arrived at the condos, I was full of food—and interest in what had gotten Julie to call me.

Plus, I was worried about the ethics of this meeting. And of my acting as attorney to the association while I investigated some of its members as possible killers. I'd therefore come up with an alternate idea for its legal representation.

I buzzed the button at the outside gate, and Julie let me through to the parking lot. I made a quick call on my cell phone, reached my friend and fellow attorney Avvie Milton, and got her go-ahead to recommend her as an attorney for the Brigadoon board. She had been my fellow lawyer at the firm of Marden, Sergement and Yurick a few years ago, and had recently left to join a boutique firm in the Valley. We had more than that in common. We'd both, at different times, been the lover of one of the firm's partners, philandering Bill Sergement.

After that call, I placed another—this one to Wanda,

to warn her what I was up to. She was off on a doggy walk with one of her clients. She didn't have any problem with what I proposed—as she shouldn't, since she wasn't on the condo board. At least not yet.

But she, too, was curious about what Julie wanted. I told her I'd fill her in later, as long as it was appropriate.

I had a feeling Julie might be about to impart her own suspicions on Margaret's murder—or to set me on someone else in an attempt to take my suspicions off her. I wasn't convinced now that Julie didn't do it. I'd see how I felt about it later.

In a little while, I was in Julie's lovely unit—the site of the condo association meeting last night.

Julie's appearance hadn't particularly struck me before. Her facial expressions said a lot—smiling or scrunched, it seemed. But today, she seemed to want to make a big impression on me. Her hair was much lighter than its prior nondescript brown, and I recalled that she was a hairstylist to the stars. Must have used a little of that magic on herself. She'd also put on more makeup than I'd seen before. Pretty, yes, but a bit much for midafternoon. Only thing ordinary about her that day was her clothes: standard blue jeans and a navy print shirt that wasn't tucked in.

I remained in the business casual I'd worn to the office, so I at least didn't feel that I embarrassed myself as we sat in her living room—looking much larger now that all the folding chairs for the meeting were removed and what must be the regular furnishings were restored. I put my big purse down beside me, then looked expectantly toward Julie, now at the other end of her big, fluffy sofa on the polished hardwood floor.

"In case you're wondering," she began, taking a sip from a mug of coffee. She'd offered me some, too, and my cup sat on an ornately carved coffee table. "You haven't met my husband, Ivan; he's away on a trip." That scrunchy look came back to her face. "He always seems to be gone when things are going on around here that I need him for." She laughed. "But that's the nature of the film industry. It calls, and people who work in it have to answer."

She seemed to await my opinion, so I nodded. "Guess so," I said. "My only real involvement has been with the *Animal Auditions* TV show, and it's filmed locally."

"Oh, that's right. I love that show!" Again her smile.

But I was starting to get irked. Why was I here?

Before I could inquire, I saw a sleek black form emerge from one of the bedrooms and pad indifferently in my direction—the cat I'd seen here before. "That's Smouser, isn't it?" I asked.

"Yes, that's my baby," Julie said in a baby-talk tone. Smouser slinked up to the sofa, levitated onto its back, and settled between the two of us, ignoring the humans who just happened to be there.

I laughed, reached out to stroke her soft back for a moment, then said, "Julie, I need to get back to my law firm soon, and then I have pet-sitting responsibilities. So—"

"Oh, yes, you're a pet-sitter like Wanda, aren't you?"

I nodded. "Which makes me partial to the current board members, who like having pets around here. I want to hear what you want to talk to me about, but I also think I'd better not take on legal representation of the board, or even any of you as individuals. I could have a conflict of interest. But I have someone I can highly recommend to you, and I've already talked to her about the possible assignment."

"That's great, Kendra."

"So," I said, "why did you want me to come here today?"

As I'd suspected, she seemed eager to talk about everyone else around, and how they hadn't liked Margaret. "I've heard that you solve murders," she said, "so I wanted to let you know what I've been thinking. Not that I have any real evidence, like on those TV shows and all. But I know the people around here, and you probably don't. Except Wanda, of course."

She sounded utterly earnest. And serious. And innocent.

And I didn't buy any of it. But I did listen.

"First, Wanda herself. You know Margaret and she were really fighting a lot about Margaret's attempts to ban pets here at Brigadoon altogether." She looked at me as if expecting an answer, and I nodded. "I've heard that the Burbank police seem to think Wanda killed Margaret, thanks to their fighting. I like Wanda, and I know she's your friend. I'd hate to think she did it, but . . . well, I actually heard them arguing the very night that Margaret died. If you're serious about learning the truth, Kendra, then don't count her out yet."

"Mmmhmm," I responded noncommittally. "Interesting. Who else is on your suspect list?"

"Well, there's James Jerome. Same motive, but maybe even stronger. He just loves his guinea pigs, and he's been fighting with Margaret at board meetings since the day she was elected, midyear."

Since this was January, I assumed Margaret had

been on the board for about six months, and Julie confirmed it.

She next turned to the other three board members: John, Sheldon, and Rick. All pro-pet, and therefore Margaret haters.

By then, my mind was saying *yeah, yeah, yeah.* And *Why am I here*? And starting to tune out.

This lady was protesting too much, and quickly vaulting to the top of my suspect list. Nothing new. Nothing—

And then she said something that made my visit worthwhile.

"I only wish my husband, Ivan, was here to help me through this hard situation with the pets and Margaret and all. We both despised what that woman was doing. But he's been gone for a week now. Won't be back till Sunday afternoon."

This was Thursday. Margaret had been dead for a week.

She had died last Thursday.

"Oh, was Ivan here to help you through the difficult time when Margaret was found dead?"

"No." Julie stared straight at me in a manner that suggested she lied. "He left on his trip just before she died."

HAD JULIE TOLD the truth about the timing, or was I reading things into her words and body language that weren't there?

Okay, I didn't know Ivan Tradeau. So what if he was on the pet-lovers' side with Julie, and didn't like Margaret? I didn't know if he had any better motive to kill her than any other pet person around there.

But he immediately latched on to at least the end of my suspect list.

And gave me a good reason to call Brody. Soon.

Of course I didn't mention my newly stirred suspicions to Julie. Instead, I thanked her for her hospitality and thoughts. And for her good wishes that I caught Margaret's killer quickly—which of course could again have been an attempt to throw me off both her and her husband as substantial possibilities.

I handed Julie the contact info for Avvie Milton, reminding her that Avvie would be the better choice for attorney in the association's legal matters regarding this pet stuff. Like me, Avvie thought like a litigator. That meant she, too, would attempt to settle disputes before they got too hot and heavy . . . if that was possible.

I gave Smouser a final pat good-bye, earning a soft purr and a glance from half-closed eyes. I smiled again. I liked this cat.

I was a lot less sure about his owners.

"Thanks for coming, Kendra," Julie said as she saw me into the hall.

My mind was awash with what I needed to do next: Return to my car. Call Brody from there. Head back to my office, for at least a few minutes, to tend to some unfinished business that shouldn't wait till tomorrow. Hurry off to do my pet-sitting.

Call Dante.

See if we were able to get together tonight. And—

Oh, hell. Just as I was about to enter the stairway, I saw a dash of golden-yellow fur. A ginger cat.

Lady Cuddles had done it again.

Chapter Seventeen

THIS SCENARIO WAS starting to feel much too familiar.

Especially when the anti-pet Bertinettis just happened to show up. They lived in another building toward the back, upstairs near James Jerome—as well as the unit Lady Cuddles called home. Why were they here, so close to Julie Tradeau's digs?

"Look, it's that creepy little cat again," huffed Teddy.

"And look who's after it . . . again." Ruth glared straight into my face.

I glanced at her for only an instant as I continued my dash down the zigzagging hallway after the fast feline.

I caught up with Lady Cuddles just as she jumped onto the sill of a window leading out to yet another balcony. I grabbed her and stuck her beneath my arm. Good thing I was wearing a jacket atop a long-sleeved shirt on this chilly January day, since the annoyed, meowing kitty stuck out her claws and raked me with them. I wrapped her close, tucked into my arms, talking to her soothingly. She must have recognized me, since she quickly relaxed.

I headed down the nearest stairway, hoping I could avoid seeing the Bertinettis again. No such luck. They stood in the downstairs hall, apparently awaiting me.

"What are you going to do now with that creature, Kendra?" Ruth demanded.

"Take her home, of course," I said sweetly.

"But you don't belong here," Teddy reminded me.

"Yes. What if you do something you shouldn't, like steal the cat?" said Ruth.

I'm a professional pet-sitter as well as a lawyer, I wanted to remind them. Plus, unlike them, I was a pet aficionado. And I was worried about this cute, elusive kitty. I wanted to ensure she got home safely and that every measure was taken to keep her enclosed there—for her sake and Wanda's, as well as for mine.

Instead, I said, "You're welcome to come along, of course. Supervise me on behalf of the residents of Brigadoon. Whatever."

"I think we'll do just that," Ruth said.

So the three of us—four, if you counted Lady Cuddles, now nestling in my arms—exited this building and headed for the one in the middle rear, where her owners, the Gustins, had their unit.

"Since you're here, would you mind opening the door?" I asked as we reached the entry to that building. Otherwise, I'd have to wait for Wanda.

I shifted Lady Cuddles while I reached into my large purse and pulled out my cell phone while the Bertinettis merely watched. Wanda was in charge of this wayward kitty, so she'd need to know anyway. Plus, she really should come back here both to let me into the unit, and to check with me to try to ensure that Lady Cuddles was enclosed in it securely this time.

I pressed in the number that called her automatically, and she answered right away. I quickly explained the situation.

"Oh, Kendra, no! Fortunately, I'm already in Burbank. I'll be there in about ten minutes."

Time I was afraid I'd have to spend with the Bertinettis hovering over me, but what choice did I have? Unless, of course, I wanted to turn Lady Cuddles over to their kind custody and care . . . not!

"Okay," I told them. "Wanda's on her way, but I'd like to go upstairs and see if I can figure out how Lady Cuddles got out this time."

Still grumbling, they at least let me in, and we climbed to the third floor. I meandered around the winding hallway past decorated doors till I got to the appropriate unit. The door was closed. And so were all the windows along the hallway that led to the outside of the building and the balconies between units, at least as far as I could see.

I hadn't a clue.

I bent my head over and whispered into Lady Cuddles's alert, pointed ears, "Won't you tell me how you did it? Especially winding up in another building."

But her only response was to start purring again in my arms. Adorable, of course, but utterly unhelpful.

Meantime, the Bertinettis still stood there, eyeing me as if they thought I might start tearing up the indoor-outdoor carpet on the floor or the wreaths, pennants, and other stuff off the doors and cram them in my pockets.

As we waited, I figured I might make a little

conversation to use the time wisely. "So," I said, "You both knew Margaret Shiler. Looked like you were good friends."

"We certainly were," Teddy said stiffly.

Ruth glanced at him, then back to me. "Yes," she agreed, then cleared her throat. "What happened to her was terrible."

The opening I'd hoped for. "Since you knew her so well, who do you think killed her?" Ruth had already accused Wanda to her face, so I suspected I knew the answer, but time had passed and maybe her opinion had shifted to someone else.

Both pairs of eyes opened wide, then narrowed angrily at me. Gee, these two had apparently been together long enough that they shared emotions and expressions, even though Teddy's face seemed more open and Ruth's more pinched.

"Everything we know or suspect, we've told the police," Teddy said.

"But who's your favorite person of interest?" I persisted.

"Any one of the people around here who didn't like her position about pets," Ruth responded. "I think the police believe it was Wanda, and I'd accept that. Second on my list would be James. Or any of the other board members." Nothing new coming out here, at least not yet.

"How about anyone else, whether residents here or not?" I asked.

"We knew her mostly because of her living here and being on the board," Ruth said. "We weren't close enough to know much about her family or friends, other than that she's divorced, I think."

"Yes," Teddy agreed.

Okay, talking to them was a definite dead end. I was delighted when Wanda finally appeared.

Once again, the window inside was open just a smidgen, but enough for this elusive little cat to climb out.

"But I checked it this morning," Wanda wailed. "She can't open it herself, and the Gustins assured me that they don't know of anyone else who has a key. I don't understand."

Neither did I, but I hoped to find out.

I'd have to ponder this mystery . . . along with Margaret's murder.

I STOPPED AT Doggy Indulgence to pick up Lexie before I hurried back to my office. When I got there, there were a few phone messages I needed to respond to, so I did, though it was late in the day and I'd have to leave soon to start my evening pet-sitting rounds.

One concerned the elder-law case for which I was soon due in court. I called back and had to leave a message for opposing counsel. No indication in his message of why he wanted to talk, but I hoped it was an opening for an opportunity to settle. As long as that meant a genuine intention to compromise, instead of an attempt to get me to back down on my client's behalf.

Since this was a suit about an ill-maintained apartment building where many residents were seniors, any settlement less than fixing the nasty problems and at least a slight reimbursement for the times my client had to stay with her children because the place was too hot, cold, or damp, simply wouldn't fly.

Then there was a call from Cornelius Eldt, who was representing the breeder against my client Joan Fieldmann in the French bulldog case. He wondered if I'd had time to read the contract, which I hadn't, and whether we could meet next Tuesday to discuss the situation, which we could. I marked the time he suggested on my calendar and called back—also having to leave a message confirming our meeting after checking with Joan.

A couple more minor calls, a stop in Elaine Aames's office to say hi to her and to Gigi, the Blue and Gold Macaw, as well as a stop to see our boss, Borden Yurick, and then Lexie and I were on our way.

On the way to my first pet-sitting stop, I called Brody. I had a good excuse, after all. I hadn't yet told him to check out Julie Tradeau's husband, Ivan.

"Glad to hear from you, Kendra," he said. "I've got some information I'll e-mail to you. Sounds like you may be in your car, considering the background noise, so I imagine you're not in a good position to take notes."

"Right you are," I told him. "And I'll look forward to that e-mail. But can you give me a rundown right now of who's top of your suspect list?"

"Hard to tell," he said. I listened carefully, glad I was stopped at a red light on Ventura Boulevard, as he went through a bunch of possibilities, from Margaret's ex-husband, Paulino, to the nasty contractor Rutley Harris, through to the guy in the picture I thought least likely to have done it, James Jerome. He'd found lots on each, but nothing that shouted, "This is definitely the killer!"

I hoped that something in writing on the Internet, in his e-mail, would somehow speak to my mind as it concentrated on something other than driving.

I mentioned Ivan Tradeau and asked Brody to check him out.

Then Brody said, "Will you be in Malibu tonight? I'm meeting Dante to talk over where we are with *Animal Auditions*. I've discussed the start of next season with our animal folks and my co-judges, plus our hosts, Rachel Preesinger and Rick Longley. Since you're a producer, too, we'll need your input."

"Oh," I said slowly. "Well, I'm pretty busy, Brody, so I don't think—" A beep sounded on my phone. "I've got another call coming in. I'll check for your e-mail. Thanks." I was stopped at another light, so it was easy enough to push buttons to end my call with him and answer the next.

"Kendra, it's Dante." The ID was unnecessary. His number was captured on my cell. More important, I knew that deep, resonant voice well.

"Hi," I said, attempting to keep the chill and hurt engendered by my previous conversation out of my voice.

"I just realized that I've been assuming that you're coming to my place tonight—only I've been so swamped I'm not sure I invited you. Can you make it? Brody'll be there for a while to talk over some *Animal Auditions* stuff, so I'll have Alfonse bring in pizza again, or something." He paused. "Damn! I know it's getting late and you have your pet-sitting to finish and I'm a jerk for not talking to you before. If you don't want to come, it's okay. I'll come up to see you over the weekend. If that's all right with you."

The megabillionaire Dante DeFrancisco, powerful pet store mogul, sounded so contrite that I had to laugh. "I'll be there," I said, "as long as you have pepperoni and mushrooms on a nice, cheesy pizza."

"Consider it done."

Chapter Eighteen

THE PIZZA WAS good. The company was better.

I knew I'd need to get to bed early so I could head back over the hill to the Valley for my first pet-sitting rounds tomorrow, but Lexie wouldn't mind a romp at dawn on the grounds of Dante's delightful Malibu estate in the mountains, overlooking the ocean. She'd especially enjoy it in the company of her friend Wagner.

And I'd be there with Dante. After a night I could only anticipate eagerly just then.

But first things first. That consisted of pizza—delicious and decadent, with the toppings I'd asked for. We all sat in his lovely living room, Dante and I on his beige-on-beige sofa that rested on an exquisite Oriental rug on the floor. Brody faced us from the chair of contrasting rust color, across the stone-topped table.

Dante's delightful, casually clad personal assistant

Alfonse hovered nearby, ensuring that we didn't lack for anything—including refreshers to our mugs of beer.

Our first topic of conversation: *Animal Auditions*. A new season was nearly set to begin. Last season we'd had two sessions, one featuring dogs and the other potbellied pigs. Both had done extraordinarily well in the ratings, which got us a lot more sponsors besides Dante's HotPets—although, in keeping with his initial orders, no other pet-supply stores could advertise on the show. That didn't preclude producers of pet foods and other compatible merchandise, and advertisers were clamoring to pay for commercials on *Animal Auditions*. A success? You bet!

The meeting that night was about how to put the scenario already chosen into effect. We'd decided on dogs again, since they were everyone's trainable favorites. The scenario involved having owners teach their pups of all sizes to be service animals. We all felt that would both attract viewers and, equally important, call attention to the need for more doggy helpers and encourage others to engage in similar acts for real.

When we'd finished talking over *Animal Auditions*, our initial topic segued into the other subject on our minds: Margaret Shiler's murder, and my investigation into it.

Dante was still awfully concerned that I was too involved, and therefore putting myself in danger. "But you've done this so much before, Kendra, that I know I can't talk you out of it this time, either. So, best I can do is to offer my help."

"And mine," Brody added. "Did you see my e-mail?"

Brody was one nice guy, never mind the secret past he had shared with Dante that I now knew about. Even better, he was great looking—definitely fit the role of movie and TV star with his sculptured facial features and gorgeous grin.

"Not yet," I admitted, though I'd been eager to see its results. "I didn't have much time at home before coming here, so I didn't look at my computer."

"Well, I already told you everything that could be important, except, of course, for the new guy you wanted me to research. And he turned out to be quite interesting. Ivan Tradeau is a stunt coordinator."

I already knew he was involved with the film industry, so I wasn't impressed.

"I hadn't run into him or his company, so I didn't know that," Brody continued, although I didn't need the reminder that he'd spent some time as a film hero himself. "And one more thing: my suspicions regarding the murder weapon in Margaret Shiler's case."

"The barbecue spit?"

Brody nodded. "Margaret did have a propane-fueled barbecue out on her balcony, so it came from there. But guess who was recently a stunt coordinator in a film where a spit was used as a murder weapon."

No guess needed. "Ivan Tradeau, I assume," I said.

He nodded. "That doesn't mean he's guilty, of course, but his hat's in the ring for being Margaret's killer, too."

"His wife's on the Brigadoon Condo Association board, isn't she?" Dante asked me.

"She sure is," I said. "She's a pet-lover, like Wanda, so she and her husband could have had just as much motive for the murder. He left town that day, and his wife said he was gone before Margaret was murdered—though I wasn't sure whether to believe her." I'd let Esther know this new bit of info regarding the barbecue spit, but it was getting a bit late to call her. It would wait until tomorrow.

Especially since Brody was about to leave.

Before he did, though . . . "By the way, Brody," I said, "have you done any background searches on Margaret Shiler herself? Her ex-husband told me she was an accountant, but not where she worked or much else about her."

"Yep, she was an accountant," Brody said. "With a major firm." He named one of the biggies. I was impressed, but wondered how someone with her miserable disposition had gotten along with clients. Maybe she just sat in a back room crunching numbers.

"She also had a successful sideline selling things on eBay and other online sites," Brody continued. "Looked as if used books were her specialty."

But neither vocation immediately led to additional suspicions about who'd offed her.

Lexie and I did stay at Dante's that night. Wagner and Lexie slept in their luxurious quarters, in special plush HotPets beds in the corner of the bedroom.

But Dante and I didn't do much sleeping.

EARLY THE NEXT a.m. Lexie and I entered our Escape and headed back toward the San Fernando Valley for my first pet-sit visits of the day. We drove on narrow, twisty Malibu Canyon Road, heading north. It was still nearly dark out. Since the month was January, daylight hours were fairly short. Streetlights and my headlights did a fine job of lighting our way.

"I'll bet I'm more tired than you, girl," I said to Lexie over my shoulder, since I'd blocked her in the backseat, as usual, for her safety. "I heard your deep breathing last night." Nearly snoring, actually, but I loved Lexie enough not to care. Wagner had slept more silently.

Dante's deep breathing wasn't snoring, but I'd listened to its rhythm, too, after our delicious lovemaking. He fell asleep much faster than me. I lay awake rehashing the delightful evening . . . and also wondering what might be next. He seemed to care deeply for me. Had even said he loved me, and I'd said it back.

I did love him. But where were we going with it? I was happy with the status quo, but felt sure Dante wanted more. If he asked, pushed for it, what would I say?

Hell if I knew.

Fortunately, as I was frazzling myself with these thoughts, my cell phone rang, and I answered.

"Kendra? It's Esther."

"Exactly the person I intended to call first thing," I told her, "but I thought this was too early."

"It would have been, except for the call I just got from Wanda."

I immediately shifted in my seat, slowing a bit so I could pay attention as the road wound right over a tall hillside. "What's going on?" I asked.

"The Burbank police want her back for further questioning this afternoon. I'll try to get it delayed until Monday. I don't suppose you'll be able to help me set them on some different suspect by then, will you?"

"Nothing definite," I said, "but that's why I was going to call you." I told her what Brody had learned about Ivan Tradeau. "It's still flimsy, but I hope to find out more."

"Flimsy is right, but at least it's something."

I promised I'd keep looking for something more meaty, then said good-bye and hung up.

And realized that I was hopping into this situation almost as if I was a licensed private investigator. But I couldn't use Jeff Hubbard's company as an alleged employer anymore.

Maybe I'd have to call him after all.

Or not. I was doing this not as a vocation, but to help a friend. No one had hired me, nor was anyone paying me. Besides, I was a lawyer. I could say I was assisting Wanda's actual counsel in this matter. I was sure Esther would vouch for me.

Which made me feel lots better. I didn't want my law license on the line for something unethical again—especially when, this time, there could be merit to the complaint.

There were other times I'd investigated murders, too, of course, but Jeff had been more ensconced in my life then—at least until the most recent cases. Oh, well.

I reached the Valley side of the hill and got onto the 101 Freeway heading south—east, rather. My phone rang again.

"Kendra, it's Darryl." He sounded frantic, and I knew why.

"I just heard from Esther," I told him. "I know that the police want to question Wanda some more."

"Can you help her?"

"I'm working on it."

He didn't press, a good thing. But he did hand the

phone over to Wanda, which told me they'd spent the night together. I was glad for both of them. The mutual support had to be at least somewhat helpful for their respective states of mind.

"I'm about to start on my pet-sitting for the day, Kendra," Wanda told me. "Esther said she'd try to get my interview with the Burbank cops delayed till next week, but if I'm stuck—whenever I'm stuck—could you please help with my pet-sitting?"

"I sure will," I told her. "Don't you worry about it."

When we hung up, I called my assistant, Rachel, who was also already on the road for her early assignments. I gave her a heads-up about possibly needing to take on additional pets to sit, depending on what happened with Wanda.

"Of course," she said, young sweetheart that she was.

I'd nearly reached the freeway exit for my first visit of the day and used that as my excuse to myself not to question Rachel about the house hunting she and her dad were doing. I didn't want to hear about it, at that moment, if they'd happened to have found the ideal situation and intended to move from my lovely main house immediately.

"That's wonderful," I said. "Thanks."

As I hung up, I decided I'd talk to Wanda a little later about my taking on some of her existing pet-sitting, to ease some of the pressures on her.

And to make it easier for me to do my own snooping. The jobs I wanted were those caring for animals at the Brigadoon condos.

I needed to spend more time there, eliciting information from all possible suspects—even though my not-so-subtle loaded questions could irritate some of those on my list, like the Bertinettis.

Too bad.

I MET WANDA at noon for lunch at a family restaurant on Ventura Boulevard, after dropping Lexie off with an assistant I like at Doggy Indulgence. Her latest brouhaha with the Burbank police was now scheduled for three that afternoon. No extension today. She looked awful. I mean, she was still the attractive, petite person I knew, and as always she wore a flowing, gauzy blouse, this one a pale peach that only served to emphasize how wan she was. There were circles under her big brown eyes, and a resigned droop in her expression.

We slid into a booth across from one another, and she immediately ordered coffee. Me, too. I wasn't exactly running on a full night's sleep, but I wouldn't have traded last night for anything.

"How are you hanging in there?" I asked, though I thought I knew the answer.

"Okay, I guess. It really helps to have Darryl on my side. As you know, he's one heck of a great guy."

I did know that, but if I didn't figure out who actually killed Margaret, and thereby clear Wanda, I had a feeling I'd better find a new doggy day care place to take Lexie.

But that petty aggravation would not begin to compare with the pain I'd feel.

"He sure is," I agreed, but decided, for my own psyche, to maneuver the subject of our conversation slightly. "So, you're okay with my helping out at Brigadoon for a few days, aren't you?"

"Absolutely, especially if you think it'll help you learn who killed Margaret."

"It may help. What would help even more is your insight." For the next few minutes, after our coffee and salads were served, I went over the people I'd met at the condo, and others Wanda thought of who didn't like pets. I made notes on a legal pad I extracted from my big purse. Listaphile that I am, I'd brought it along for just this purpose.

Wanda was a genuinely nice human being, despite her occasional, understandable, and excusable moodiness lately. Each time she talked about someone and his or her foibles, even those at the complex who weren't overly fond of animals, she came up with reasons why that person couldn't be a killer.

In exasperation, I finally blurted, "I don't want to hear how wonderful everyone is. Tell me who you think could have killed Margaret—assuming it wasn't you. And if it was you, tell me who I should concentrate on blaming it on."

Her eyes wide with apparent horror, she stopped eating her salad and stared at me. Then, her voice low and her body hunched, she said, "If you really think I could have done it, Kendra, maybe I'd better ask someone else to help me."

"Did you do it?" I asked point-blank.

"No, I didn't murder Margaret," she practically shouted.

Ignoring the glances from our fellow restaurant patrons, I smiled. "I didn't think so. Okay, then, who's your top suspect?"

Her expression softened. "You were just trying to get me mad, weren't you, so I'd accuse someone?"

"Something like that."

"Well . . . if I had to guess, and I really hate to do it, my vote is still for that terrible contractor who did work around our condo complex: Rutley Harris."

Chapter Nineteen

WISHFUL THINKING, SINCE Rutley wasn't a Brigadoon resident? Or was Wanda extra perceptive, recognizing that a dispute over poor construction timing and workmanship had somehow escalated enough that Harris turned killer?

Or did she know that Margaret and Harris had slept together?

No matter. He was already high on my suspect list, too.

I accepted the condo keys for her current clients from Wanda, along with a list of who and where they were and what care they required. With luck, I'd be caring for her animal charges only this afternoon so she could keep her mind and time free.

Good luck, that is. Bad luck, and she'd be stuck in the Burbank jail, but I wasn't about to mention that.

After we split our bill and walked into the parking lot, she stopped beside my Escape and we hugged.

"Let me know how everything goes this afternoon," I told her.

"You, too."

As I slid into the driver's seat, I sent her a cheerful wave. But when I put my hands on the steering wheel after starting the engine, I thought about letting my head droop in concern.

Nope. Instead, I turned east out of the parking lot, toward Burbank.

NO PROBLEM GETTING through the condo complex's main gate. I simply followed someone in, although I again had a security card from Wanda. The fact that I entered so easily indicated that the killer didn't necessarily need to be a resident to reach Margaret's apartment.

I parked, then headed for one of the first buildings, the one where the Tradeaus had their huge unit. They weren't on my list to visit, but one of their near neighbors was.

Only a couple of weeks had passed since I'd last been here helping Wanda with her pet-sitting. Then, she'd been on a romantic weekend with Darryl. Now, she was awaiting an ugly interrogation by the cops. Not exactly comparable. And my main reason for being there wasn't confined to animal care this time.

I needed more information to figure out who might have despised Margaret Shiler enough to more than just wish her dead.

I hadn't even started onto another avenue filled with suspects—like disgruntled fellow employees at her accounting firm. Or a boss who decided to get rid of her in a way more permanent than firing. Her ex-husband might know of something like that, but Paulino hadn't suggested it. And I knew about the contentiousness here. Even so, I might soon have to branch out to be successful.

I used a key to let myself into the building and mounted the steps to the second floor.

Happily, no one like Margaret—or the Bertinettis— stopped my progress and demanded to know why I was there.

The pets in the unit I headed for were a couple of tabby cats. Both were utterly charming and seemed glad for some human company. This was not a condo I'd visited the last time I'd taken over Wanda's pet- sitting duties at Brigadoon. According to her, their owners were out of town for a week, and all seemed well with the felines.

I strolled through this building as if I belonged there. On my next stop, a little bichon frise mix required some loving and a nice long walk, which I gave her with no hesitation and lots of attention. I did run into a middle- aged male resident who said hi and looked puzzled, and I explained without further detail I was there as a backup pet-sitter. He seemed okay with it.

As he turned to leave, I asked, as an afterthought, "Have you by any chance had any work done on your unit by Harris Commercial Construction? I live near here and need some remodeling, and I've heard they're good."

He said he'd heard of them but knew little about them. Not enough info to assist me in the least.

Two more dogs and a cat later, I was ready to enter the back building where Wanda lived. James, too, and the Bertinettis. And, formerly, Margaret. The few residents I'd run into didn't know much about Harris Construction.

The back building was another matter, though. I decided first to stop in to see my buddy Basil, Wanda's Cavalier King Charles spaniel. I proudly paraded Basil outside, toward the parklike area behind the building— all the while keeping an eye open for the wayward Lady Cuddles, since this was also her territory. Her family, Wanda had warned me, was remaining on a filming location for an extra week, so she was still in charge of the escape artist kitty.

As I went outside, board member John was just entering. I hadn't paid a lot of attention to his appearance before, mixing him up with the other men running the condo association. He looked like the oldest, with short salt-and-pepper hair and matching goatee that I assumed was designed to hide the wattle beneath his chin. "Hi," he said, stooping down to pet the pup. "Is this Basil?"

I nodded, and explained that Wanda had some business to attend to that afternoon, and I was helping out with her animal charges—including her own. I had no intention of describing her business. If she wanted to relate her difficulties to other board members, that was up to her.

But there was a topic of conversation I could broach with John: Rutley Harris. I obliquely hinted that I might have some remodeling at my home to hire the guy for.

"Why, sure, Rutley is doing some work for me. Margaret recommended him highly . . . though I know something went wrong there. I don't know what. But if you want to talk to him, he's here now. I'm having him upgrade the bathroom in my master suite."

Talk to him now? Why not?

Maybe my memory of what a jerk he was had been exaggerated over the few days since I'd seen him.

John showed me along the zigzagging hallways with windows overlooking patios and gardens, past other units with decorations on the doors, to his first-floor unit. He opened the door and let Basil and me enter. "He should be right through there." He pointed to a door down an internal hallway, from which emanated hammer blows and low conversation.

I entered. Sure enough, there was Rutley Harris inside a generous-sized master bath, along with a couple of other guys. "Hey, Rutley," John said, "Kendra wants to check with you about a remodeling job she has."

"No kidding."

I winced beneath the suggestive leer on this louse's face. He wore a sleeveless muscle shirt today, and he did in fact brandish big biceps. But there was nothing sexy about the way he looked me up and down. I shuddered . . . and considered kicking him where he'd notice I wasn't interested.

For the moment, I just said, "Looks like you're pretty busy here. Doing a good job, I'm sure. So . . . you remodel bathrooms. And I know you've done some replastering and painting in the condo halls. Tell me more about what kind of work you did for Margaret Shiler."

"Like I told you before, Kendra, I remodeled for her, I screwed her, but I didn't kill her."

"That's not what she meant," John interjected, obviously attempting to keep the peace as Rutley's two large employees seemed ready to come over to defend his honor. "But . . . you . . . er, were with her?"

"Just once. It was a mistake."

Enough of a mistake that he'd killed her? I kinda hoped so, but didn't expect Harris to change his tune at this instant and confess—even though he was the one I hoped had done it. And right about now, I regretted even instigating this conversation. Rutley was running it in an entirely different direction from where I'd intended it to go

"Anyway, if you actually want me to do some work where you live, Kendra, give me a call." He gave me an awfully lewd wink along with his business card, which I handled as gingerly as if it contained contaminants. "I'd be glad to take care of it . . . and you."

John was extremely apologetic as he led me from his unit, with Basil, on his leash, prancing happily at my side. "I didn't know about Margaret and Rutley. And he was out of line talking to you that way, Kendra."

"I'll say." But Harris's protestations made me move him a notch higher on my suspect list—not easy to do, since he was already at the top.

"Anyway, I'm sorry. But I need to dash off to meet someone now. And I'm sure you have more animals to visit for Wanda, right?"

I assured him I did, and bade him good-bye at the downstairs door.

I took Basil home and fed him his dinner early, then left Wanda a note, hoping that she'd be home soon to see it.

Then I went upstairs to James's unit and knocked on the door, but he apparently wasn't home, so I was unable to say hi to him and his guinea pigs.

Okay, time to go see Lady Cuddles. I looked forward to this visit, since I actually enjoyed the elusive kitty.

I only hoped she was at home where she belonged.

Good thing was, she was.

Bad thing was, as soon as I opened the door, she dashed past me down the hallway.

"Lady Cuddles!" I cried, and hurried after her along the zigzagging hall, where it was hard to keep her in view.

I looked with uneasiness as I passed the Bertinetti unit, but fortunately no one came out.

"Please stop," I called to the kitty, but she continued to ignore me.

And then I turned a corner—and no longer saw her ahead of me. I immediately began to despair.

"Lady Cuddles, where are you?" I cried.

I was in an area that, unfortunately, had become familiar—the one where Margaret Shiler had lived.

Her unit was on the right. I didn't see crime scene tape on the door any longer. I started to dart by it, hoping I'd spot Lady Cuddles around the next corner.

Only . . . the door to Margaret's unit was ajar. Was that where the kitty had disappeared?

I stopped outside, ready to push the door open a little and call out . . . only I heard some thumping and rustling from inside. Too much of it for a small cat to generate.

Were the police there, looking for further clues to the killing?

I figured I'd better butt out.

But I still needed to find Lady Cuddles.

Carefully, I pushed the door open a little more. I called out, "Hello? Anybody here?"

I half expected some loud voice of authority to shout something like, "This is the police."

Instead, as I looked inside, I saw a figure sneaking into the other room.

A kinda familiar figure. Someone I'd only recently met, but I'd definitely seen him before.

It was Paulino Shiler, Margaret's ex.

What the hell was he doing here?

Chapter Twenty

"WHAT ARE YOU doing here?" Nope, that wasn't me talking, but Paulino.

I'd always understood that a good offense is the best defense, and I assumed that's what he was up to.

"I'm helping to take care of some of the pets in the complex," I responded. He blocked my entrance, which I didn't like at all. "Including Lady Cuddles, the kitten who just slipped in there. Please let me by. I need to go get her."

And see if I could figure out what Paulino was up to.

I did take a brief look around to ensure that Paulino hadn't brought his boxer-mix pups along. They might be cute, and well adapted to the dog park where I'd first met him, but they didn't belong in this apartment that had been the scene of a crime.

Nor did I want them ganging up on Lady Cuddles. Even though I thought the cute kitten could elude two determined dogs.

I found no canines loose in the unit. Nor did I immediately spot Lady Cuddles. What I did see, though, was a bunch of boxes from one of the big office-supply chains—not collapsed ones, but expanded into crate shapes with lids on them.

Should I assume they were filled? If so, with what?

I kinda thought I knew.

"Are you still Margaret's heir?" I asked her ex-husband, pivoting to face him. He stood behind me, his arms crossed, his face sullen. I'd found him an athletic sort before—at least a runner, with his thin frame and tanned skin. Now, his complexion was red, especially against his shining buck teeth.

"I'm just here after some things that are mine," he retorted. "Margaret hung on to them for a while after our divorce, but she promised I'd get them back."

"When she died?" My turn to cross my arms and glare. And wish I'd left the door open wider, only I hadn't wanted Lady Cuddles to escape again.

Was this guy dangerous when angered? I didn't exactly want to find out.

"Whenever." He shrugged. "As if it's any business of yours."

"You're right. Just let me find Lady Cuddles, and I'll leave you alone." But I wouldn't leave the Burbank cops alone. In fact, I thought I'd give Detective Candace Melamed a call as soon as I exited this unit. Just in case no one was allowed to take anything yet from the crime scene.

Like an ex-husband who just might be attempting to steal whatever he could from Margaret's estate.

Which got me wondering—who actually were her heirs?

"Are your kids coming to help you move this stuff?"
I asked, figuring his response would help answer some
of my questions. Like, did they have kids? How old?
Where did they live?

And was he attempting to steal this stuff from
them?

I'd guessed Margaret to be in her early fifties, and
maybe Paulino, too, although he was in better shape
and appeared younger. That would mean any kids could
be adults.

"I gather what you're asking is if I'm helping my
kids, or stealing from them? The answer is the former,
if either. I had kids, and so did Margaret, both from
prior marriages, but none together. My stuff is my stuff,
and if my kids want it after I'm gone, they're welcome
to it. Not hers, though. They were miserable little turds
while we were together. No way do I want them to
inherit what's mine."

"Sounds fair," I said. As long as the stuff was truly
his. Which I definitely doubted.

But would he have killed Margaret for whatever
was in those boxes? For them and some other as yet
unspecified reason? For a motive I hadn't yet figured
out? Maybe.

I kept him on my list along with Rutley Harris. And
others.

We were still standing near the entryway. "Excuse
me," I said. "I need to find the cat."

He still blocked my path, but I managed to slip
by him into the living room. I wasn't exactly certain
where Margaret had been murdered, but it had most
likely been here—big swatches had been cut from the
carpet in the middle of the room, and there wasn't much

furniture there, either. Some or all of it might have been removed as possible evidence.

A few more boxes sat on the floor there. I pretended to slip sideways and "accidentally" knock the top off one.

A stack of books lay inside. Old books. Probably first editions.

The kinds of books I'd been told were the ones Margaret sold for a healthy profit as an Internet sideline.

Paulino claimed they were his? I'd heard that he, too, was an accountant. I pictured him as running around the dog park in off-hours for fun. Not as a reader.

Especially of classics.

But I could visualize him on eBay selling stuff for as healthy a price as people would pay. After Margaret gave him instructions on how she did it.

That was, of course, simply jumping to a conclusion. Could be *he* had taught *her* how to establish an adjunct career online. I'd check into it. It could provide a motive for murder—if they argued over possession of some valuable stuff she was selling. Or about who had taught whom what. Or even pirated accounting clients.

Or not. That was jumping to another conclusion. What I needed was facts, if I wanted to get Wanda off the suspect hook.

I was sure Paulino wasn't about to confess any sins, whether anger with his wife, or murder, or acting as a carrion eater by engulfing his ex's possessions to the detriment of her actual heirs.

What I needed even more, at this moment, was to locate Lady Cuddles.

No sign of her at the moment.

"Lady Cuddles," I called, standing in the middle of Margaret's messed-up living room. "Where are you?"

I heard something from elsewhere in the unit, a small cry that could have been a kitty. I headed in that direction.

Paulino was right behind me, which made me even more uneasy. I genuinely began to dislike the guy. Didn't trust him.

Wanted to leave.

But not without the elusive kitty who'd brought me here.

A doorway led into a short hall, and I heard the noise again. I wound up in the kitchen. There, on the counter, stood Lady Cuddles. She sat down when she saw me, and I saw her sort of smile. Or at least that was the expression I assumed she'd intended. Like, Gotcha again!

She stayed right there, and I picked her up, noticing yet again the rather bland ID tag on her new collar. I was delighted, though, that Wanda had replaced what was missing.

What if I hadn't been able to find her? What kind of pet-sitter would I be if I lost a charge, no matter how elusive?

What kind of friend would I be to Wanda if, as I took over for her during her several hours of need, I screwed up?

As it was, I still could only hope I'd solve Margaret's murder and free Wanda from suspicion.

"Okay, young lady," I said to the purring kitten in my arms. "Time for you to go home."

"Yeah," said Paulino. "Time for both of you to get the hell out of here."

As if he owned the place. Or the stuff he was most likely attempting to steal from there.

Not if I could help it.

"By the way," I found myself saying, "Do you know of anyone at Margaret's accounting office who might have wanted to kill her?"

"No! For some damned reason, they seemed to like her. Now leave!"

"Thanks for letting me in," I responded on the way out the front door. Okay, so I was overly polite, considering his rudeness. But I wasn't about to tell him I was going to call the cops on him.

Lady Cuddles stirred in my arms as we got into the hallway, as if she intended to leap down.

Not if I could help it.

I snuggled her closer, my fingers locking beneath her collar. Touching that ID tag.

As I walked down the zigzag hallway toward the unit Lady Cuddles would call home, if she could speak, my mind started puzzling over something.

Not that it was necessarily significant.

But it was a question I had to ask Wanda.

I WAITED TILL I'd let myself into the unit owned by the Gustins, Lady Cuddles's owners.

Okay, around the angles in the halls, I wouldn't be able to see if Paulino Shiler was hauling boxes out of his ex-wife's place. By the time anything happened, he and the crates could be long gone.

Even so, after ensuring that the door was closed behind me, and checking out the unit's windows to be sure none was ajar, I sat down in the kitchen, not far from the fragrant box of kitty litter, and used my cell phone to call Detective Melamed of the Burbank PD.

Lady Cuddles sat down on the floor beside me,

nonchalantly washing her little kitty paws with her long tongue, as if she'd been the picture of feline innocence all day. Not! But she was so cute, it was hard to stay annoyed with her.

I didn't know if Wanda was still at the Burbank police station under interrogation. Or whether this little piece of info I intended to impart could have any bearing on the murder case.

But I figured the detective needed to know.

I hoped she'd do something to stop that darned Paulino. Not that I'd any info about Margaret's kids, her presumed heirs. And I certainly hadn't adored Margaret. Still, her kids didn't necessarily deserve to be robbed by their former stepdad. The fact that he liked dogs better than his deceased ex might work a little in his favor, but taking valuables from her apartment erased any benefit he might otherwise have achieved in my mind.

I checked my recent phone call history since I hadn't programmed in the number of the Burbank authorities. I called, and asked for Detective Candace Melamed.

She didn't take long to get on the phone. "So, Ms. Ballantyne, I've spoken with your friend Detective Noralles of the LAPD. Are you calling—again—to try to solve this case for me?"

"Not at all," I said. At least not now. Okay, I shouldn't ask, but I did anyway. "Is Wanda still there?"

"Do you mean, did I arrest her? Not yet." She practically sang the last couple of words, obviously proud of herself.

And probably intentionally goading me.

"Glad to hear it. I genuinely don't think she's guilty, although I know you care about that as much as you care about what I intend to eat for dinner. But that's not why I called."

"Okay, tell me fast. I've got things to do."

I told her about my excursion into Margaret's no longer taped apartment, thanks to Lady Cuddles, and what—who—I'd found there.

"He's removing articles from that condo?" she practically shouted into the phone.

"Yep," I replied.

"Thanks for calling and telling me, Ms. Ballantyne. It doesn't make him guilty of the murder, even if what you've alleged is completely true. But if it is, I'll be glad to arrest the SOB—er, burglary suspect—and take a harder look at him for the murder, too." She paused. "You know, Detective Noralles thinks a lot of you."

"He's a good guy," I responded.

"Look . . . We don't need any official help in this matter. We've narrowed our suspicions down to a few suspects, and the matter is still under investigation. I won't tell you anything about our work. But if you happen to learn anything else useful . . . well, I won't mind at all if you share it with me. Unofficially, of course."

Startled, I thanked her and hung up.

I didn't believe that a detective on an active murder case, one I hadn't actually worked with before, was encouraging me to do my own investigation.

But it had sure sounded that way.

Now, all I had to do was solve the murder.

Chapter Twenty-one

I HAD SOME more pet-sitting stuff to do before picking up Lexie at Doggy Indulgence. I stopped to take excellent care of some pet charges in North Hollywood and other areas nearby, and eventually it was time to head for nearby Studio City.

I entered the door of the doggy day care facility, and as always ensured it closed snugly behind me. Lots of barks and cavorting canines greeted me inside. A few animals attempted to sleep in the area filled with people furniture, but a lot more seemed to be engaged in an intense game of chase-the-balls.

I smiled as I watched, but my happy look faded as I failed to immediately see Lexie.

Not again.

I did see Kiki. She was at the vanguard of caretakers playing with the pups. She tossed balls of various shapes and sizes, encouraging dogs to dash after them and bring them back.

I doubted that Darryl was here. He'd most likely been in Burbank with Wanda, and probably remained in her company, attempting to cheer her after whatever hell she'd been put through during her interrogation.

That meant I wouldn't have him to intervene in case my impending conversation with Kiki went awry.

Well, so what? I wanted to know where Lexie was. I considered asking Lila, the attendant who'd been so sympathetic last time, but she was busy playing with pups.

The simplest possibility was that Lexie was once again in Darryl's office, as she had been the last time she had apparently disappeared. That was the direction I headed.

I knocked first. Unsurprisingly not hearing Darryl's directive to enter, I nevertheless opened the door—unlocked again.

Sure enough, Lexie was on the floor nearby. She stood on her hind legs, greeting me eagerly, as if in thanks, then hurried toward where her comrades were playing.

So why had she been excluded from the games?

I turned, ready to go to the middle of the floor to get Kiki's attention, but didn't have to. She was right behind me.

"Why was Lexie in here again?" I demanded with no preamble.

"She deserved a time-out. She was playing too rough with the other dogs." Kiki's supposedly pretty film star wannabe face was stiff, her eyes glaring, as she responded icily.

"And do you give some of the bigger dogs, like the Labs or Dobie mixes, time-outs, too?" I demanded.

"They're more likely to hurt the other dogs if they get too physically assertive."

"I do what works best for the dogs around here," she said defensively. "I always do."

"Even if it's not something your boss approves of?" I knew Darryl would be peeved when I told him about this latest mistreatment of my pup. Fortunately, isolation for a short while might be hard for Lexie to deal with, but it wasn't permanently harmful. Even so, I continued, "You need to be careful about what you do and who you hurt, Kiki. I'm not just talking about your taking whatever you have against me out on Lexie. And I'll bet she's not the only one you go after in response to a slight by someone else. I know you're upset about Darryl's being so close to Wanda now. And what you've done to retaliate for that, well—"

"What do you know about that?" she asked immediately. Her already pale face had drained of all color, and her widened blue eyes were those of the proverbial scared doe captured in an auto's headlights.

I'd only been guessing that she had done something. Now I was extremely curious about what it was. "More than you think I do," I lied.

"I know you solve murders." Her voice, usually projected as if she was onstage, was suddenly soft and raspy. "But I know I didn't—I mean, you don't actually have a clue about me . . . do you?"

By now, the word "curiosity" had become one huge understatement for describing my state of mind. What the heck was Kiki talking about? A "clue" about her crazy infatuation with Darryl? Or a "clue" about her involvement in the case? Or none of the above?

My thoughts scrambled for a solution. The only

murder I was looking into was Margaret Shiler's. Wanda, whom Kiki obviously disliked, was apparently the cops' favorite suspect.

Had Kiki killed the woman and framed Wanda?

Hell, that was a stretch even for my overactive imagination.

"Oh, I have a pretty good idea," I said, persisting in my prevarication. "But why don't you just admit it to me?"

"You're lying!" she finally accused. "You don't know anything, do you? You bitch!"

Before I could attempt to convince her otherwise— despite the truth in what she said—she turned her back and joined the doggy ball game once more.

I watched her for a while, also keeping an eye on Lexie and her excited participation in what was going on.

Kiki once again cheered canines right and left, tossing and rolling balls and laughing along with the other attendants as they all encouraged the game.

But every once in a while, Kiki cast a furtive glance in my direction, as if she were attempting to read my mind and learn if whatever she didn't want me to know had actually shown up there.

I wished it had.

And somehow, I would ensure it eventually did.

I FINISHED THE remainder of my day's pet-sitting with Lexie's company. She was used to my uneven commands of sometimes staying in the car with the windows cracked. I was always careful, of course, but at least, at this time of year, I didn't have to worry about her dehydrating or turning into roast rack of Cavalier.

On other visits, she was invited inside to play while I did the cleaning and feeding before I could join in the charming canine games. I noted everything, as always, in my pet-sitting journal after returning to my car.

Eventually, we were back inside the security gate at home. I looked toward the main house, and the lights were low. Apparently neither Russ nor Rachel was there; I wasn't sure about Beggar.

Lexie and I headed up the stairs to our home-sweet-garage, and as I walked, I called Rachel to see how she was doing with her pet-sitting assignments of the day.

"Hi, Kendra!" she enthused as I reached into my pants pocket and extracted the door key I'd stuck into it. "I'm on my way home. I've finished up for today." She gave me a rundown of all the pets she'd visited and cosseted that day as Lexie and I entered our apartment.

"Sounds good." I stuck my large purse in the same spot I always did these days—on a shelf at the bottom of the small decorative table in my tiny entry. I waited before saying good-bye, just in case Rachel had something else to tell me—like, she and her dad had located the perfect house to buy and they'd be leaving next week.

I'd been assuming that was coming any moment lately. But she didn't say it tonight.

I breathed a sigh of relief. Then I went into the kitchen to feed Lexie her dinner. I wasn't sure what to do about mine, though it was late enough that I doubted I'd have a date tonight.

Even so, I called the only person in my date book these days.

"Hi, Kendra." Dante's warm, deep voice sounded like he was happy to hear from me.

"Hi, yourself. Any chance of us getting together tonight?" Like, was he in the mood for a nice, romantic dinner and some quality time? I didn't say all that, but figured he could hear it in my purposely throaty tone.

"I'd love it, but I can't. Unless you can come here, but even then—I've another early morning video conference with the East Coast. And right after that, some potential suppliers are coming to my office to pitch some new products that actually sound quite good. And—"

"I get it."

I had sunk into one of the chairs around my minuscule, round kitchen table. My heart had sunk as well. No Dante tonight.

Was he starting to make excuses?

Not that I expected to see him every night.

And then a fact I hadn't considered dawned on me. "Tomorrow's Saturday," I suddenly reminded him.

"Don't I know it." He sounded neither surprised nor happy about it. "A corporate executive's job is never done, just like a pet-sitter's. Or a lawyer's, for that matter."

"But what about your employees? Don't they get Saturdays off?"

"You forget—we're in retail. Doesn't matter if we're office types. We need to stay available. My conference call will include a few store managers to get their input, and the sales reps know that to encourage people to buy the products they represent, you meet them at their convenience."

"Right." I attempted to interject cheerfulness into my tone. "So, well . . . have fun." Like, *see ya. Whenever.*

"I don't like this, Kendra," Dante growled into my ear. "You know, if we were living together, we'd see a lot more of each other, even at our busiest times."

I couldn't think of anything frothy and pithy to say, so I stayed quiet. I had too much on my mind already to deal with this issue now.

"No response?" he asked with a sigh. "I figured. Okay, how about this: Can we get together for dinner tomorrow night? You choose the location, near your place or mine. We can spend the night together, too, if you're all right with that."

"I'm more than all right with it, Dante," I told him from deep inside my heart.

I would definitely look forward to it.

I DIDN'T EXPECT to speak with anyone else that night. I watched some interesting but unrealistic dramas on TV, then some news—equally interesting and unrealistic.

As I started thinking about bed, my cell phone rang. Had Dante called to say good night?

Nope. The number wasn't his, but Althea's. Her boss, Jeff, used to call around the same time when we were together and he was out of town. Was this an attempt to remind me of him?

"Hi, Kendra," she said when I answered. "How've you been? Where've you been? Solved your latest murder?"

"How did you know I'm working on one?" I demanded.

I had of course considered asking Althea to assist me soon after Margaret's murder, but after that I'd begun to depend on Brody. And he had been enlisted by Dante for this duty.

"Just guessing," she said with a laugh. "But I've missed hearing from you. Need any computer research done on this one?"

"Thanks for asking," I said. "I've been trying to approach research from a different angle, but of course no one is as great as you at finding stuff."

A compliment that might not be entirely true. Dante depended on Brody, and from what I'd learned about him, Brody was probably as thorough online as Althea. That probably meant, even if he wasn't as fast, that he was an equivalently skilled hacker. Not to mention film star, judge on *Animal Auditions*, and former underground government agent.

My lovely grandmother-age friend Althea couldn't compete with all of that, but neither did she have to.

"Oh," she said. "Well, I mostly just called to say hi. And to let you know that if you do need any research, I'd be glad to help. Just so you know, Jeff's out of town for a couple of weeks, so I can't even charge you a fee of getting together with him."

"Who's watching Odin?" I asked without thinking. Odin was Jeff's wonderful Akita, the reason I'd met Jeff in the first place. They'd been my initial pet-sitting clients when I'd needed a second career after my law license was suspended.

"Oh . . ." I could hear the hesitation in Althea's voice, although I suspected this was the underlying reason for her call. I had to assume Jeff had enlisted a different pet-sitter. Which might be a good thing. He'd seemed inclined to attempt to win me back, but I'd remained adamantly against the idea for a while, instead acting as if we were friends. "Well, he hired someone else to stay in his home while he's gone. I don't think she's a member of your pet-sitting club, but you'll have to ask him."

"That's fine, as long as whoever it is takes good care of my buddy Odin."

There was a slight pause in the conversation as I sought something else to say. I assumed Althea did, too.

I hated that. We'd been friends for a while. I might have hurt her feelings by asking for someone else's help, and she probably thought she'd hurt mine by telling me obliquely that Jeff was finally moving on—at least as far as pet-sitting went.

But I was fine. And I didn't want to lose her as a friend. And . . .

Hey! There *was* someone I needed information on, whom Brody so far knew nothing about.

"You know, there *is* one person I wanted to ask you to check on for me, Althea."

"Yes?" She sounded excited.

"The thing is, I only recently realized that even though I've been acquainted with her for a while, I don't know her last name. But knowing you, you'll figure it out. Could you please give me all you can find about a woman named Kiki? She's a sometime actress, although I don't know any roles she might have gotten. Her current job is as an animal caretaker at Doggy Indulgence Day Resort."

"That's the place you take Lexie, isn't it? Your friend Darryl owns it. Can you ask him Kiki's last name?"

"I don't want him to know what I'm up to, Althea, or even suspect it. Please just see if, even without her last name, you can find anything at all on Kiki."

Chapter Twenty-two

ON SATURDAY MORNING, I brought Lexie along as I accomplished my earliest pet-sitting visits. Then we headed for Burbank. I needed to hand the keys back to Wanda for the condos where I'd pet-sat yesterday on my friend's behalf, though I thought some of those she'd handed me might be duplicates.

"Thanks, Kendra," Wanda said, meeting me at the door to her condo unit after buzzing me in. "Hi, Lexie." She made a fuss over my adorable Cavalier, and I did the same with her Basil. I drew the line at hugging and petting Darryl, though, when he appeared behind them in the entry.

"Have you figured out yet who killed Margaret?" he asked with obvious hope.

Even if I hadn't already known how hard this all was on him, I'd have guessed it from the bags beneath my buddy's eyes.

"Still working on it," I assured him.

"Would you mind coming along with me on a couple of visits, Kendra?" Wanda asked. "Lexie can stay here with Basil." And with Darryl, which was, I assumed, the main reason she'd invited me—for a discussion out of his earshot.

"Fine," I said. I couldn't stay long, since I still had the rest of my own morning pet-sitting visits to do, but I'd hang out as long as possible to lend any moral support I could to my friend. I had some questions for her, too. Like what did Detective Melamed ask her yesterday? Did she happen to mention my call about Paulino Shiler? Had Wanda been finally dismissed from the suspect list?

We walked down the hall, heading, it appeared, toward Lady Cuddles's unit. "Yesterday was the pits," Wanda began, slowing her pace.

"I'll bet," I responded encouragingly.

The questions she'd been asked this time weren't much different from the last time—more about why she just happened to go into Margaret's apartment, where she had discovered her dead body. Why they'd been arguing, since their verbal feud, commonly known around the condos, had been reported by a rash of residents. Where she had been earlier on the night Margaret was killed, which I had subtly inquired about before, too. She'd told me she was doing her regular pet-sitting, at Brigadoon and elsewhere, although the animals couldn't give her much of an alibi. Presumably that's what she'd also told the cops, too. Wow, they apparently hoped she'd step all over what she had answered before, so they could leap on that as a sign of her guilt.

But, she confirmed, nothing in her responses had changed.

The detective hadn't mentioned Paulino's attempted burglary yesterday. The first Wanda heard about it was when I had called early that morning to let her know I would be at her unit soon.

Wanda was still, apparently, a suspect. The detective had assured Wanda she'd be in touch again soon.

Some action on my part was needed, and I'd been working on ideas for what that should be.

We had just reached the door to the unit containing Lady Cuddles. I backed up a little so I'd be primed to catch the elusive kitty if she happened to get by Wanda, who unlocked the door.

As soon as she pulled it open, though, it wasn't a zooming Lady Cuddles who greeted us, but a tall guy frowning behind his glasses. He wore khaki shorts and no shirt, strange on this cool January day. "Wanda!" he exclaimed.

At the same time, she squeaked, "Jamiel." They obviously knew each other. I hoped they'd fill me in soon, though I had more than a hunch who the guy was: Lady Cuddles's owner, and therefore the resident of this unit, finally home from his trip.

"Sorry we didn't call you," Jamiel said. "We took an overnight flight from Honolulu and just got back." He turned and called behind him, "Trudy, Wanda's here." He then looked at me, then, expectantly, to Wanda.

She hastily introduced us. "Kendra helped me take care of Lady Cuddles a couple of times. She's the one I mentioned to you by e-mail."

"Great. Good to meet you." Jamiel waved us into the unit, which I'd visited before. In layout, it resembled the others I'd seen in this building: Wanda's and James's and the one previously belonging to Margaret Shiler.

It had a small entry leading into the living room, with a hallway to one side. Its furnishings were pleasant but not necessarily plush, with an ornate set of wooden shelves along one wall containing bric-a-brac and a TV. The hardwood floor, partly covered by a rug, was much more decorative than those I'd seen in other Brigadoon units.

Jamiel asked us to sit down. Before we did, a woman entered from behind us, Lady Cuddles snuggled in her arms. Jamiel's turn to make some introductions.

Trudy Gustin was clearly of Asian ancestry, with thin, dark brows over lovely almond eyes, and facial features that suggested she could easily win beauty contests. She was clad in a slinky silken robe. "Thank you both for taking care of our little one, here. Only . . ."

Uh-oh. Was she about to castigate us for allowing Lady Cuddles to run around the condo complex? Other residents could have filled her in. Or, more likely, Wanda had kept her informed.

"Is something wrong?" Wanda sounded fearful that she had indeed done something to hurt the kitty. She sank onto a chair.

"Not really." But Trudy's questioning tone suggested otherwise. "But—well, she's wearing a different collar and name tag. What happened to the ones she had before?"

Ah! I'd intended to quiz Wanda just a bit about the timing of when Lady Cuddles's gear had gone missing. Now I didn't have to bring it up myself.

"Actually," Wanda said, "I don't know where they went. She was wearing them on the first days I took care of her, and then . . . well, on one of her runs through the condo she appeared to have lost them."

"I'm so glad Wanda replaced them so quickly," I interjected on her behalf, sitting on a chair next to Wanda. "With Lady Cuddles escaping from here as much as she did, I'd hate to think what could have happened if she'd been out without any identification at all."

"True," Trudy said thoughtfully, heading gracefully toward the sofa. "I liked her original stuff better, but it won't hurt to have a backup if I try to replace the original ones."

"Right," I said. "And while we're on the subject . . . Wanda, do you happen to remember when you first noticed that Lady Cuddles's collar was missing?"

I held my breath. Would she remember—and would it be the timing I was counting on?

"Absolutely," she said. "I can't forget anything about that evening. It was one of the times Lady Cuddles had gotten out of here, and I was hunting for her. I found her." Wanda shuddered. "I also found Margaret Shiler's body. Of course I told you about that," she said to the Gustins, "since the reason I was even in her unit was because the door was open and I was afraid Lady Cuddles had gotten inside. Which she had, the poor thing."

The Gustins were suddenly close together, looking sad and solemn and supportive of one another, which was sweet. They, unlike almost everyone else in the complex, weren't on my suspect list. Far as I knew, they had indeed been on their extended trip to Hawaii when Margaret was killed.

"I'm just glad she was okay," Trudy said. "She might have seen the killer, right?"

Wanda nodded. "As I told you on the phone, she seemed freaked out. Even scratched me a little when I picked her up. I had to leave her for a while when the police came, since I was supposed to keep the crime scene just as it was when I entered."

"My poor baby," Trudy said.

Said baby seemed to snuggle even closer into Trudy's arms, as if she understood the conversation, the cute kitten.

"But when you first walked in, saw Margaret, and found Lady Cuddles in her unit," I prompted, "was Lady Cuddles wearing her collar then?"

"No, that's what I meant, Kendra. I won't forget anything about that night. That's the first I noticed that the collar and name tag were missing."

"Did you tell the police?" I asked.

"Sure, when they questioned me that night—not that they seemed impressed. I can't imagine it had anything to do with what happened to Margaret, either." She looked earnestly toward Trudy. "But I do feel responsible that it was missing. I'm still looking for it, and I've asked around the condos, too. No one seems to have seen it. I even asked Detective Melamed again yesterday if they happened to find the collar and name tag in the unit when they investigated the crime scene. She looked at me like I was crazy for asking anything about their investigation."

"Did she happen to answer?" I inquired.

Wanda shrugged. "No, and I got the sense that she thought I was insulting her by suggesting she hadn't done a thorough search of Margaret's unit."

Had she, and had the crime scene techs?

The idea niggling at the edges of my brain was now swirling full-force through my consciousness.

It might be utterly asinine, and get me nowhere

because the doggy sense inside me was barking up an absolutely wrong tree.

But I'd never know unless I tried.

WE SOON LEFT the Gustins' unit. Wanda had animals in other units to check on before heading out to see more pet-sitting clients, and I needed to get on with my critter visits, too.

I stopped at her unit, said 'bye to Darryl and Basil, and picked up Lexie.

Wanda accompanied us out. As we walked, with Lexie on the leash at my side, I got further input from Wanda about what the police had actually asked her. She'd shown she was attempting to cooperate by answering as well as she could, not simply clamming up because her counsel was present.

"Esther encouraged me, though I know she was worried about what I might inadvertently say that could hurt me."

"What all did they go over?"

"Same as before. They wanted my time line, what I'd done before, why I happened to go into Margaret's unit, how Margaret and I got along, and why we weren't best buddies. They didn't get into pushing me harder for a confession, so I assume they were still fishing for inconsistencies. I don't think I gave them any, at least none of significance."

"Did Esther tell you afterward that anything seemed off to her?" We'd reached my Escape, and I encouraged Lexie to get in the backseat.

Wanda shook her head, her pretty face looking utterly downcast. "But I'm getting so frazzled by all this, Kendra, I'm liable to turn everything upside down if they question me again. They'll think that's a sign of guilt, not nervousness. And Darryl—well, he's been such wonderful support. But our relationship's so new . . . I'm afraid of what the stress will do to it. That's why I wanted to talk to you alone, not in front of him. Give him time to think of something else for a few minutes."

"Darryl's a special guy," I assured her, but she already knew that. "He'll be there for you."

I hoped. My own experience with men hadn't been so wonderful. But then the men I'd fallen for weren't as steadfast as my fast friend Darryl. Or at least the way he used to be toward me.

"One final question, then I've got to go," I told her. "Lady Cuddles's collar and name tag. I gather the cops either aren't attaching any significance to their disappearance, or they're not letting you in on it. Do you recall any reaction at all when you brought them up?"

"Well . . . in some ways that Detective Melamed reacted less to it than to anything else I said."

Which could mean she was hiding what she really thought.

"I can't promise anything," I told Wanda, "but I've an idea that just might help us find who killed Margaret."

Chapter Twenty-three

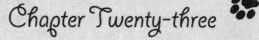

ON MY WAY to my next pet-sitting place, I got a call. "Hi, Kendra," said Althea's familiar voice. "I've found some stuff for you."

"On Kiki?" I inquired, stopping at a red light. I glanced into my rearview mirror and saw that Lexie was lying down. Evidently her stay with Basil had worn her out—not a bad thing.

"That's Kiona Kistner to you."

"No kidding? That's her real name?" The light turned green, and the Escape headed forward, with my assistance. Only a few more blocks, and we'd be in the Encino residential area that was our goal.

"Assuming she's the employee of Doggy Indulgence Day Resort, and she's also an actress represented by the Imminent Stars Film Agency, that's her."

"I don't know the name of her agent, or even if she has one, but I know she's a wannabe actress. And, yes,

she unfortunately works for Doggy Indulgence. So . . .
I guess she is—what was it?"

"Kiona Kistner. I've got a bunch of additional info
on her for you—address, phone number, and all of
that—the easy stuff to find, and even more, though I
don't think you need her Social Security number. But
there's something else."

I was always curious about how Althea made finding
anything on anyone so easy. Superhacker? Sure, but I
suspected there were some resources available to those
in the security industry that, if the rest of us knew the
extent of the supposedly private info they could access,
we'd feel far from secure.

"Like what else?" I asked her.

"She's been talking to some real estate agents in the
Valley about a commercial site."

"Interesting." I drew out the word, wondering what
the woman was up to. And why it caused her to resent
Wanda's getting close to Darryl. I still wasn't sure if
she had any romantic interest in my good friend. "What
kinds of property is she looking at?"

"Still checking, but it seems to be storefront property in visible locations."

I'd reached the curb outside the home of Mountie, a
Greater Swiss Mountain dog who'd been my client for a
while. I especially liked Mountie because his coloration
was similar to Lexie's—black and white with auburn
trim—but he was a whole lot bigger. Fortunately, he
was a sweetie, so I intended to bring Lexie in while I
tended to and played with him.

I waited for a minute, though, since I was still speaking with Althea. "Kiki—Kiona—wants to open a store?"

"Unfortunately," said Althea in one of her driest tones, "even my best research doesn't give up what's in someone's mind, unless they've conveyed the information in a manner I can find."

Something I'd have to check into. Did it have something to do with Kiki's recent snit, her obvious irritation with Wanda, her fear I'd found out something about her—and the seed she'd planted in my mind about possibly being so riled that she'd even considered killing a person Wanda didn't get along with, like Margaret, to frame her for it?

Far-fetched? Yes, but feasible.

"Thanks, Althea," I finally said. "As always, I owe you." I cringed slightly, awaiting her usual fee these days: insisting that I get together with her boss, Jeff Hubbard, for a meal, in case seeing him again made me yearn for the old days when he and I were an item. She wasn't the one necessarily exacting that payment. I knew that Jeff had told her to insist on it. Even if he was out of town, I might still be obligated on his return.

"Yep, you do," she said—but she didn't add a demand on Jeff's part.

I wondered why.

"Bye, Kendra," she finished, and was first to hang up.

Leaving my curiosity hanging. But Lexie and I needed to go in to see Mountie, so I didn't worry about it . . . much.

AFTER FINISHING OUR sitting, standing, walking, and playing with the rest of my pet charges for the day, Lexie and I headed somewhere I'd visited only infrequently: Dante's corporate headquarters in Beverly Hills.

I needed something from him. Mostly information this time, but I figured he, or his company, would be the perfect source.

So what if it was Saturday afternoon? That's where he was. I called from my car, just in case, and he confirmed his official location.

"Any of your staff around, too?" I inquired as I entered a ramp onto the San Diego Freeway heading south.

"A few. I cracked my whip a couple of times, so those wanting to get furthest in the company decided to drop in to humor me." His tone made it evident that he was attempting to be funny, not some hard-hearted executive who expected his peons to be at his beck and call at every moment.

In his retail business, I knew it wasn't unusual for employees to be busy on weekends. He'd even confirmed it. On the other hand, I was talking about the main office, not a store that the public would soon stop patronizing if its hours weren't convenient.

In any event, Lexie and I soon arrived at his building, parked in the nearly empty underground garage, and headed up on the elevator. In the lobby, I was quickly permitted in by the security guard, whom I'd met before and who expected me. Lexie and I headed for the next bank of elevators and were soon at the door to the headquarters of HotPets.

I pushed the button on the security system outside and gave my name when someone responded. A guy I hadn't met before immediately opened the door. He was young and smiling, dressed in a white shirt and black slacks despite this being a weekend, and all but bowed to me. "Kendra? I'm Stan. Dante told me to let you in. Can I get you coffee? What a cute dog. Can I get her a biscuit? Some water?" I figured he'd go far in the HotPets organization, assuming no one despised him for trying too hard.

I said yes to everything offered, then let him usher me to the office I knew was Dante's.

Unsurprisingly, the gorgeous guy was inside. Also unsurprisingly, he was on the phone. He smiled as I entered and waved his hand toward an antique chair facing his elegant desk.

I glanced around the room before obeying, in case he happened to have some suppliers' catalogs on the polished wooden shelves along one wall. That would probably have been too tacky, though—or more in the realm of some underling purchasing agent. Instead, there were framed photos of lots of HotPets stores, most likely taken on their opening days.

Then I took a seat, and Lexie lay down on the floor beside me.

I blatantly eavesdropped, but the conversation wasn't especially interesting. I gathered that Dante was talking to the manager of an Arizona store about a complaint the company had received. He clearly wasn't pleased, but kept his cool while saying firmly that a dissatisfied customer was unacceptable. The manager needed to check into the situation, fix it if possible, and report back either way.

He hung up his landline and looked at me with those deep, dark, delectable eyes. "This is a pleasant surprise, Kendra."

"I called first," I reminded him.

"Sure, but that was the surprise—that you wanted to get together this afternoon."

"Right now, it's business," I informed him. "Later, though . . . well, I wouldn't mind a little pleasure."

I felt myself flush at his sexy smile. "Same here. Okay, let's get the business out of the way."

"You came through before, when I needed some specific animal gear to help solve a murder," I told him.

"This is about the Margaret Shiler situation." That wasn't a question but a statement.

"That's right."

He shook his head slowly, his lips folding into a straight line that I wanted to kiss to unravel. Or to kiss just because they were there and attracting me. The rest of his chiseled features seemed almost to freeze while he clearly weighed his words. "Kendra, I care for you because of who you are. Everything about you. But I worry about you when you're out solving murders as a sideline. I know you've even helped absolve me. But—"

"But you're going to tell me again to butt out this time."

"Exactly."

"You also know what I'm going to say."

This time those lips pursed ruefully. "You'll tell me to do the same."

My turn to smile.

"You know I was in a dangerous game in the past," he said, "and I got out. I knew how to handle myself, and it still became too hot for me. Some day . . ." He stood and approached me around his desk. Lexie sat up and watched him.

Me, too.

"The thing is," he continued, "now that I love you, I want to take care of you. I hate the idea that you might get hurt."

I stood, and was soon in his arms. "I appreciate that, Dante," I told him. "I'll be careful. I promise."

"So did . . ." He stopped speaking.

"The woman you cared about who got into a car accident?"

"Yeah."

"I'm not her, Dante. And this is a very different situation. I'll be fine." Interesting that he'd alluded to her. Kinda supported my theory of the timing of his concern. Was it due to his own now-healed injury? Because his feelings for me were growing?

A combo thereof?

Scary.

We kissed. It lasted a long and sexy time, and got my knees so weak and my insides so hot that I could have sunk onto the floor right there, and taken Dante with me.

But that wasn't the time or place. I soon got hold of myself and whispered against his mouth, "Later. Right now . . . are any of your purchasing people around? I need to order some pet stuff."

MY ORDER PLACED—and put on rush—I still hung around, chatting with the purchasing folks, learning interesting info about how they found new products to place in HotPets stores—most of it run, at least quickly, by Dante. With asterisks, of course, calling his attention to items of particular interest. A new flavor of the same old food wouldn't necessarily excite him, but a new brand, or new technological gadget such as a doggy or kitty GPS system, would really get his attention, especially if the wholesale cost was decent.

Mostly, Lexie and I were killing time, since I didn't have law work to accomplish that day, but I still needed to do another round of late-day pet-sitting. I spoke with my assistant, Rachel, and she was well on schedule, too.

All was good. Except that I'm much too impatient to enjoy waiting.

Eventually, Lexie and I headed off. After our pet-sitting visits, we headed home.

Where I saw Dante already inside the security gate. He must have headed to his home after his day at the office, since his adorable German shepherd, Wagner, romped in the yard in front of my large, rented-out house with its current, but not future, occupant, Beggar.

Russ Preesinger stood watching, alongside Dante. Had they been discussing Russ's and Rachel's impending vacating of the site?

The topic didn't come up as I joined them and Lexie joined the pups. A short while later, Rachel came home, too. We were all together like one big happy family—one about to split up, at least physically, I feared, not long from now.

A bit later, Dante and I went out for dinner. When we came back . . . well, he stayed the night, as presaged by our kissing at his office.

It was an intense, heated, and altogether delightful interlude.

But many interesting questions awaited me, and I hoped most of them would be addressed in the coming week.

Chapter Twenty-four

I SPENT MUCH of Sunday with Dante. Or, rather, he spent much of it with me, since I was the one with the more pressing agenda: pet-sitting.

I felt sure that Dante, megamogul of the pet industry that he was, could have found a lot to do relating to his company had he chosen to. Or it might have found him, had he not elected to focus so much on me.

So it was with some sadness that I faced Monday morning. Dante had stayed at my apartment on Sunday night, too, which was especially sweet, considering that we had both dogs with us and my entire place would have fit in his posh Malibu living room. We'd spent a couple of days together, almost inseparable, and now we were about to separate.

How ludicrous that it should bother me so much. It wasn't as if I hadn't spent nearly all of my adult life on my own. Nevertheless, I knew I'd miss him.

I managed to move my mind off him—mostly—as Lexie and I leaped into morning pet-sitting rounds. Wanting to check in on Darryl and how he was doing, I decided that Lexie would spend another fun day at Doggy Indulgence Day Resort.

Kiki was the doggy indulger nearest the door when we walked in—which worried me, after her giving my pup unwarranted time-outs in Darryl's office. I nearly called her Kiona for the sheer surprise value, but didn't want to have to explain how I knew her real name or where I'd gotten the information.

Instead, I merely said, "Hi, Kiki," in a friendly voice.

"Hi, Kendra," she said in return, a lot less amiably. But at least she greeted Lexie lovingly, as she did all her canine charges. It was people that she had problems with.

Especially me, just now. Maybe, in her mind, I was a surrogate for my friend Wanda, or was too associated with Wanda and whatever there was about her that irked Kiki so much.

I just hoped she didn't take it out on Lexie again— even though my pup was none the worse for wear having been isolated for those couple of visits here.

But exactly why was Kiki researching storefront rentals in the San Fernando Valley?

Not that I was about to ask . . . now. Instead, I inquired, "Is Darryl here?" Almost at the same moment, I saw him walk out of his office toward me, as always carefully skirting the playing canines at his feet.

I didn't spend much time there. I had things to do, including an upcoming meeting at my law office. I soon said good-bye to Lexie, who had curled up on a sofa in

the people-furniture part of the room. I figured she was
saving her strength for an upcoming doggy game.

As Darryl walked me to my car, I inquired how he
was holding up.

"Well enough, I guess," he fibbed. "Wanda, too.
But . . ."

He didn't have to finish. I filled in that he wanted this
nightmare over as soon as humanly possible.

So did I, for their sake. And also so I wouldn't have
to worry Dante so much about what I was doing.

"I'm working on something to try to solve Margaret's murder," I assured him as we reached my Escape.
"At least part of it should come together this week. No
guarantees, of course."

"Of course. But . . . well, thanks, Kendra. I still feel
bad that I blamed you at first. Although . . ." His eyes
clouded over behind his wire-rims as he continued to
look at me.

"Although you still wonder whether all this would
have happened to Wanda and you if I weren't a murder
magnet," I filled in. "No answer on that, either, but I
know you realize there are things in life that are beyond
our control. And just remember that I've solved all the
situations my friends have been involved in."

I stopped right there without adding the obvious "so
far." I absolutely intended to do all I could to fix this
one, too.

I kissed Darryl on the cheek and said I'd chat with
him soon.

I wasn't about to tell him the plan I'd put together . . .
or that the first person I intended to test it on was one
of his employees.

I didn't really believe Kiki was so outrageously

angry with Wanda, whatever her rationale, that she had killed Margaret simply to pin it on Darryl's lady love.

But in case I was wrong, I would start my scenario by trying it on her—hopefully to rule her out.

THAT AFTERNOON, I had a meeting scheduled with Joan Fieldmann. She arrived at the Yurick firm offices at twelve thirty, and was announced by a call from our cheerful receptionist, Mignon.

I walked out to the entry and greeted Joan. She looked nervous and drawn, which called attention to her puggish facial features that resembled Pierre's. She'd brought her pet along and hugged him tightly, as if remaining close to the white-and-black French bulldog with the big ears gave her courage.

"Come on into my office," I said cheerfully. "We'll talk." And I'd try to prep her for our meeting with the breeder and her attorney, and perhaps even help her to relax a little.

I'd reviewed the breeder's contract that Joan had signed, and had the file on the side of my usually cluttered desk that I had nearly cleared for the occasion. I opened it and again scanned some of the most onerous provisions.

Meanwhile, she had settled into one of the chairs across from my desk, then helped Pierre into the other one. When Joan, who wore navy slacks and a flowered shirt, crossed one leg over the other, Pierre, who was lying down, crossed his forepaws. Coincidence, or were they connected that closely?

I talked to Joan soothingly, assuring her that this meeting was intended to make introductions all around and to ensure that we all understood the issues. I hoped it wouldn't get too contentious, but I wanted to make sure that the other side was fully aware of our concerns about contract clauses, particularly some that I hoped to dissect and show to be somewhat ambiguous.

Even though, in fact, they seemed much too clear, and much too clearly against my client's position.

At precisely one o'clock, Mignon called once more and chirped that Mr. Eldt and Ms. Irving were there.

"Please see them into the conference room," I told her, then glanced at Joan. Her face had relaxed some during our preliminary session, but now she looked nervous all over again. "Just relax," I told her. "We'll see if we can understand Ms. Irving's position, and make sure that she and her attorney understand yours—especially the fact that your goal is to fulfill the contract and show Pierre, and at the same time take the best care of him possible."

She nodded and smiled, and put Pierre back on the floor. On his blue leash again, he trotted beside us as I led them along the corridor between enclosed offices on the outer perimeter of the building and shielded cubicles of secretaries and paralegals on the inner side.

I looked questioningly toward Mignon as we reached the entry area, and she smiled and inclined her head toward the door to the bar-conference room. I led Joan and Pierre inside.

There, two people sat at the elongated table in the middle of the room. The actual bar was still along the inside wall, but it was used only for decoration these days. Same thing went for the tall-backed booths closer to the windows. But the center was all business.

As we entered, both people stood. Cornelius Eldt appeared to be of an age that would fit in well at the Yurick firm—Borden Yurick had mostly hired other senior attorneys who weren't ready to retire despite their prior employers' assumptions. They all tended to represent senior clients in the matters they had specialized in before. I was half the age of some, and enjoyed both working with them and helping with elder-law matters when I wasn't working on cases of my own— which, unsurprisingly, considering my other vocation of pet-sitting, tended to involve animal law.

Cornelius looked courtly, with bright white hair, a handsome yet wrinkly face, and dark suit, white shirt, and red tie.

His client, Elmira Irving, was fiftyish and very attractive, her blond hair styled in a becoming layered look slicked behind her ears, revealing lovely yet small diamond studs. She, too, wore a dark suit and looked as dressed up as a seasoned lawyer heading for court to argue a case before a judge with a difficult reputation. Only when she stood did I realize she had brought a French bulldog along, this one entirely black and sitting patiently at her feet.

Of course the interested Pierre had to pull his leash in that direction so he could sniff his greetings.

"This is Cosette," Elmira said with obvious pride. "She's Pierre's mama. She's also one of my prize-winning French bulls." She looked directly at Joan. "Like Pierre could be, if you showed him correctly—or, better yet, complied with our contract and let me take him back to do it right. And—"

Before my client, who was clearly starting to steam,

said anything incendiary, I broke in. "Let's not get ahead of ourselves," I said smoothly, earning not a glower but a small smile from the woman I'd interrupted.

"I'm sorry," she said. "It's just that my Frenchies are like my children, and I definitely want what's best for them. Keeping my kennel name—MirVilous Kennels—out there with dogs who do well in shows is good for them and for me. Some of the dogs in Pierre's litter didn't turn out as well as I'd hoped, but Pierre is definitely show quality. I'm convinced he's championship material, if shown to his best advantage. By me. I'm still part owner, after all, and—"

I again started to interrupt, but this time it was her attorney who spoke. Cornelius Eldt touched his client gently on the arm and said, "We understand your enthusiasm, Elmira. And the contract between Ms. Fieldmann and you doesn't leave room for argument against your position."

He looked at me expectantly, knowing I had to respond with an opposite position in order to represent my client best.

"Of course there are arguments," I said. "Ones I don't need to get into now, but I certainly will if we wind up going to court over this. That would be time-consuming and expensive, so my suggestion is to see if we can work this out among ourselves rather than via litigation."

"May I speak?" said Joan. I almost said no, since despite my preparation of my client, I wasn't sure what she'd say or how she'd say it. This wasn't a good time for her to try to explain why she signed such an onerous contract. Or to admit anything against her interest.

"Just remember that we don't want to get contentious here," I cautioned her.

"Of course not. I just wanted to make sure that Elmira understands how much I love Pierre. I think he's beautiful. And I've gone to shows, including ones for amateurs, to learn the techniques of showing. I don't know why Pierre didn't do better in the show I took him to—although I know you have your opinion, Elmira— but I intend to keep trying, as best I can."

"I watched you." Elmira sounded sour. "As I told you then, the lessons you took clearly weren't enough to teach you the techniques of showing Pierre to his best advantage. And the way you've trained him—he's much smarter than that."

"Yes, you've told me all that," Joan said dryly. "More than once."

"It's clear to me that you have some mistaken ideas about how shows work," Elmira said. "And it's not like you listened to me. You still have to—"

Once again, Cornelius calmed his client, this time before she came out with some command aimed at my client.

"Sorry," she said, then bent down to pick up pretty Cosette. When she was again sitting in her chair, I saw tears in her eyes. "The thing is, I'm really proud of my kennel. And disappointed that the others in Pierre's litter didn't turn out better. Cosette's a little older, and I'm ready for another champion. That could be Pierre—if he's shown correctly." The tears were gone, replaced by an angry glare.

Hmmm. This was one of those situations where I could see both sides—kinda. Not that I was exactly sympathetic to Elmira. Especially considering her awful attitude. Plus, my loyalty was to my client, so I would definitely act as her advocate.

I glanced at Cornelius. "I think both parties have given their opinions," I told him. "Let's mull this over for a day or so, then talk about logistics of your client's claim—and whether we're talking about a pending lawsuit here."

"Fine by me," he said, and he, Elmira, and Cosette said relatively congenial good-byes.

I was left alone in the conference room with Joan and Pierre.

"That was awful!" she said with a soft wail. "That woman can't really take Pierre back to show him, can she?"

"She has an argument to that effect," I answered. "His full registration won't be transferred to you until you've supposedly fulfilled the terms of your contract. That means Pierre either has to achieve championship status or Elmira acknowledges he's gone as far as he can. And till then, she may be able to take him back to show—or even permanently."

"But I'm trying to comply. And I won't give Pierre back, ever. Please fix that damned contract so I can tell that terrible woman where to go."

"Contracts don't exactly work that way," I countered softly. "But give me some time to think about this and talk to Mr. Eldt about where we go from here. I'll let you know if we come up with anything."

I didn't get into the more onerous clauses of the contract. It did contain an arbitration provision, which could be a good thing—as long as the arbitrators saw the situation rationally. But if they followed the letter of the contract, which arbitrators certainly could do, Joan would most likely lose.

I said my good-byes to Joan in an upbeat and optimistic manner. But as she left, I hoped I'd develop an animal dispute resolution solution that would work for everyone, Pierre, and even Cosette, included.

Chapter Twenty-five

DANTE DIDN'T SHOW up on my doorstep that night. Nor did I make the trek to his Malibu digs.

Damn, but I missed him!

Still, instead of giving in to angst, I took Lexie on an extra long walk along our narrow, twisty street after we got home. At this time of year, the sky darkened early, and there weren't a lot of streetlights around. Fortunately, though, most neighbors and I promoted area security by leaving at least some outside lights on nearly all night.

Seeing illumination in my main house, I placed a cell phone call to Rachel as I re-entered my property. She was already preparing for bed, but she gave me a rundown of that day's pet-sitting, all of it good.

Plus, she said she'd heard from some of the production people on *Animal Auditions*, and preparations for the next season were progressing well.

She didn't mention any house hunting by her or her dad, and neither did I.

When we hung up, I glanced at the time, which appeared on my cell phone. It wasn't really so late . . . but it soon would be. I'd been putting off a call that I'd better make now.

Lexie and I were on the stairway outside our apartment by now, and I unlocked the door and let us in. Then I went into the living room and sat down, steeling myself for a potentially difficult phone discussion.

LAPD Detective Ned Noralles answered nearly immediately. "Hi, Kendra. I'd like to assume this is a social call, but I imagine you have something else on your mind. Right?"

"It's always good to talk to you, Ned," I said, "but, yes, there is something I wanted to ask you."

I explained that I wanted to meet with Detective Candace Melamed of the Burbank police, and why. "If you could act as intermediary, I'd really appreciate it."

"You haven't been shy about facing down cops before," he reminded me. "Why now?"

"Don't you think that what I want to try is a little off-the-wall?"

"No more so than the ploy you used to solve the murder when my sister Nita and I were suspects," he responded. "But, you're right. I already know you and your . . . well, unorthodox methods of butting in and getting answers." And he had helped me deal with other detectives before, too. "Since it's you, I'll do it."

"Thanks, Ned."

NED DID, IN fact, come through. He called me early the next morning, while I was out on my pet-sitting rounds, to tell me to be at the main Burbank PD station at ten that morning.

"You're the greatest," I told him. "Will you be there?"

"I'd better be. Otherwise, I suspect one of you will kill the other."

I got there before Ned. The main Burbank police station is an interesting building, with its primary entrance up some steps beside a tall, rounded structure that extends from the more ordinary part and has a whole lot of windows.

Inside the high-ceilinged entry, I let the cop behind the enclosed counter know I was there, but said I'd wait till everyone was ready for the scheduled meeting before going farther inside.

To my delight and relief, Ned soon arrived. I assumed he was on duty that morning, since he wore the kind of suit he always did when involved in a homicide investigation. Its dark shade looked good on him. But, then, he was one good-looking cop.

In a short while, we were waved inside—after appropriate security screening—and shown to a small meeting room. It was probably used for interrogation of suspects, and might even have been the place Wanda was taken for her sessions there.

Detective Melamed strode in at about the same time we did. She wore a gray suit and a suspicious expression behind her narrow glasses as she waved us toward the chairs around the table.

I sat beside Ned, facing the lady cop. I was about to start talking when she asked Ned, "So, Ned, why are you so interested in this case?"

"I explained before, Candace. For a long time, I

considered Kendra, here, an interfering b—er, civilian. Which she is." He shot a look toward me that I assumed was intended to be fond, but I was already glaring at him. "The thing is," he continued, "her unorthodox methods have actually helped to solve some cases. In a few instances, I was already focused on the actual perpetrator as my key suspect." Not necessarily true, but I wasn't about to contradict him when he was, presumably, helping me. "In a couple, I wasn't. But by the time Kendra did her stuff, I was convinced she had gotten it right each time."

"I'm sure you did, when she helped to clear your sister and you in the murder of that reality show judge." Candace's tone was utterly dry. Apparently her throat was, too, since she took a sip from a mug of coffee she had brought in.

Unfortunately, she didn't offer to get us any.

"That was one instance," Ned acknowledged. "Anyway, she has an idea now that might help you to get results faster."

"Will it draw my attention away from Wanda Villareal?" Her icy blue eyes were now narrowed on me.

"I hope so. But I can try my experiment on her, too, if you'd like," I replied.

"And what experiment might that be?" Even more skepticism oozed from her voice. Her body language, as she sat up even straighter in the wooden chair like the one I sat in—awfully uncomfortable—suggested she'd rather be nearly anywhere than this small room.

"Before I explain," I said, "I want to ask a few questions about your investigation so far." That was one reason I'd asked for Ned's assistance. Fortunately, Detective Melamed apparently hadn't considered me much of a suspect, even though I'd been at Brigadoon a few days before the murder and had argued with the victim.

If I now started making waves about the investigation, her focus might start including me, even if simply out of spite.

But hopefully she was more likely to discuss what she'd found with a fellow cop than with an interfering pet-sitter who also happened to be a lawyer.

"I don't imagine you'll just go away if I tell you I don't want to answer, will you?" At least this time her nasty tone was accompanied by a slight smile—snide or not, I couldn't quite tell.

"Nope," I acknowledged. "So . . . here's my question. You're aware of the cat that was in Margaret Shiler's apartment when Wanda found her, aren't you?"

"My response is yes. So now I've answered. Are you going to leave?" This time her smile was broader, as if she was actually enjoying herself.

I smiled back. "Nope. I've got several more questions."

"I figured."

I asked her if there had been any blood on Lady Cuddles, and her answer again was yes. "On her claws," she acknowledged. "Initial DNA testing indicated it was Wanda's, and she admitted to being scratched when she picked up the cat."

"Was there anyone else's blood?" Ned got into the act.

"The victim's. And, yes, before you ask, there may have been more, but that's not certain."

"Okay, let's move on," I said. "Did you notice, or did

Wanda mention, that Lady Cuddles had been wearing a collar with a name tag?"

Candace nodded. "Wanda said she wasn't sure when she saw it last, but when the first officers arrived and began locking down the site, they saw her with the cat and took her aside. The crime scene folks talked to her a little while later, and they took photos. The cat wasn't wearing the collar then." She leaned over the table toward us. "One thing, though. We've been careful not to mention the cat or the collar to anyone—especially the media. Wanda knows, and I asked her not to discuss it. I suppose some people she'd already talked to are aware of at least the presence of that kitten. Because of the apparent timing of when the collar went missing, we know it might have significance in the murder, without knowing what that significance might be yet. So I'm instructing you, Kendra, not to start talking about it. If you do, you'll be obstructing justice." And thereby vulnerable to her arresting me.

"I understand," I said. "But here's the thing I want to do, Candace." She hadn't told me to call her by her first name, but Ned had done so, and we seemed fairly friendly now.

I described what I had in mind, and who I had in mind to try it on. It was contrived, absolutely. But I explained how I'd seen such a silly scenario work in a case somewhat similar to this one, and Ned—sort of enthusiastically, bless him—backed me up.

I didn't mention my first intended victim, Kiki, but I didn't actually expect the results to cast all suspicion suddenly onto her.

"That's right!" Candace exclaimed part way through

my presentation. "You're a friend of Dante DeFrancisco's. No wonder you came up with this strange idea. Cat collars? Of course he can supply them, and fast . . . right?"

I nodded, hoping speed was high on Dante's agenda.

I soon finished my explanation, then said, "There are no guarantees of results, of course. But just in case, I'll keep you informed. If you want to have someone there, fine.

"Otherwise, I'll just work out a way to record what goes on. I'm not a criminal law expert, but I doubt the kind of entrapment I have in mind would be admissible at trial. Even so, it might really help you narrow down your list of suspects."

"Interesting idea, Kendra, if a bit bizarre," Candace said. "But okay, I guess, especially since Ned vouches for you." The two of them exchanged coplike narrow grins.

I tossed a grin of my own back at them both, actually quite surprised that Candace had agreed.

But then she said, "I've read about you in some of that tabloid reporter Corina Carey's stuff. I realize that, if I agree to go along with this, you'll be skirting around my directive not to mention the collar to anyone, but I assume you won't talk to the media about it—especially her. And if what you're suggesting yields results, credit should be given where it's due—the Burbank PD."

Namely her, I was sure, but that was okay. I didn't want publicity or pats on the back, only the truth—which I was sure would clear Wanda.

I soon said good-bye to both cops. I was nearly ready to set my experiment in motion.

All I needed was the stuff I'd ordered from HotPets.

I WAS BACK at my law office later that afternoon, almost ready to leave for my end-of-day pet-sitting. I'd left a message for Dante on his cell phone, and had also called the supply people in his head office. No word yet about my order.

Except . . . as I was extracting my purse from my desk, my interoffice phone rang. When I answered, Mignon chirped into my ear with more exuberance than ever, "You've got a visitor, Kendra."

"Who is it?" I asked, then saw my closed office door start to open.

In an instant, Dante appeared. He closed the door behind him, strode in, and urged me to my feet.

The kiss he gave me curled my toes and singed the rest of my body.

"Hi," I whispered when he moved away a little.

"Special delivery," he said, and held out a large package he'd been holding behind his back.

Chapter Twenty-six

THE PACKAGE CONTAINED exactly what I'd ordered. Of course. Even though the supplier wasn't one of HotPets' normal sources, no one in the business would dare to do anything less for the megamogul Dante DeFrancisco, whose company undoubtedly ordered more of whatever a company's wares were than any other firm in the world.

Of course, someone in their order fulfillment department might be wondering how many kitties there were named Lady Cuddles who needed a new collar and name tag.

I hugged Dante again and laughed. He looked as if he'd been dressed for work, minus any jacket or tie. "I won't even ask how much this cost you—both to get the stuff and have it shipped here so quickly."

"Good idea," he said.

I'd offer to pay, of course, if I thought he wanted me

to. But I knew this was intended to be a favor. I'd add it to the list.

"So . . . are you going to tell me exactly what you're planning to do with all this?" He backed away a bit, and I missed him already, though he planted that outstanding butt of his on the edge of my messy desk.

"Sure," I replied. After all, I'd already revealed it, more or less, to Detective Melamed. Even gotten her blessing—sorta.

And much to my surprise. But Ned's presence and support had undoubtedly helped. "You'll need to keep it quiet, though."

When I was done describing, he laughed aloud. "You're somewhat predictable, Kendra, you know that?"

I immediately felt defensive, crossing my arms over my ruffled blue shirt. "A good lawyer learns which techniques tend to work best. A good pet-sitter, too."

"Not to mention a murder magnet. But I've come to appreciate how you get the animals around you, or things connected with them, involved in figuring out what happened."

"Thanks," I said. "I guess. So . . . would you like to observe my very first trial? I don't think it'll net me the murderer, but I'll probably be able to rule someone out—a person I almost wish was the genuine culprit."

"I'm yours to command," he said with one of those steamy smiles that got my insides percolating all over again. "At least for this afternoon. Let's do it."

I called Darryl first. Didn't exactly tell him what I was up to or how I'd do it, but I did let him know who I was about to practice on.

"Why Kiki?" He must have been in his office and able to talk about her without her eavesdropping.

This was slightly knotty. I didn't want him to fire her, but neither did I want her to get away with bad-mouthing Wanda for no reason. "Just to rule her out," I said. "She . . . well, she seems a little unhappy about your relationship with Wanda—which isn't really her business or mine. I don't think her attitude is bad enough for her to want to frame Wanda for murder, but—"

"But you've considered it," Darryl finished. Still seated behind my desk, I looked up and saw Dante watching me with apparent interest.

"I just want to rule it out," I repeated, "and practice my snooping technique in the meantime."

"Okay." Darryl drew out the word, though, and I could tell he was thinking. "I'm not exactly sure why Kiki would resent Wanda. Maybe, as part of whatever you're doing, you can find that out, at least. Kiki's been a good employee, especially with the dogs. She's a bit miffed with *me* now over some management issues, but nothing major."

Maybe. Did he know, though, about Kiki's property search? This probably wasn't the time to inform him.

"Of course, if it ever comes down to choosing between her keeping her job here and Wanda . . ."

"Hopefully, that won't happen. I'll need to meet with her in private, and then I'll see what I can learn."

Since I hadn't had Darryl on my speakerphone, I gave Dante the gist of our conversation.

"More than one mystery around here," Dante observed mildly. "First thing to resolve, I'd imagine, is what's really going on in Kiki's mind."

"Exactly," I said. "Ready to help me find out? I assume you'll want to observe."

"Absolutely."

We stood up to leave. I took my package, retrieved my purse from the drawer, then drew near Dante on my way to the door. Which meant another delicious delay . . . in his arms.

"Okay," I finally said, attempting to catch my breath. "Let's do it."

"It?" he inquired, his dark and delightful eyebrows raised.

"Head to Doggy Indulgence."

DANTE DROVE US in his sleek Mercedes. No need to take both vehicles, although I'd want to stop back at the office later to grab my Ford before doing my evening's pet-sitting. But I didn't want to wait any longer to start my scenario.

"Okay, I've played along this far," Dante said as he pulled onto the 101 Freeway, heading east toward Studio City. "You told me before *what* you intend to do with those collars and tags. I've got a good guess about the *why*, but you weren't really clear on that. So how about letting me in on it while we drive?"

Why not? The guy beside me was damned smart, and he'd have my back more than the Burbank police, even assuming Detective Melamed provided backup to earn her possible murder-solving credit. Plus, he knew enough for me to be sure that his guess was more than an educated one.

So I explained. "Well, you already know that the reason Wanda found Margaret Shiler's body was that the elusive Lady Cuddles had escaped and Wanda saw the apartment door open. She went inside to look. Sure enough, the kitten was there. So was a very dead, and bloody, Margaret."

Dante nodded. "Got that."

"Wanda noticed that night that Lady Cuddles's collar and name tag were missing. While she waited for the cops to arrive, she did nothing to mess up the crime scene—other than pick up Lady Cuddles, which probably helped to prevent more bloody kitty paw prints. That's when she got scratched. She also looked for the collar and tag, but saw no sign of them. She bought Lady Cuddles another collar and name tag the next day—from HotPets, of course—but duplicates of the originals weren't immediately available in the store. And that was that, as far as she was concerned. But I wondered about the missing collar and tag. Could the killer have taken them away? If so, why? And where are they now? Far as I know, and the Burbank police have confirmed it, they're still missing. It's not too much of a leap to think the killer might have removed them."

"Another *why* comes to mind here. What was the killer's motive to grab them from the cat in the first place?"

"Only a guess, but what if the white collar became covered in blood after the killing? If it was only Margaret's blood, that wouldn't be a big deal to the killer. But what if he or she wasn't sure whose blood it was?"

"The killer's own could be a possibility," Dante acknowledged. He had exited the freeway on Laurel Canyon and was now waiting for a light to change. He looked at me grimly, and I looked back.

"Exactly. So . . ."

"So you're going to use these new ones to watch your suspects' reactions to seeing the collar and tag."

"You got it," I said, smiling at him.

"I just hope what you've got isn't going to hurt you."

DEAR DARRYL HAD set things up by the time I got to Doggy Indulgence.

I didn't see Lexie at first, and after Kiki's recent nasty pranks, I had some concerns whether she had somehow gotten the word about what I was about to do. But then Darryl's office door opened, and both Lexie and he emerged.

Near the main desk at the entry, he greeted Dante and me. He gave me a hug, and at the same time whispered into my ear, "Kiki's on assignment in the kitchen. I've taken the liberty of borrowing her purse. It's in my office, and once you've stuck your little present into it, I'll make sure it's returned to the area where employees keep their belongings."

"You're a dear, Darryl." I kissed him on the cheek, then glanced at Dante. He didn't seem daunted by the show of affection. But then, he already knew I had a thing for Darryl—namely, long-term and really deep friendship.

In a while, everything was set up. I went into the kitchen while Darryl worked the magic of returning Kiki's purse to its original location. Meantime, I'd transferred my little present into it.

"Hi," I said to Kiki, who was busy scrubbing a small area of the floor. Beside her was a big plastic garbage bag that didn't smell especially good, and I assumed that Darryl had somehow gotten one of the doggies to leave its duty where it didn't belong.

Kiki turned to glare up at me, as if I'd done whatever caused her to be on cleanup detail. She wore a Doggy Indulgence knit shirt—this one a shocking pink—over skinny jeans. Her bleached blond hair appeared a trifle damp—from either cleaning or perspiring.

"Can I talk to you for a minute?" I asked.

"No."

I pulled a chair from behind the table where employees ate lunch and sat on it, watching her. "Guess what. I'm going to talk anyway. I'd really like to know why you're so upset about Wanda, and therefore about me."

"Not your business." She returned to her scrubbing.

"Oh, but I think it is. Wanda's my friend. Besides that—well, as I'm sure you know, she's on the Burbank police's suspect list for the murder of Margaret Shiler, who lived in her condo complex. They were arguing over pets. But I'm certain someone has set Wanda up. I don't know why yet, but there's a particular clue that'll at least help me find out who."

I proceeded to tell her all about the disappearing Lady Cuddles. Interestingly, she turned around, sat on a dry area of the floor, and listened. Nodded her head, as if this wasn't a new story to her.

Might my original suspicions about her actually be correct?

I then got into my theory about the killer taking Lady Cuddles's collar and name tag because they contained a clue about that person's identity. "So far, the police aren't convinced, but I'm trying to rule suspects out."

Darryl and Dante wandered in just then, as if their timing was one big coincidence. I'd asked for exactly five minutes before their big entrance.

Darryl held Kiki's purse.

"I'm sure Kendra's told you her theory by now," Kiki's calm employer said. "Please empty your purse so we can be sure you aren't hiding the missing stuff."

"How dumb!" she exclaimed with a sniff, standing at last. "Number one, it's not me. Number two, whoever killed that woman would have gotten rid of the collar by now if it could point to them."

"Humor us." Dante had been here with me before, so Kiki knew who he was. Otherwise, since he tended to eschew on-air media interviews, or even paparazzi photos in the papers, she'd certainly have heard of him but wouldn't have known what he looked like.

The man had a magic way with women. Maybe it was his absolutely sexy male looks. Or their knowledge that this guy had a whole lot of money.

Whatever it was, Kiki said, "Well, all right. For you, Dante."

Just like that, she took the purse and turned it over, dumping its contents on the floor. Out rained makeup, a comb, a wallet, and lots of not-unexpected stuff.

Almost last, the collar and name tag slid out and sat on top of the rest.

I watched as her eyes widened. And blinked. Then narrowed. "You set this up, Kendra. I know you did. Well, here's my answer, even though it's not what you're looking for. I was serious when I said I didn't know anything about that damned cat or its missing collar and stuff. I didn't kill that Margaret woman. As much as I'm angry with Wanda for interfering with what I've been trying to discuss with Darryl, it's a real stretch to think I'd kill someone I didn't even know, in the hope that the cops would blame her, don't you think?"

"Exactly what did you want to discuss with Darryl?" I asked before anyone else—including said Doggy Indulgence owner—could do so.

"I want a lot more responsibility, since I'm around here more than getting acting gigs. I want to become manager. I'm good with dogs, and he knows it. I need more money. That's it."

"We've talked a little about your latest ideas," Darryl said. "How did Wanda prevent you from discussing the rest?"

"She's either here with you or you're on the phone with her. Or thinking about her. The few times I've tried to talk to you about everything, you were in a hurry to see her and seemed too distracted to really listen to me or to take me seriously. So . . . Here's the thing, Darryl. I didn't kill anyone. I didn't do anything to hurt Wanda. But I will hurt you."

"What!" I exclaimed, leaping to my feet, ready to defend my dear friend from whatever this woman had in mind.

"Not physically," she said scornfully, standing there with hands on her hips. "If I don't get what I want from you, Darryl, I'm starting my own doggy day care facility. A lot of your customers really like me, so you'll lose business. It's as simple as that. You can ignore me to go snuggle with your Wanda, or you can talk to me."

With that, she stalked out of the kitchen.

I looked from one of the men to the other. "Well," I said, "the good thing is that we learned what she wants from you, Darryl, although why she's blaming Wanda for any of it doesn't exactly make sense."

"I suspect she needs a scapegoat," Dante responded wisely.

"The other good thing is that I did get a reaction from her about my fishing for a suspect in Margaret's murder—and the items I used as bait."

"Do you think she did it?" To my surprise, Darryl sounded almost hopeful as he stared at me through his wire-rims.

"Nope," I said. "I'm still looking. Kiki's first reaction convinced me she isn't guilty—not that I really suspected her. But as silly as my set-up is, I believe it'll catch a killer."

Chapter Twenty-seven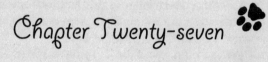

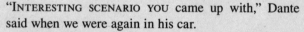

"INTERESTING SCENARIO YOU came up with," Dante said when we were again in his car.

Lexie was lying in the backseat, evidently exhausted despite her day at Doggy Indulgence having been somewhat abbreviated. Either that, or she'd been freaked out by the kitchen scenario. Or maybe she simply hadn't finished her afternoon nap.

We were heading back to my office, already on the freeway heading west.

Then Dante said exactly what had been on my mind. "But do you think it'll really be effective in helping you find the killer?"

I shrugged sadly. "Honestly? I don't know. But I'm hopeful, and I've got to do something." We went over the short list of persons I wanted to attempt to unnerve with the collars and tags, and how I'd maneuver each into a position of vulnerability. I could only hope that

if the guilty one was among them, he or she would go
bonkers when the cat stuff mysteriously reappeared.

Assuming he/she had made it disappear in the first
place.

A single replacement set might have sufficed, but I'd
wanted extras in case someone kept one—or in case
I needed to modify the appearance now and then for
my scenario to get serious. If, of course, one could ever
look at something so off-the-wall as serious. But I'd
used others equally strange and gotten useful results.

Dante, of course, attempted to insist that he be present each time I experimented. "We'll see," I said.

"If not me, then Brody." He stopped speaking then,
as if he'd had the last word on the subject.

The last word? Perhaps. But not necessarily the final
result.

We chatted about other stuff on the drive to my
office. I wasn't certain what Dante was doing while I
finished the rest of my day there. He spent it in the bar-
conference room with his smart phone, since there were
no meetings scheduled there for the afternoon. Lexie
seemed eager to check on him, so now and then she and
I would walk there to say hello.

While I was in my office alone, I went through
some files I needed for the upcoming week, including
a motion and supporting documents that I'd need for a
scheduled court appearance.

I also stewed over the situation with Pierre and his
breeder's overreaching contract. I even did some initial
online research, although I didn't want to spend a lot of
time on it and have to bill Joan.

It didn't necessarily matter how any similar disputes

had been resolved in court, since there was a pretty strong arbitration provision in this particular contract. Fortunately, arbitrators had more latitude in resolving a dispute, needing to consider the law but also attempting to ascertain the parties' intentions and consider that information as well.

They could follow the actual language of a disputed contract, or make a Solomon-like attempt to "split the baby"—in other words, reach a compromise that most likely neither party would be entirely pleased with.

This agreement's arbitration provision stated that it was binding, so even if Joan, not liking the result, wanted to incur the time and expense of attempting to prevail another forum, a successful appeal was unlikely, absent something egregious on the arbitrator's part.

As I read again through the contract language, it appeared fairly clear—and not in my client's favor. The best course would be a settlement that both sides agreed to.

I thought hard, made notes, and arrived at suggestions that, maybe, Joan could at least live with instead of being forced either to follow everything in the contract exactly . . . or to wind up having to return adorable Pierre to his breeder.

I called Joan and somberly told her the direction of the dilemma I'd now zeroed in on.

"Oh, Kendra, I was afraid of that."

"But compromise is always possible, if we come up with a settlement proposition that Elmira would agree to." I didn't mention that I hadn't completely hated Elmira, despite her being our opposition. Maybe, unlike most people on the opposite side of a negotiating table from me, she'd actually be reasonable.

I told Joan the way my other thoughts had been heading. When I was done, I asked, "Do you think you could live with that as a compromise?"

"It's a lot better than most of the other possibilities," she said. "And it might actually be of some benefit to me. Let's give it a try."

I called Elmira's attorney, Cornelius Eldt, and left a message asking if we could set up another meeting.

DANTE DID MORE than stay near me for the rest of the day. That evening, he had Alfonse, his personal assistant, deliver his doggy Wagner to my place so the four of us could spend the night together. Dante, Wagner, Lexie, and me, that is. Alfonse returned to Dante's Malibu digs.

While engaging in delightful conversation with Dante, before and after dinner, I silently pondered my next move in the Margaret murder investigation. I definitely intended to impose my scenario on all suspects on my list. First one—second, if I counted Kiki— would most likely be Margaret's ex-husband. He was less likely to be in contact with any of the other suspects to give them a heads-up about what I was doing.

When bedtime rolled around, my mind, and the rest of me, were absolutely focused on other activities . . .

I WOKE FIRST in the morning, even before my clock radio startled me. I was locked in Dante's arms—not a bad place to be.

But I had a big day ahead of me, and so I stirred. That, of course, woke him. Our nearness suggested getting even closer, and soon, as my body sang, angels also started singing in my ear. No, that was a current music sensation. My clock radio had finally gone off.

"Good morning, Kendra," Dante said as he nibbled my ear.

I purred, then pulled away. "Time to get dressed."

"Too bad."

But dress we did. We took the dogs out for a short but energetic romp along my street, ate an abbreviated breakfast, and then it was time to go our separate ways.

"Are you going to pull one of your capers today?" Dante stood beside my Escape, Wagner at his side. He wore the same clothes as yesterday. No spares at my home. Yet. Although he had moved miscellaneous items in, like an electric razor and a toothbrush. I knew he kept extra stuff at his office, so he'd be able to change there.

"You mean with the collars?" I asked innocently.

"Exactly." His glare suggested I didn't dare do it without him.

Thing was, I'd contemplated how to achieve my objective all alone, and realized how hard that might be. I needed a distraction.

And there was no better distraction than Dante.

"I hope to," I admitted. "I'll have to make a call first. If it works out and I can schedule something, I'll let you know. Then, it'll be fine if you can make it." I acted as if I was granting him a favor, when actually he'd be doing the favor for me.

"If I can't be there, I'll make sure Brody is." He leaned in my open window and gave me a kiss—just missing Lexie's eager face as she tried to stick her nose between us from the backseat.

Dante laughed, and I drove out, waving at Rachel. I spoke to my assistant on my hands-free device as I cruised toward my first pet-sitting of the day, to make sure we were in sync about who was caring for which animal clients. All was well on that front.

I decided to keep Lexie with me at my office, in case what I hoped to accomplish at short notice happened to materialize.

It did. I reached Margaret's ex, Paulino Shiler, when I called him first thing from the office. Since I had to look up his phone number, and knew I'd need to concentrate on what he had to say, I hadn't wanted to phone him from the car. Turned out he intended to take his beautiful part-boxer pups to the dog park that very afternoon, since rain was predicted for the next couple of days.

I told him I had a couple more questions, so I'd be there, too. Would even have my own pup along, so maybe the three canines could cavort around the park together.

Neither of us mentioned our ugly little interlude in Margaret's apartment.

I quickly called Dante. He sounded a little distracted— gee, did he actually have to run his business empire even when I called him?—but confirmed that either Brody or he would be there on time.

I also let Detective Melamed know what I was up to. She muttered something, then thanked me—and said she'd spoken again with Ned. She only hoped he wasn't just yanking her chain about me—and could keep his mouth shut so she wouldn't look like an ass to her coworkers and superiors for agreeing to such lunacy.

Unless, of course, it garnered quick results.

I soon said good-bye, then I waited for afternoon to arrive.

TURNED OUT IT was Brody who joined me. I liked Brody, especially since he was an amazingly popular judge on *Animal Auditions*. I remained terribly fond of that show, since I'd helped to found it.

I tried hard not to show my disappointment that he wasn't Dante.

We'd both parked on the hillside leading down to the park. Even in grungy jeans and a T-shirt with the sleeves torn out, the guy was movie-star gorgeous. Or maybe the casual clothes enhanced his he-man appearance.

I'd purposely worn nice slacks that day and exchanged my nicer shoes for sneakers I'd stored in my Escape. Lexie leaped excitedly at my side, clearly knowing where we were, whether from the scents of other doggies in the air or the occasional excited barks from the fenced-in area where canines roamed free.

"Hi, Kendra." Falling into step with my pup and me, Brody gave me a quick hug and a kiss on the cheek. "Dante made it clear I'd better do a great job of helping you this afternoon. He told me what it would entail, but you'd better fill me in on details."

Which I did. Fast. We'd already reached the entrance gate, and we carefully edged our ways inside, ensuring that it latched behind us so no dogs could escape.

I looked around and saw that Paulino and his boxer-mix pups were already there. "Let me introduce you," I told Brody.

We approached Paulino, and I saw that the thin forty-to-fifty-something guy, again in workout clothes, once more wore his large, dark backpack. He was engaged in a game of catch with his two dogs, who excitedly dashed after each ball he threw.

I smiled as we drew close. Paulino clearly recognized Brody, since he grinned broadly, revealing the gap between his front teeth, and extended his hand for a substantial shake. "It's really great to meet you," he said. "I like your attitude on *Animal Auditions*. I've also seen your movie about K-9 Marines probably a dozen times."

"I'll let Lexie loose," I told him. "Mind sitting over there for a little chat?" I pointed to a bench that wasn't far away, and we three humans all headed there.

As he had the last time, Paulino put his backpack on the ground. "What's up?" he asked. "I haven't seen anything new on TV about the investigation into Margaret's death."

I shook my head sadly. "They don't exactly keep me in the loop." I didn't even know what they'd said or done to Paulino in response to his raiding Margaret's condo unit, but doubted he was about to tell me.

I noticed a guy come through the gate with a German shepherd resembling Wagner. The dog stayed at his side despite the distraction of all the other pups in the park, obviously well-trained. Like a K-9. Had Candace Melamed sent him as an undercover observer?

We chatted a little more before I said, "I mostly just wanted to touch base with you, see if you had any more ideas about who might have wanted to hurt Margaret.

The police haven't let go of the idea of my friend Wanda, and though it's really up to them to solve the case, I still would like to help."

"I've told them all I know. And you, too."

"That's what I figured. Look at our dogs." I pointed a little distance away, where his pups seemed to be playing a game of keep-away with Lexie, using a rag toy as bait. "That's so cute!" I reached into my purse and brought out my cell phone. "I'll get a picture. Hey, come over here and you can help me pose them."

Which he did. Both of us played for a short while with the dogs, tossing the toy between us so the pups kept dashing from one of us to the other.

They eventually grew bored, and so did I. Besides, I believed my objective had been achieved. I led Paulino back toward the bench, where Brody had remained, cheering us on.

"There's one more thing I wanted to run by you," I told Paulino. "Did you know there was a runaway kitten that was in Margaret's apartment before anyone found her body?" He didn't. I explained the whole bit about the missing collar and name tag. "Her name is Lady Cuddles. It just seemed much too coincidental that her identification disappeared around the same time Margaret died. There's some speculation that the killer stole them. Maybe they contained a clue, like a bit of blood."

"Strange," Paulino said, not sounding especially interested.

We talked for a little while longer, Brody easily answering Paulino's questions about his acting career—and, yes, he already had an accountant, so unfortunately didn't need Paulino's services.

Then I said, "Know what? I forgot to bring any treats for Lexie. Do you have any extra in there?" I motioned toward his backpack, which was still on the ground.

"Sure." He lifted it and unzipped the top.

I leaped up and sideways and said, "Hey, look at that!" as I shoved my way toward Paulino, my hand beneath his backpack. I upended it, and a bunch of contents tumbled to the ground.

Including a small white cat collar with a little blue name tag.

"What's that?" Brody asked.

I gasped. "It looks like Lady Cuddles's!" I pulled a tissue from my purse and picked it up, as though attempting to ensure I didn't erase any evidence. I'd been observing that guy with the shepherd staying somewhat nearby, so I spoke loudly enough to provide a clue, if needed. I checked the name tag. "It says Lady Cuddles," I confirmed, sounding quite shaken. "Paulino, I thought you said you didn't know the kitten. And—"

"I didn't. I don't. And I don't know how that got there." He sounded panicked. Was this proof—or at least an indication—of his guilt?

And then he looked at Brody and grinned. "How'd I do, Mr. Avilla? Did I pass your audition? I assume you stuck it there to see how I'd react, in case you needed someone to act in one of your films. Or an *Animal Auditions* show. 'Cause I didn't put it there, and I certainly didn't kill Margaret."

Thing was, I believed him. About not killing Margaret, I mean. I already knew he didn't shove the collar into his backpack. Brody had done that while Paulino and I were playing with the dogs, using one of the new ones that I'd stuck into my purse.

Interesting reaction, though. I caught the disgusted sneer and shake of the head on the guy I figured was sent by Detective Melamed. He and his dog headed toward the exit.

So did Brody, Lexie, and I, soon afterward. We didn't exactly admit our rationale to Paulino. Maybe he guessed the truth but decided to turn it around in his favor.

Brody, good sport that he was, even said he'd keep Paulino and his excellent reaction in mind for future productions he was involved in.

So far, I'd gotten two entirely different reactions by using the new collar for bait. Would it really help me figure out who'd killed Margaret?

At this point, I didn't know. And I still had a cast of thousands—well, at least several other potential suspects—to try it on.

Chapter Twenty-eight

PROBLEM WAS, MY scenario could get awfully time-consuming. But till I figured out the actual killer, I'd need to stay involved.

Plus, as I kept pushing at people for reactions, they might start chatting to one another and spoil the surprise. If that happened, the guilty party could pull off a perfectly calm response and potentially throw me off his or her trail.

But even with all the energy I anticipated spending in a short while, I didn't need to use up a lot of Dante's or Brody's time.

Brody and I met on the Valley side of the hill for a quick cup of coffee. We sat outside at one of the chains, Lexie lying at my feet. We humans rehashed what had happened and got a good laugh out of it.

"Who's next?" he asked, and I told him the next couple of people on my agenda. "Sounds promising.

Have you figured out when you'll try your charade on them?"

"I need to schedule a visit to each. But really, Brody, don't worry about it. I can handle it, especially since I intend to keep the cops informed."

He called Dante, and together they read me the riot act. I *would* keep them in the loop. And allow at least one to accompany me to each meeting.

I sheepishly agreed, rather misty-eyed about how much they seemed to care.

In any event, my ensuing call, with Brody observing, was to Wanda. I filled her in and told her that the next person I hoped to eliminate from my list was her friend and neighbor James Jerome.

After we hung up, she called back almost immediately. "He's home now and expecting us," she said. "I won't be able to stay long because I need to take a Rottweiler for a walk, but if you can come right away . . ."

"Sure." My mind raced a bit. I could call Detective Melamed, but having her send someone to observe inside James's unit wasn't going to happen. Still, I could figure out a way to shoot pictures, just in case. Plus, I'd have two other people as backup. Wanda would be there—and I could tell from Brody's interested expression that he would be, too. "What does James do for a living?" I asked. I hadn't inquired before, but his being home on a weekday, even so late in the afternoon, suggested he was either unemployed or worked from his condo.

Turned out to be the latter. "He has an okay business buying and selling guinea pig items on the Internet," Wanda replied.

A kinda competitor to Dante's HotPets' Web site,

I assumed, on a small scale. I wondered how much money he made with such a limited market. Or maybe there was more to it than Wanda knew.

I did call Detective Melamed. Rather, I left a message. She hadn't told me how to contact her guy in the field, and I didn't think she'd want me to explain all to the officer who answered. I left my number and the address where I was heading. She'd understand.

Brody and I soon headed toward Burbank in separate cars. I'd have preferred not taking Lexie along on this particular outing, but didn't want to take the time to drop her off either at home or at Doggy Indulgence.

What I could do, though, was leave her in Wanda's apartment with her friend and fellow Cavalier, Basil. Wanda was fine with that. Then the three of us humans headed through the zigzag halls to James's.

He opened the door immediately. "Great to see you, Kendra." He gave me a hug and looked suitably impressed when I introduced him to Brody. "I'm a real fan," he said as they shook hands.

"Did Wanda tell you I'm still digging for details about Margaret's murder?" I asked as he showed us into his sparsely furnished living room. The slight rodent odor managed to break through the scent of cleaning solutions in the air. I went straight for his amazing maze of guinea pig habitat and smiled at the wiggling noses of the inhabitants.

"Yes, she did," James said. Like Wanda and Brody, I took a seat on the threadbare sofa. James wasn't wearing one of his usual guinea pig shirts that day, but a button-down that suggested he was going, or had been, out and about.

We chatted about how the investigation was going.

"Too bad Lady Cuddles can't talk," I told him. "We don't know exactly what she saw, but she might be able to ID the killer. And . . . well, there is one way she could actually be of assistance." I described the missing collar and ID tag. "The cops seem to think that the murderer might have made off with them, assuming blood got on the collar or whatever."

"Interesting," James said. "Haven't seen anything like that around here." His dipping eyebrows raised toward his receding hairline in apparent sincerity. He was another one I hoped wasn't guilty, but who knew?

In any event, the trap was baited. Now it just had to be set.

We talked next about how things were around Brigadoon, with restless residents still concerned about how the pet issues might wind up being resolved.

"With Margaret out of the picture, are there still a lot of folks besides the Bertinettis who want to rule out pets?" I asked.

There were a few, and we discussed that for a while. I soon inquired if I could use his bathroom. "I can find it," I said with a grin. "All these units have the same layout, though some are mirror images of the others."

Which also meant I knew the location of both bedrooms in this unit—down the same hallway that contained the non-master bath. Only a small part of the hall was visible through the living room doorway, so I made sure I was out of sight as I peeked into the other chambers.

One was James's bedroom, as sparsely furnished with stuff that looked as if it had been bought used from a charitable organization as the living room was. The other bedroom was clearly his office. The desk wasn't any better than the rest of the furniture, but the computer appeared to be state-of-the-art.

I popped carefully inside and pulled the latest collar and ID tag from my pocket, hiding it behind the desk.

I then went down the hall for my stated destination, and flushed with the door open so all could hear.

No one had resolved how to deal with the pet-haters by the time I returned to the living room. I stayed on that topic for a while, fed by comments and questions from both Brody and Wanda. Then I said, "James, Wanda said you have an online business selling guinea pig products. Is that true? I'm fascinated by the idea and would love for you to show me how you do it."

"Me, too," Brody said, with a cherubic smile that would probably cause thousands of female film fans to faint. "I've got this idea of selling showbiz memorabilia online as a sideline. But it always seems so challenging. Maybe you could show us how."

James seemed pleased by the interest and showed us down the hall and into his office. We stood in a group behind him as he logged on and displayed a few pages of stuff he sold: guinea pig food, treats, toys, and even cages, as well as shirts, notepaper, pens, banners, and blankets depicting guinea pigs. For the large items, he said he had an arrangement with wholesalers who would drop-ship the stuff when orders came in. He also showed us his pages on eBay.

As he talked and demonstrated, I started edging around the room as if I needed to see the screen from a different angle. I wasn't sure whether he was watching me, but I'd occasionally say something admiring so he'd at least know where I was.

·

And then I gasped aloud. "What's that?" I exclaimed, pointing to a spot behind the desk.

"What's what?" Brody asked, playing along.

"Is something wrong, Kendra?" Wanda asked, also on the same wavelength.

Only James seemed oblivious. "It's my favorite guinea pig harness-and-leash set." He pointed to the screen.

"Oh, maybe that's what it is," I said in exaggerated relief. Then I bent and gingerly lifted the white cat collar from the floor, dangling it from my index finger. "No, it isn't. It's Lady Cuddles's missing collar! The ID tag has her name and address on it."

"What?" James's eyes went suddenly wide, as if he was finally tuning in to our conversation. "Not possible. I'm all for pets, but I'm not a cat person. I wouldn't allow one in here, anyway, 'cause it would bother my guinea pigs."

"The point isn't that Lady Cuddles might have been in here," I responded patiently. "But like I said, there's some suspicion that the murderer might have stolen her collar and ID when he murdered Margaret, to hide evidence that could incriminate him or her."

"Oh." He looked at me blankly, as if he couldn't quite get his mind to grasp what I was aiming at.

Which told me how unlikely he was as a viable murder suspect. The killer, whoever it was, would surely be keeping his or her mind, eyes, and ears open for any suspicions people had about Margaret's murderer and any potential evidence.

I aimed a brief smile toward Brody and Wanda. Brody's confirming nod ended in an instant, and

Wanda's pretty face appeared relieved. We were all apparently on the same page.

"I don't remember ever seeing that before," James continued. "How could it have gotten in here?" He looked and sounded befuddled. And then he looked straight at me. "Oh, my lord, you said that the police thought the killer stole that collar. Someone must have planted it here. I didn't like Margaret, sure, but kill her? No way! Now what am I going to do?"

"It's no big deal," I assured him softly. "I'll talk to Detective Melamed, who's in charge of the investigation. I don't think you'll wind up any higher on her suspect list than you already are."

His puzzled expression segued into a glare. "You put it there, didn't you, Kendra? You wanted to see what I'd do, if I'd act guilty."

"Yep, I'm guilty of that. And my opinion is that you acted innocent. I can't guarantee what the cops will do. But at least we can vouch for you." I glanced toward Wanda, then Brody, and they both expressed concurrence.

We left soon after. "I don't think James is very happy with me," Wanda said with a sigh as we walked to her apartment so I could retrieve Lexie.

"You two are still on the same side on the pet issue around here," I reminded her. "I think he'll forgive you."

Especially when the killer was finally caught.

As Brody, Lexie, and I left Brigadoon for the day, I said, "There are a few other folks around here I need to try this on."

Brody nodded. "So I gathered. Are there any others

you're just hoping to eliminate this way as possible suspects?"

"No," I said. "Now I'm going to have to get down to the people I really think could have killed Margaret."

Chapter Twenty-nine

MY NEXT TEST of a suspect couldn't be until late the next afternoon, I learned after making some phone calls.

Which worked out okay. For one thing, I again had a delightful evening with Dante after ending my pet-sitting. Brody came to my place, too, and we informed Dante about our visit to James's.

Good excuse—since he happened to be there—for Dante to stay the night. He didn't have Alfonse bring Wagner this time, though, and Lexie acted lonesome. At least I got her a late-evening romp through my ample yard along with Beggar—which gave me a chance to talk with Rachel and her dad, Russ, while Dante egged on the dogs. Fortunately, although it was chilly, the predicted precipitation had been delayed.

"We've found a place we like, Kendra," Russ told me solemnly. "We're going to make an offer on it."

"Oh," I said stupidly. "That's great." I tried, unsuccessfully, to interject enthusiasm into my tone. I'd known this day—er, night—was coming.

Rachel threw her arms around me. "It's not far from here. I'll still do whatever you want me to for Critter TLC, LLC. And of course I'll continue to be the hostess on *Animal Auditions* as long as you want me." She hesitated. "Will you be okay without us here?"

"What an ego!" I exclaimed, clearly jesting. "Of course I will." But my heartiness didn't fool her, and she hugged me again.

When I turned, I saw that Dante had stopped near us on the driveway, the two dogs playing at his feet. His eyes were on me, his expression one of those he gets when he's in his mysterious former government agent mode—in other words, unreadable.

Had he heard, and did he feel sorry for me, too? Or was he plotting, in his smart, wealthy mind, how to manipulate things to save my house for me? He'd already worked around me to finance my recently purchased Ford Escape.

I'd made it clear, when I learned of it, that although I appreciated the gesture, I didn't want him doing stuff behind my back, even if he thought it was for my own good.

I hoped my return glare gave him the message to bug off—in the nicest manner, of course.

Later, when we lay in bed, I half expected him to broach the subject. He didn't.

I wasn't sure whether I was glad or sorry. But I knew I was happy to be treated once more to one heck of an enjoyable night.

●　　●　　●

I ALWAYS LIKE to take advantage of any information I learn. As a result, I used my tenants' impending vacating of the main house as an excuse to call my next suspect.

I, of course, let Russ and Rachel know I'd be taking a few folks into the house when they weren't around. "It's mostly to check out a guy I met who does contracting work," I told them early in the morning while the dogs were again enjoying the yard. Nope, none of the predicted rainstorms yet. And Dante had already left for his office.

But I knew he'd be back. And there'd be someone ostensibly working in my yard that afternoon. It would actually be an undercover sort sent by Detective Candace Melamed while I checked out—who else? Rutley Harris.

Before that, though, I had pet-sitting to perform, and so did Rachel.

Then, to my surprise, I had a meeting scheduled in my office regarding Pierre, the French bulldog.

Cornelius Eldt, the attorney representing the breeder, Elmira Irving, hadn't bothered to return my phone call till that morning—and that happened only after my client, Joan Fieldmann, set up the meeting time with Elmira.

Joan arrived at the firm a few minutes before eleven o'clock, the time set for the conclave. I'd checked with Mignon, and fortunately the conference room was available. I talked with Joan first in my office.

She was wearing a nice black dress, and had put on enough makeup to make her look attractive, in contrast to her usual frumpiness. Black-and-white and beautiful Pierre, sitting on her lap, could pass for her accessory.

Joan appeared ready to impress her adversary.

I inquired why she had called Elmira directly, and what she'd said. I'd need to know if they had talked about anything adverse to my client's interests, so I could explain it away in the meeting.

"Well, you and I talked about a possible solution on the phone yesterday. You know I'm used to making sales calls, addressing questions directly. This disagreement has gone on long enough. I don't want to go to court over it. The compromise you suggested . . . well, I think I can live with it."

"Good girl," I said. The words made Pierre sit up and wiggle his big, pointed ears at me, and I laughed. "Not you, guy. Anyway, let's see if Elmira will go along."

Mignon chirped into the phone a few minutes later that the other members of my meeting were there, so I led Joan and Pierre toward the conference room. It took a little while, since the secretaries and paralegals were drawn to the cute French bulldog. They'd gotten used to my bringing Lexie and didn't always pop out to say hi to her, and they knew not to bother Gigi, the Blue and Gold Macaw owned by Elaine Aames that was frequently present, too.

Pierre took it all in like the adorable gentleman . . . er, gentle dog . . . he was. In a few minutes, the three of us joined the others in the former bar that was now our firm's main meeting room.

I exchanged handshakes with Cornelius, who was again dressed for the olden days when attorneys always wore suits for meetings, not just court. I'd dressed up some that day, but my nice blouse and slacks still looked more business casual than formal.

Cornelius waved us to our seats around the

conference table, though it wasn't easy to convince his client. Attractive, middle-aged Elmira, despite her own nice suit, knelt on the shiny wooden floor, fussing over Pierre, and Joan observed with a smile and teary eyes.

Soon, though, we were seated around the large oval table, Joan beside me with Pierre again on her lap, and the others facing us.

"So, Kendra," Cornelius began. "I heard you had a settlement proposition."

I nodded. "Word travels fast." I started by saying how difficult it could be for everyone to have to rely on an arbitrator, as required by the contract, to choose one position or the other. I held my hand up to silence Cornelius when he started to speak, figuring what he intended to say. "Yes, I know you believe your client's contract is ironclad. Plus, we both know that an arbitrator can come up with a solution that might make both parties miserable. So let's see if we can work things out so we're the only ones who're miserable, Cornelius, since our legal fees will stop sooner."

I then stated succinctly what I believed both parties' positions to be. "Elmira considers Pierre a perfect representative of MirVilous Kennels. Her contract purports to maintain certain ownership rights, including keeping her on Pierre's registration and requiring Joan to show him in a manner Elmira approves of. And if she doesn't approve, she can allegedly take over the showing and, if she chooses, take Pierre back. Is that your basic understanding?"

After quick consultation with his client, Cornelius acknowledged I'd gotten it more or less right.

"Joan's essential position is that she is complying in all ways with the contract," I continued, "which has an implied reasonability standard. She loves Pierre, enjoys showing him, and wants to do it herself. She's taken lessons and believes she is handling him fine for a beginner." I held up my hand as Elmira opened her mouth to comment. "Elmira does not agree. Right?"

Both women nodded.

"So here's what we suggest." I went through the scenario we'd discussed. "Elmira may choose the number of shows she wants for Pierre over the next six months, preferably close to the L.A. area. She will solely handle Pierre at first, but will also work with Joan to train her. If Pierre starts amassing enough points to suggest he could achieve a championship, Elmira will stay in the equation, still showing Pierre and working with Joan. This scenario will continue, and Elmira will mostly show while training Joan, till championship is achieved, if ever. But if, even with Elmira's handling, championship doesn't seem in the cards, her showing will stop and Pierre's registration will revert to Joan alone. In that case, Joan can show him or not, as she pleases."

"That will be hard to administer," Cornelius sniffed dubiously.

"We'll let Elmira stay mostly in charge till she stops showing Pierre and he gets his championship," I said, "or not. We'll also hire a mutually acceptable, major handler who's a member of the Professional Handlers Association"—I'd asked around the Pet-Sitters Club of SoCal till I got that name from someone knowledgeable—"at their joint expense to monitor what's going on and determine when, if ever, Joan can take over some or all of the showing. That handler's determination will be final and binding."

I'd been watching Elmira's face as I proposed all this. She looked pensive, and I wasn't sure what she thought of it. But when I was done, Cornelius took her to a side of the room, and Joan and I left for a few minutes— allowing Elmira a little more time with Pierre.

We stayed outside, talking a little nervously with Mignon and my senior counsel, Borden, who'd come to join us. As always, he was clad in a Hawaiian aloha shirt—this one green with pink flowers. Both of them were filled with concern and sympathy.

Soon, Cornelius came out to the firm's entry area. He motioned for us to return, and Joan and I did.

Elmira was standing near the doorway, hugging Pierre. She smiled as we came in and, relieved, I knew their answer.

"As long as we can agree on written terms and a PHA handler to advise them," Cornelius said, "we have a deal."

I FELT GOOD and jazzed after that session, so I was utterly optimistic when I went home to wait for Rutley Harris.

I realized, of course, that giving him my home address wasn't necessarily the wisest course of action. On the other hand, if he clearly responded as if he was the killer, he'd be picked up by the yardman who'd be right outside—the undercover cop Detective Melamed had promised to send. Plus, Dante had insisted on dropping everything to be there for this scenario, so I'd never be alone with Rutley.

I hoped. I didn't like the guy, whether or not he turned out to be guilty.

Dante arrived a few minutes early, calling me from his car to open the security gate so he could drive right in. A couple of guys, dressed in grungy jeans beneath zippered sweatshirts, walked in after him. They introduced themselves and showed me their IDs—undercover cops from the Burbank PD. They asked where I kept my gardening equipment, and they soon were shuffling around the front lawn, acting as if they were raking up dead grass.

A good thing, since soon a red pickup truck pulled up to the closed front gate. After our hello kiss, Dante had spent the time going over our intended setup and chiding me—again—for dreaming up this scenario.

My landline soon rang. "Kendra? It's Rutley Harris. I'm right outside."

"I'll let you in." I left Lexie inside, not wanting her to be involved if things got ugly. I considered saying the same to Dante, who viewed me with his assessing dark eyes as if he was thinking identical thoughts about me. I smiled at him. "Show time."

I'd put another of the cat collars with name tag attached into my jeans pocket. I still wondered if I'd need as many as I'd ordered. I'd smeared a smidgen of tomato sauce on this collar for effect. Dante followed me down the stairs from my apartment, and I saw Rutley emerge from his truck.

He was dressed for the cooler January weather, so he wasn't showing off his extensive muscles. He eyed me up and down as if my clothes didn't exist, which made me want to go shower immediately.

Dante saw it, too, and stepped protectively beside me, putting an arm around my shoulder. Rutley didn't seem at all cowed, but regarded tall, well-built Dante, in his business shirt with the top buttons undone, as if he were a teenage runt.

Uh-oh. This session wasn't intended to be a testosterone skirmish.

I made myself smile and say, "Glad you could come. As I said on the phone, I own this property—well, the bank and I do." I didn't want this cockroach to get the idea I had more assets than I did. "The tenants are moving out, so I thought I'd do some remodeling before looking for replacements."

If Dante hadn't heard before, he definitely knew my tenant situation now.

Beggar was the only one home, and Rachel and Russ had done as I asked and confined him in the den. He wasn't happy about the intrusion, but I got him to stop barking by patting his head and handing him a treat.

For the next ten minutes, I walked Rutley around the house and made comments about upgrading the bathrooms and a few other changes I really wasn't about to undertake.

Dante stayed right with me, offering suggestions, some of which made sense. Others didn't, but I knew his intent was to remind Rutley of his presence.

I left the two of them talking about possible tile work in an upstairs bath, excusing myself ostensibly to make a quick phone call. Which took me outside. Near Rutley's truck.

The supposed gardeners stayed in character and nodded at me without approaching, and I nodded in return.

I went back inside, and soon our discussion ended. We walked Rutley outside once more. On the driveway, I said to him, "Thanks for coming. I'm eager to get your estimate for the work. Oh, by the way, have you heard anything more about suspects in Margaret's murder? You know, Wanda's a friend of mine, and I'm hoping she's dropped from suspicion soon."

"The damned cops keep questioning me now, too." Rutley's thick jaw tightened and his eyes grew dark.

"What I'd really love is to get Lady Cuddles, the kitten, to tell me what she saw. You know, she was there when Wanda found Margaret's body."

"Yeah. That cat may be cute, but it's into everything."

"You didn't happen to find her collar and name tag while you were working on any of the Brigadoon units, did you?" I asked, attempting to sound all innocence.

"Sure didn't," he said. "But I've heard something about them disappearing the night Margaret died, and that there's some thought that the killer took them."

Interesting. I would have to finish up my little skits soon, before the world figured out not only the significance of the collar, but what I was doing about it.

"Yes, I've heard that," I said. "Do you suppose the murderer's blood is on them or something?"

"Who knows? Anyway, I'll send you an e-mail with my estimates on that work. Good seeing you, Kendra. And keep me in mind for any construction work you want done, Dante." He must know who Dante was, with a comment like that, which was also interesting. He hadn't acted impressed at all during our house walk-through and discussion.

He opened the door of his truck. It was one of those with four doors and a large seating area inside, and a smaller cargo area in back. I looked into it through the back window. "Oh, is that a sample of some tile you're installing somewhere?" I'd spotted some boxes before. "Could I take a look at it?"

"Sure. I got it for one of the units at Brigadoon."

He pulled open the back door and moved around some tools and boxes . . . and that was when I gasped. "Is that what I think it is?" I pointed to a short white strap smeared with red that had a bright blue metal tag in the shape of a cat's head on it.

"What the hell?" Rutley grabbed it in his thick hand and yanked it out. "Where did this come from?"

I looked at him, attempting to gauge his craftiness quotient. What would he say next?

"Damn it all, someone must have planted it there. Like I said, the cops haven't left me alone. I argued with Margaret, sure. Didn't like the bitch. She kept telling me my work was too slow, not right, too expensive. Threatened to have me blackballed from the condos. And all because I screwed her once—literally—then wouldn't again. But I didn't kill her—and whoever did it must want to make it look like I did."

He actually sounded sincere. I glanced at Dante, and saw that his expression was rueful. I guessed that he had wanted it to be Rutley, just to get this awful example of the male sex off the streets.

I sighed inside, noting in my peripheral vision that my two "yardmen" were taking all this in, too.

"Well, we'd better turn this over to Detective Melamed," I told Rutley. "Wish I could do it with some evidence of who actually did kill Margaret. Any ideas?"

"Yeah. I even gave the cops my list. Not only that, but I'd had a key to Margaret's apartment for the work I was doing there, and I lost it. Another one, too. Thought

I had them both with all the others when I was working on a bunch of units at the same time, but they weren't there. I also told the cops that. Since whoever killed Margaret did it at her place, maybe he found them and let himself in with her key."

"It could have been someone she knew, someone she let in herself," I said.

"Maybe, but the cops let it drop that that particular key might have been right there, in the unit, when they started collecting evidence. Only one, though."

Hmmm. That might be an even more telling clue than the missing collar. But only if whoever found it had used it to get into Margaret's condo.

That was when I knew who the next target of my suspect-weeding scenario would be.

Chapter Thirty

Dante and I sat on the sofa in my small living room. Soft, furry Lexie was on my lap. I'd made my necessary calls, and was waiting now till it made sense to start visiting my pet charges for the last time that day.

I wished I could start my next suspect setup earlier. But even if I'd been able to get Rachel to pick up most of my evening pet-sitting, I still had to wait until Wanda was available.

As for my lawyering, when I filled Borden in on what appeared to be my resolution of the Pierre problem, he was happy. I didn't have anything else pressing that day, so he seemed okay with my not coming in till the next day.

"Don't you have some executive stuff to take care of?" I asked Dante, who sat there asserting dominion over my TV remote. I had satellite service, and he'd found a business channel that he'd put on mute, staring at the streaming stock prices at the bottom of the

screen. Since we were on the West Coast, I wasn't sure
what the amounts signified so late in the day, when the
stock market was already closed in New York.

Not of huge interest to me. I'd invested what little
extra money I'd been able to save in bank CDs and con-
servative mutual funds. I was considering liquidating it
all to pay down more on my mortgage. But I wasn't sure
it was the wisest thing to do.

Instead of worrying about that for the moment, I
stared at Dante, on the far side of my sectional sofa. I
felt restless. Ready to do something. But all I could do
just then was wait.

Dante must have felt my stare, since in an instant he
returned it. Then he wasn't at the far end of the sofa any
longer, and Lexie was on the floor.

DANTE DIDN'T COME pet-sitting with me. He simply
sent me on my way after retrieving a laptop computer
from the trunk of his Mercedes. I'd given him an extra
key to my apartment, so he could lock up when he left.
He also knew the security system code.

"I'll be at Brigadoon by seven o'clock," he told me.

"Me, too." I gave him a good-bye kiss, patted Lexie,
and left.

Fortunately, all my animal charges were in excellent
condition, a little needy of attention, but I absolutely
could deal with that. And did. Despite my feeling
stressed for time, I spent a sufficient amount of it walking, feeding, playing, hugging, and whatever it took to
ensure that the pets all got plenty of TLC.

When I was done, it was time to head to Burbank
and Brigadoon.

I called Wanda on the way. As I'd requested, she had set up the meeting that I'd hoped for.

"I don't think it'll be particularly pleasant, though," she warned. "I got a pretty cold reception when I called, especially since I structured my request around the issue of whether people should still be able to keep pets at the condo, and, if so, whether the rules should be amended."

"As long as we've been granted an audience," I told her, "that's perfect. And if my suspicions are correct, having a pleasant time definitely won't be in the cards . . . although, with luck, we'll have a finale to our search for someone to replace you in the cops' eyes as top suspect."

"Really?" she inquired, then said, "Interesting possibility. See you in a little while." She hung up.

I called Dante. He was nearly there, having stayed at my place till it was time to go. "Started negotiations for any more perfect pet food to carry in your stores, or to acquire more sites to build them?"

"That'll happen tomorrow," he said, and I heard the smile in his voice. "Today I just sent some encouraging e-mails to my best store managers."

Which might partly explain why the HotPets chain was so successful. It definitely had one hot, kind, and astute dude at the reins.

Soon I was outside the condo complex. I saw Dante's car parked on the street, and he came over and got into the Escape's passenger side. I called Wanda, and she performed her buzzer magic to open the outside gate and let us in.

A janitorial truck rolled in behind us. What a surprise. I felt sure it had originated in Burbank's city center.

I parked near Wanda's building, quietly approached the truck, and confirmed that these were the cops.

Wanda buzzed us all into the building, cops included. Since they were invited by a resident, they might not require a warrant for the condo, although that might not be true for individual units.

Dante and I headed to Wanda's apartment, where she waited at the door. I wasn't exactly sure where the cops went, but they'd told me to record my meeting with a high-tech gizmo that they handed me. Best I could tell, it was a radio of sorts so the cops would be able to eavesdrop. Maybe it even contained a teensy camera. I wore a jacket with a breast pocket, and the part hanging out resembled a pen flashlight.

My petite friend Wanda didn't look particularly perky these days, but she'd spiced up her appearance with a bright orange gauzy top.

I peered around her into her unit. "Darryl's not here?"

She shook her head. "Still at Doggy Indulgence. I'm not sure what's going on, but he said he had a late meeting today with one of his employees—that nasty little Kiki, I think."

Interesting. Maybe two issues would come to a head tonight—assuming that my assumptions about who killed Margaret were now correct, and I got the kind of reaction I anticipated from my main suspects.

"So, are we ready?" I asked Dante and Wanda.

We were, and my gang headed to the unit near Margaret's where Ruth and Teddy Bertinetti lived.

Yes, they had rushed to the top of my suspect list, even though I didn't know their motive. Of course I could be misinterpreting what I thought had become a big clue.

I'd find out soon.

We walked along the zigzag hall, at one point passing the Gustins' unit. "Seen Lady Cuddles lately?" I asked Wanda.

"Only professionally. I visited the Gustins to talk about plans for their next trip, probably in a month or so. That cute little kitty came over and made a fuss over me, like I was family."

"Were the Gustins okay with that, or did they get jealous?"

"They seemed relieved, since it sounds like both Trudy and Jamiel have extensive stays planned in other towns on film shoots."

"Good deal. We'll have to give Lady Cuddles some extra catnip if it turns out this ploy solves Margaret's murder." I glanced at Dante, and he grinned.

"Yes, HotPets has a good supply of cat toys containing catnip," he said.

We were soon at the Bertinettis' door. The decorative wreath I'd seen before was gone—a stark omen of what we'd find inside?

Teddy greeted us none too enthusiastically. "Come in." He stepped aside so we could obey. The entry looked like most others in the condos that I had visited—wooden floor, and an open doorway into the living room on one side.

Ruth was already there, sitting on a sofa with black upholstery that matched a couple of chairs facing it. None looked especially comfortable, but that seemed appropriate for the choices made by these two. The room also contained some large potted plants, shelves built into the wall containing a huge HDTV, and a small upright piano. I wondered which one played the piano. Maybe they both did.

I also wondered whether the community association had any rules about when they could play it—and whether the Bertinettis, who were such sticklers for pet rules, obeyed those regarding music.

Once more I was struck by how much these two appeared to be in sync with one another. Teddy wore a casual blue striped shirt tucked into jeans. Ruth's outfit was quite similar, although her shirt had a few more buttons open, revealing a diamond pendant. "Nice shelves," I said to start the conversation. "Did that contractor Rutley Harris build them for you recently?"

"Yes," Ruth replied, "But what's this all about? I gather you want to discuss the shameful pet situation around here, but I'm not on the board . . . yet. I have no control over it at the moment. Although I'm definitely running for the vacant seat."

"Wanda was just hoping that if we talked about it, we could change your mind. Have you met Dante?" I introduced him, stressing his significance in the pet community, including HotPets.

"You know, Ruth and Teddy, that there are all kinds of pets," he said smoothly. "Not everybody has to love them, of course, but those who do, really consider their pets part of the family. Would you want to deprive the people who live here of their kids?"

"Pets are just animals," Ruth spat, making me strongly consider standing and smacking the nasty woman. But of course I didn't. As a lawyer, I knew better than to engage in assault and battery.

Even so . . .

"The thing is"—I gestured a warning to Wanda, who also looked as if she considered committing mayhem—"since the biggest advocate of changing the rules concerning pets isn't around any longer, we were hoping to lobby some of her supporters and get you to change your minds." I took a seat on one of the chairs, as if I'd been invited to, and Dante and Wanda did likewise.

"Forget it," Teddy said staunchly, standing beside his wife with his arms crossed.

"You're certainly entitled to your opinion," I said in a tone I intended to sound charming. "And I have to admit that there have been some animals around here who've been permitted to break the rules."

"Like the cat I heard about," Dante tossed in, as if he'd been coached. Which he had been. "That little kitten who seems to always be running around, instead of being confined in her unit. What's her name?" He looked at Wanda.

"Lady Cuddles," she responded.

"Right," I agreed, before the Bertinettis could interrupt. "Did you know that Wanda found Lady Cuddles right there with poor Margaret, the night she was murdered?"

"We heard." Ruth's generally pinched expression grew even uglier, as if she were disgusted.

"Did you also know that Lady Cuddles lost her collar with her name tag that night?" Wanda asked. "I happened to notice that it was gone. The police seem to think it could have been taken by the killer, perhaps because it had blood on it. Isn't that awful?" She gave a sweet little shudder.

But my attention was focused more on the Bertinet-tis, who now were both on the couch. Ruth's expression seemed to harden. Teddy's usually squinty blue eyes widened as if he was trying to assume an expression of innocence.

So far, they were still my top suspects. Especially considering their response to one of my questions.

"Anyway, since you were such good friends with Margaret, maybe you could ask some of your other friends at Brigadoon if they happened to have seen the missing collar," I said. "Although I assume most of your friends took Margaret's side on the anti-pet issue, so they wouldn't have much reason to kill her."

So, I thought, *why did you?* Not that they'd officially admitted it—yet. I hoped they would when they found the collar they'd most likely thought they tossed away.

Time to set that up.

I glanced at Dante, who gave a conspiratorial little nod. He was set up to be our gardener this time—to plant our little item of evidence.

"Would you two mind if I got myself a glass of water?" he asked. "My throat's really dry." He stood to head for the kitchen. When Ruth started to stand, he said, "No, I didn't mean to interrupt the conversation. I can get it myself, really."

But of course she went with him. We'd sort of assumed she would accompany him—or at least one of the Bertinettis would.

"I guess this is a good time for me to leave," Wanda said. "I'm sure you won't want to hear this, Teddy, but I have a little more pet-sitting here at the condos to do tonight. I can see myself out."

But Teddy went toward the front door with her.

Our plans for planting the collar actually had three possibilities, depending on which of us was left alone by the Bertinettis. Dante could have hidden one in the kitchen, or Wanda could have stuck one behind a door off the entry.

So my ordering multiple collars and tags had the clearest purpose yet.

But now it was left to me, and I'd already scoped out a suitable spot: inside the piano. I headed there, my hand in my pants pocket, and made sure no one was in the room when I lifted the lid and carefully placed the collar inside.

I was standing by the piano seat when everyone but Wanda returned to the room. "Is it okay if I play something?" I asked, and, not waiting for an answer, sat down and started playing a rousing version of "Chopsticks."

Except that when I got to the part past the chorus, where the highest notes were played, they turned out sour. As if something restricted the piano strings.

"What's the matter?" I asked innocently. "Isn't your piano in tune?"

"Of course it is," exploded Ruth. I had the impression that everything around her, like her dark, perfectly placed furniture, had to be flawless. She'd been standing near the doorway by Dante, who had a glass of water in his hands, and she now hurried over to where I was.

"I wonder, though . . . ," I said thoughtfully, and lifted the lid hiding the piano's innards. And gasped. "What's that?" I asked as I peered in.

"What's what?" demanded Teddy.

All four of us were suddenly staring in. Then I

backed up for a moment to ensure that any photos or recordings being made by the gadget sticking out of my shirt pocket took in as much of this as possible.

"I'd better call the police," I said sternly. "That looks like Lady Cuddles's missing ID stuff."

"How did it get in there, Teddy?" Ruth shrieked, suddenly becoming unhinged.. "Did you mess up with that, like everything else?"

"No, I—hell, that's enough. I'm not saying another word. I think I'd better—"

I expected him to finish that statement with something like "call my lawyer."

Instead, I turned and saw that Teddy Bertinetti was aiming a lethal-looking handgun toward all of us.

His hand was unsteady enough to keep it waving. And I suddenly became afraid it might go off whether Teddy intended it to or not.

Chapter Thirty-one

"OKAY," I SAID loudly, practically aiming my boob, where the cops' gadget was located, toward Teddy. "You're pointing a gun at us. Is that a confession that you killed Margaret?"

"I was afraid you did, Teddy," wailed Ruth, wringing her hands as she stood off to one side of the living room.

"What the hell are you doing, Ruth?" Teddy demanded, backing up enough so that every other human being in the room, including his wife, was within range of his weapon. That meant he had to sidestep the matching sofa and chairs. I kept half hoping he'd trip over something, but that could mean he'd fire the gun wildly and hit someone. I didn't care a whole heck of a lot about Ruth, but I definitely didn't want him to hurt Dante. Or me, for that matter.

"You know exactly what I'm doing," Ruth said softly.

"Yeah, I do, you bitch."

"What do you mean?" Ruth's voice was now raised a humongous number of decibels. "You're the one who had an affair with her."

Ahhh. The motive was now making its presence known. But was it Ruth's motive, or Teddy's, or both? Either way, why murder someone over it? Damned if I knew.

Interesting, though, that the not-so-attractive dead lady had slept with both Rutley and Teddy.

"And you're the one who killed her, because of that," stormed Teddy. His gun hand was waving, which made me more than a little nervous.

Dante, too, apparently, since he gallantly stepped closer and shielded me with his big, beautiful masculine body.

Not that I allowed him to. I moved aside, which seemed to make Teddy's gun hand shake even more, back and forth, between us. Dante shot a glower at me, and I attempted a brave but determined smile back.

"You're so horrible!" screamed Ruth. "First you start an affair with that woman. When I caught you, you promised to back off. You said you'd just been doing it because you and she were so simpatico about that stupid no-pets-allowed position. But did you stop? No! I should have killed you instead of her."

Okay, now that sounded pretty much like a confession to me. But Dante and I were still in a dangerous situation.

Where were the cops?

I decided to try to buy some time. "So, Ruth, why did you take Lady Cuddles's collar off?"

She'd been staring with hatred toward the man she'd married and lived with in Brigadoon. The look she shot toward me then wasn't exactly adoring. "I didn't hate cats before—not like Teddy does. One scratched him when he was a little kid, and he's loathed them ever since. I didn't care too much, though I wouldn't have minded having one before. But to try to keep our marriage together, I thought that if I got onto the condo association board with Margaret, I'd be able to help sway things the way Teddy wanted even more than she did. I planned to run for the next open seat. I started suspecting they had something going . . . and when I accused her, she laughed about it. Said that I hadn't done a great job teaching my husband how to really please a woman. In fact, he was pretty rotten at it."

"Hey!" Teddy roared, pointing the gun decidedly in his wife's direction. "That's a lie!"

"It's what your mistress said, dear," Ruth said sweetly. "I wanted to kick her teeth in then, but decided to wait and see. After all, if she taught you better, you might use some of your lessons the next time you touched me . . . if I ever let you."

"You've always been a cold bitch!" Teddy shouted, but at least he didn't shoot.

And Ruth didn't shut up, still speaking to her husband. "Even after that, Margaret kept goading me about being an awful wife, in so many ways. And about how she was sure she could convince you to divorce me. I just couldn't take it anymore. I went to her place that night ready to confront her one final time and insist that she back off. I found her in her kitchen, and did she act nervous? No! She started making fun of me . . . Even showed me the key to the Gustins' condo that she used to let that cat out and make trouble in a way you approved of, like you approved of everything about her. She even encouraged that stupid cat to creep into all the buildings at Brigadoon when it was loose. That night, she had a nasty-looking barbecue spit in her sink, with one hell of a point on it. Guess she was planning a cookout, but I cooked her goose first."

Lovely image, but I didn't say a word. Listening worked a whole lot better. Apparently, Ruth hadn't been happy holding everything inside, and now it was in everyone's best interests to let her vent her hysteria as much as she wanted. As long as it was verbal and not physical, at least.

"So," Ruth continued, "when what happened, happened, in Margaret's apartment, that damned kitten was there and saw it all. I'd already wiped the spit clean, so it wouldn't have had any fingerprints. But the cat had blood on her, and I picked her up to try to rinse it off her—and she clawed me. I bled, too, then, and I saw that some of the blood was on that white collar. I'd dropped her, and she'd nearly gotten away, but I figured I'd better take the collar off. She might wipe off the blood on her paws and fur as she ran around the condos, but the blood that was on that white thing might be partly mine. The thing is . . . Hell!"

Ruth ran across the room toward the piano, and Teddy looked even more unnerved, as if ready to shoot her.

"What's wrong now?" Teddy bellowed.

Ruth raised the lid of the piano again and looked in. "The blood was near the buckle on that collar, not in the center. I'll bet . . ." She ran at Dante with her own claws outstretched. "I'll bet this came from one of your stores, you damned interfering bastard. It isn't the one I took off that kitten at all. I knew I did a good job getting rid of it."

"In the complex's garbage?" Dante inquired calmly, catching Ruth by her wrists and turning her so she'd be a shield if Teddy happened to shoot.

"Of course not. I put it in a plastic bag and took it to the Dumpster at a supermarket near here."

Which meant it was unlikely to be found easily, if at all, depending on how often the Dumpster contents were hauled off, and where they were taken.

But there could be another clue that might be found more easily. "So, Ruth, did you steal the key to Margaret's unit from Teddy, to get in there that night? One of those he'd sneaked away from the contractor Rutley Harris—at Margaret's request, I assume?"

"That's what happened to Margaret's key?" Teddy squeaked.

"How did you know about that?" Ruth demanded at the same time.

It had been the clue that had made me assume one of the Bertinettis was guilty. A while back, I'd seen Teddy try to open the door to their unit with a key that he'd assumed would work, since it was the same kind used for all the condos. But it hadn't worked, and he'd had to dig out another one. Rutley's telling me about the keys that went missing had gotten my mind spinning around several possibilities.

"I assume, Teddy, that Margaret asked you to retrieve her key from Rutley Harris, after they started arguing and you began seeing her on the side. That way you could visit her at any time, right? And, while you were at it, you were to 'borrow' Rutley's key to the Gustins' unit—the one Margaret started using to let Lady Cuddles out now and then to bolster her point about pets being out of control around here." No answer. I'd assumed that Rutley had received a copy of the Gustins' key when he had updated their shelves and hardwood floor. "Ruth found out about Margaret's key when she learned the two of you were seeing each other. Her turn to 'borrow' a key—yes? And, Ruth, I'll bet you took the Gustins' key that night but left Margaret's in its place—after removing any fingerprints, probably—and that you're now the one letting Lady Cuddles out and about to help make the anti-pet point."

"I still wanted to help Teddy." There were tears in Ruth's eyes.

Which was when a knock finally sounded on the outside door. "Police," called a brusque voice. "Open up."

The look on Teddy's face suggested he was weighing whether to shoot first and open up second. But he quickly realized the futility of that . . . for him. It wouldn't have done us any good, either.

Soon as he lowered his weapon an iota, Dante rushed forward to grab it, and him, just as the door splintered open and the Burbank police, in gardening gear, poured in with their weapons drawn.

Ruth melted onto the floor, sobbing hysterically. "He killed Margaret," she shrieked. "My husband's a murderer."

OF COURSE THE statements given by Dante and me to Detective Candace Melamed, who arrived a few minutes later, contradicted Ruth's last allegations.

"Not that I'm certain," I told the detective as we stood out on the patio, where she used a more obvious recording device to take my statement, "but I think you'll hear on the recordings your nifty little device made that Ruth pretty much admitted her guilt; that last claim was probably an attempt to shift suspicion back on her husband, the way she'd started before." I also mentioned how fascinating I found it that Ruth, whom I now believed to be the killer, had accused Wanda so quickly right after she'd found Margaret's body.

This was the first time I saw the detective in something other than a formal suit. Today, she wore a Burbank PD T-shirt over jeans. I assumed it might have been her day off.

Her icy blue eyes looked almost warm for a change. Why not? I'd solved her case for her and had promised that she could take credit.

"I know you were narrowing your suspicions down on these two," she told me. "Why did you think it was them—or one of them?"

I described my thought processes on the scenario about the key to Margaret's unit—and the Gustins', too.

"It wasn't a certainty, of course," I admitted. "In fact, it was a pretty sketchy reason to suspect them. But when the contractor Rutley Harris admitted losing a couple of keys to units around here, that made me really consider that incident with Teddy and focus on the Bertinettis more strongly than anyone else I was wondering about."

I didn't bother to mention that had I not obtained a confession from one Bertinetti or the other, I'd planned to try my scenario on Ivan Tradeau. He had, after all, once used a barbecue spit as a prop in a film he worked on. But now, he was exonerated. And Ruth had apparently used the spit simply because it was convenient.

"I'm glad you came through on this, Kendra," Detective Melamed said as she prepared to let me leave. "Ned Noralles' vouching for you notwithstanding, I really stuck my neck out here, letting you play your little games with the police department's tacit approval."

I thought the approval was a little more than tacit,

but I didn't tell her that. Plus, the credit she'd been searching for would be all hers. I'd even say so to my reporter friend Corina Carey.

I waited in the winding hallway while Candace took Dante's statement. I saw a bunch of crime scene sorts going in and out of the Bertinettis' unit, and some of the same condo residents who'd been around Margaret's unit stood outside the tape barrier, exchanging gasps and comments and nods of their heads.

One of them was James Jerome, who came up to me and asked what was going on.

"I think Margaret's killer has been apprehended by the cops," I said, then added, good lawyer that I am, "allegedly."

"Was it Teddy or Ruth?"

"I think they'll have to sort that out," I said tactfully, although I knew the answer: the wronged wife. Even so, Teddy was a possible accomplice after the fact, and he'd definitely held Dante and me at gunpoint. There were certainly charges that could be brought against him for that.

Wanda joined us, too. "Is it over?" she asked almost fearfully.

"I think so," I said. "At least as far as you're concerned."

"Kendra, you're the best," she said, and hugged me.

I noticed then that the Gustins were among the people milling in the hall and mulling over what was going on.

As Dante and Candace Melamed reentered the hall, I turned toward them . . . which was when I saw a yellow streak stream past, through the open door of the Bertinettis' unit.

"Lady Cuddles!" I shouted. And then I started laughing.

Chapter Thirty-two

SINCE IT WAS a crime scene, the cops had to be the ones to round up and boot Lady Cuddles from the Bertinettis' condo unit. They seemed none too pleased that the elusive little kitty had once more potentially messed up parts of their investigation.

"But she helped to solve Margaret's murder," I reminded Candace Melamed when the detective was ultimately the one to carry the kitten into the hall and hand her to me. "Did you thank her?"

Candace glared through her glasses with her again chilly blue eyes, then smiled. "Don't press your luck."

Standing beside Wanda were the Gustins, and I handed their sweet, if slippery, pet back to them—without telling them, just then, about the stolen key. Some condo residents in the hall laughed and cheered. I figured they were among the pet-loving contingent.

I wondered what would happen to the pet-haters, with three of their most vocal supporters now out of the picture. At least I assumed that was so, with the Bertinettis in such trouble.

"You're a heroine of this tale," I assured the cute ginger kitten, who looked up at me with big blue feline eyes, the picture of utter innocence, and I couldn't help smiling at her.

"Mew," she responded.

I wasn't the only human in the area to laugh.

LATER IN THE evening, we were in Dante's car. We'd undergone further interrogation by Detective Melamed and her folks, who'd had additional inquiries after rerunning their recordings from the equipment they'd attached to me and, fortunately, monitored while we were in the Bertinettis' condo unit.

I had a sense that they were fairly pleased with the results. At least they had a viable suspect or two to focus on in their ongoing investigation.

I'd done my duty and called Corina Carey—and given her an off-the-record exclusive for her tabloid TV show, *National NewsShakers*. In the brief interview, I'd extolled how well Detective Melamed of the Burbank PD had handled the investigation. Did Corina buy it? Who knew? But I believed she'd handle it the way I wanted.

I also called Esther Ickes to let her know that her criminal-law client Wanda might not need her much longer. Nice lady that she is, she applauded me, and we made arrangements to have lunch together soon— somewhere that I could meet her new kitty, Sacha.

Now, Dante and I were off to meet Wanda and Darryl for a late possible-victory dinner.

"I never knew you played the piano," Dante said.

"It was 'Chopsticks,' not Chopin," I reminded him. "Not that hard to learn or play. Most kids do."

"I'm glad to say you're not a kid anymore." We were stopped at a light, and the look he aimed at me positively smoldered.

It made me simmer, even as I laughed.

"Me, too. Besides, amateur piano playing isn't the only thing. There's a lot about me you don't know."

"Yet."

That single word also brought a reaction from me as the light turned green and we continued. It suggested that we'd be together longer. That he'd have time to learn lots about me in the future.

Fortunately, our conversation lightened up, and we soon reached the Italian restaurant on Ventura Boulevard that was our destination.

Wanda had gone ahead of us to meet Darryl, and they were already seated when we got there. The restaurant was one that had been there for a while, and it was filled with customers and aromas of garlic and the delightful sauces for which its food was known.

Darryl stood immediately and gave me a huge hug. Embracing my lanky friend was like hugging a sapling tree, but with a whole lot more fervor since he returned it, hard. "You did it, Kendra! I knew you'd figure out this murder, too—and save my Wanda."

I didn't bother to remind him that there'd been a time he had been peeved with me for supposedly causing the situation in the first place, simply by being a murder magnet.

This evening, Darryl wasn't wearing a Doggy Indulgence knit shirt. Instead, it was a plain blue button-down.

Wanda, too, wasn't dressed characteristically. Instead of one of her gauzy tops, she'd donned a scoop-necked dress.

Dante and I hadn't taken the time to change, but our attire was sufficiently casual for the restaurant.

We all sat down, and ordered a bottle of Chianti in celebration. Then I gave my friends a better rundown of all that had occurred than I'd been able to impart to Wanda while still at Brigadoon being interrogated.

"It's all over then?" inquired Wanda in a tone that suggested she still didn't believe it.

"No guarantees." I'd seen cops choose not to accept the obvious, at least not at first. "But I'd say one or both of the Bertinettis are subject to imminent arrest—and my bet is on Ruth being found guilty of murdering Margaret."

"Yay!" Darryl exclaimed, then proposed a toast. "To Kendra Ballantyne, exceptionally great attorney, pet-sitter, and murder magnet."

"And murder solver," I added.

"Hopefully for the last time," Dante said, his glass lifted high. "As long as that's the way she wants it."

Hey! He'd gotten the message. He might have his own druthers about me and my life, but he couldn't control it.

"It's never exactly been within my control," I said, "but that's certainly my preference." Our eyes met in a long and lengthy silent conversation.

Darryl cleared his throat. "Anyone interested in hearing about my conversation before with Kiki?"

I pulled my eyes away and raised my hand. "I am. What's with her, the way she seemed so . . . well, bitchy about Wanda and you? Did she suddenly get the hots for you?"

No answer immediately. A server put a basket of rolls on the table, along with some interesting-looking sauce that smelled of garlic. We passed them all around, each of us indulging.

Then Darryl said, "No hots, fortunately. I guess I was just too preoccupied to pay enough attention to her, what she wants, and how badly she wants it." This time, it was Darryl's and Wanda's eyes that caught and held, and I laughed. Darryl looked around in apparent embarrassment, giving a brief laugh. "Okay, the thing is that she felt like I wasn't giving her enough responsibility. She wants to be a manager of Doggy Indulgence."

Which was part of what she had told me.

"She wants more authority over who does what when," Darryl continued. "Which dogs get special attention, who walks them, redesign of our play areas. All that. She'd also like more money. I told her that the reality of it all is that I'm the boss, she's an employee, and though I'll try to add some responsibility to what she has, and even give her a raise, it'll be more a pat on the back than anything sizeable. So . . . well, she says she's going to show me how dumb I am by starting her own pet daycare center somewhere near Doggy Indulgence." He looked rather rueful. "I really don't need the competition."

"But you shouldn't let her extort what she wants from you either," Wanda interjected, then looked at me. "That is a form of extortion, isn't it, Kendra?"

"Sounds like it to me," I responded. "Stick to your guns, Darryl. I always talk up what a wonderful facility Doggy Indulgence is, and now I'll do it even more."

"Thanks," he said glumly. "I may need all the extra endorsements I can get."

• • •

BEFORE WE LEFT, I gave Wanda the extra white collars and name tags—those that I hadn't stained with ketchup for catching the killer. Since Trudy, Lady Cuddles's owner, had liked her original collar and tag, these could now be substituted for the missing one. Hopefully, the Gustins would soon get their key back from the cops. In any event, Lady Cuddles's roaming days would soon be over . . . I hoped.

Wanda also told me she'd all but decided not to run for the vacant board seat. "Let someone else get involved in that nasty quagmire instead of me," she said with a smile. "But rumor has it around there that the pet faction is gaining back all the strength it lost."

"Great news!" I said.

Dante came home again with me that night. Not too big a surprise, since my place was a lot closer than his, and it was late. Plus, a lot had happened that day. I felt exhausted, and imagined he did, too.

Lexie greeted us eagerly at the door. But though she seemed quite happy to jump on Dante in greeting, she looked around him, as if expecting Wagner to appear and lead her into a chase around the yard, even so late at night.

Didn't happen, of course. I was glad Dante had his assistant Alfonse at home to care for his dear German shepherd, but it wasn't the same as Wagner having his master around. Nor Dante having his own, bigger dog to roughhouse with.

Our personal celebration that night was amazing. And exhausting. I fell asleep cradled in Dante's arms.

Morning came early, and with it came additional

celebration. We eventually had to hurry to get dressed.
I gave Lexie a quick constitutional in the yard, and she
was soon joined by Beggar. And I was joined both by
Dante and Rachel.

"I'm really going to miss this," Rachel said with a
sigh. "Beggar will, too. We'll have to schedule a lot of
play dates. Our new place isn't very far from here." She
looked at me then, her big brown eyes even larger than
usual. They darted sidelong toward Dante, who was
standing right beside me. "I hope I didn't give anything
away that I wasn't supposed to."

"No," I said as cheerfully as I could muster. "I think
Dante knows." I believed he'd overheard the conversation I'd had with my tenants right out here in my yard,
even if we hadn't gotten around to discussing it. And
all I'd said to Rutley Harris, when I'd invited him to
check the place out for a non-existent remodeling, had
clinched it. It could all have been lies, in my attempt to
catch him. But that part wasn't.

Rachel looked at me expectantly, as if she figured
he'd have worked out a solution for me.

Which he most likely would have, had I elected to
allow him to control my life.

Instead of assuaging her conscience, I went over a
few pet-sitting issues with my assistant, and then we
went our respective ways. I brought Lexie along, since
after my first few pet-sitting stops I intended to take her
to Darryl's. Rachel headed toward her own clients.

I took my time, as always, enjoying every one of my
pet charges and trying to ensure that they each enjoyed
my visit. Lexie, too—at least in the homes where
canines resided.

I'd soon finished my visits in areas beyond Studio

City and made my way back in that direction. Time to drop Lexie at Doggy Indulgence.

To my surprise, Dante was there, standing at the greeting desk with Darryl. No sign of the dreaded Kiki anywhere, but that was fine with me.

Darryl was smiling so hard that the edges of his lips nearly seemed to reach the frames of his wire-rimmed · glasses. "Come into my office for a minute. You, too, Dante." He put his arm around my shoulder and steered me there, saying with obvious delight, "You'll never guess what Dante did to solve my problem, Kendra."

The only problem I could think of was the one about Kiki. But what could Dante have done about that? With Darryl directing me, I couldn't easily turn to see if I could read it in Dante's dark eyes, so I just went along.

I didn't have to wait long to find out what Dante had done. He and I were soon sitting in the chairs facing Darryl's cluttered desk.

"Tell her, Dante," Darryl said with a laugh.

"Why don't you?" said the guy beside me—who always seemed to have an answer for anything. Was I glad about that or irritated?

That might depend on his solution here.

"Well, you know Kiki said she intended to start her own doggy day care facility to compete with me." Darryl's face clouded slightly, and I nodded. "She isn't going to start it. Dante is."

"What!" I exclaimed, wondering why Darryl seemed so pleased about the idea.

"You know that some HotPets include sideline businesses, depending on the location," Dante said calmly as I glared at him. "Some of them have grooming facilities, others have boarding kennels, and others—sometimes the same ones—also have day care. I've decided to open a day care facility and hire Kiki to manage it. I've seen her here. She seems quite good at caring for animals, and Darryl is giving her a glowing reference."

I felt utterly confused. What were these men doing?

And then the explanation became evident.

"Where, exactly, will this day care facility be?" I inquired.

"Santa Monica," Dante said with a smile.

Which was when I joined these two with a smile of my own. Santa Monica was sufficiently far away from Studio City. The new facility wouldn't compete directly with Darryl, and it would make Kiki happy enough to keep her out of his hair.

I jumped up, grabbed Dante till he stood, too, and gave him a great big kiss. "You rock!" I told him.

"I like to think so," he said.

THAT DAY, I called Althea to fill her in on what had transpired.

"Another murder solved!" said my favorite security company employee and computer hacker. "You're amazing, Kendra."

I had to ask. "Will you tell Jeff?" I'd felt as if I hadn't reached full closure with my former lover—at least not from his perspective.

"Next time I talk to him. Would you believe—" She stopped.

"What?" I urged.

"Turns out the new pet-sitter he's got staying at his house was referred to him by his dear ex-wife, Amanda, who apparently preferred not hiring you anymore for her cats. And—"

"And?" But I thought I knew the answer.

"She's joined him on his business trip to Atlanta."

I'd known how eager she was to get back into his life. And now that I wasn't around for him, she'd made her move.

Was that good for Jeff? Not my call. Maybe it was all for the best.

For now, at least.

"Say hi to them both for me." I thanked Althea once more before saying good-bye.

EVENING APPROACHED AGAIN, and I hadn't talked to Dante since the morning. Would we be together tonight? Hell if I knew.

But that's what I wanted. In fact, I'd been pondering some possibilities and wanted to run them by him. So I called him.

"Hi, Kendra." He sounded so warm that my toes tingled. "I was just about to call. I've finished up for the day and wanted to know if Wagner and I could head your way this evening."

"Sounds good to me," I said, attempting to sound casual.

Inside, though, everything started percolating. Did I want him to come? Did I really want to initiate the conversation I'd been contemplating?

I could always change my mind.

They arrived about an hour later, bearing pizza. After letting the dogs romp through the yard together— only Lexie and Wagner, since Russ and Rachel weren't home—we went upstairs into my small kitchen. I popped the cork on some wine Dante had brought me sometime earlier.

We fed the dogs first, then we humans sat down at my small table and started to eat. Of course the pups hovered at our feet, begging.

Almost at the same time, I said, "Dante, I've been thinking—"

And he said, "Kendra, you may not want to hear this, but—"

I stopped, my heart plummeting, and looked into his solemn, dark eyes. Uh-oh. Was I totally wrong?

"You first," I said, attempting to smile.

"No, you."

What I had to say might make no sense in light of what I thought he was about to say. Even so, I'd convinced myself I wasn't a wimp. Might as well get it out on the table along with the delicious pizza and wonderful wine. Two out of three was okay, wasn't it?

"All right," I said firmly, looking over his shoulder at the door to the rest of my apartment. "Here's the thing. You know my tenants are leaving. I've been thinking about what to do then, and my simply refinancing the place with the bank—again—probably won't work, considering how much money I'm making now."

I glanced at him. Nothing legible on his face. Did he know where I was going with this?

Did I?

Well, sure. "I really don't want to give it up," I continued. This time, I kept my gaze fastened on his. "You'd indicated before that you'd be willing to help me." He neither nodded nor shook his head. I sighed inside but kept going. "You said you love me. And since I love you, too—"

That got a reaction. He put his piece of pizza on the plate and stood. I did likewise. I was suddenly in his arms and sharing a hot kiss spiced by the taste of pizza sauce. "I'm so glad to hear you say that," he whispered. "Now, continue."

The dogs sat up beside us, as if listening to our every word. Well, what was going on could affect both of them.

"Not much left to say, except . . . well, how would you feel about us sharing my mansion? We'd work out the financial details, but you'd need to pay more than me—which, believe me, still hurts. But I'd get over it, if we could be together. If you wanted, Alfonse could move into my apartment over the garage, so you'd still have your personal assistant on the premises. And—"

"Sounds as if you've been giving this a lot of thought," he said.

"Yeah, I have." I'd also been fretting about what it meant in terms of the future.

"I've been thinking about it, too," Dante said. "I was even considering giving you an ultimatum tonight—but I knew how well that would sit with you. Yes, Kendra, I'll move into your house with you and take care of the finances however we ultimately decide that'll be. I could pay for it all, you know."

"Yes, I know, but that's not how I want it."

"I figured." He hugged me fiercely. "Your obstinacy is one of the things I love about you—even though it sometimes drives me nuts. Okay, so we know there are a lot of details to work out, but I'm willing to compromise. You, too?"

"Me, too. As long as you understand that the rest of my life can't be affected by this. I'll still be a lawyer working at Yurick & Associates, and I'll still pet-sit. And even though I'm not thrilled to be a murder magnet, that could wind up being part of the package, too."

"I get it." He kissed me again in acknowledgment. "You've driven me crazy since we first met. Might as well own up to it now, before you change your mind. As long as you're serious." He pulled back and looked deeply into my eyes.

"I'm serious," I said.

And I wouldn't change my mind.